PLAY IT AGAIN

Tracy Krauss

by

Tracy Krauss

Strategic Book Publishing and Rights Co.

Strategic Book Publishing and Rights Co.
12620 FM 1960, Suite A4-507
Houston, TX 77065
www.sbpra.com

ISBN: 978-1-61204-392-0

Introduction
and
Acknowledgements

This book represents a slight departure from my usual romantic suspense genre in that it is a romance, plain and simple. Hopefully, it does incorporate some of the 'edge' that I try to put into my writing, which comes unapologetically from a Christian worldview. *Play It Again* also represents the resurrection of a dream since the original manuscript was the first novel I ever completed. It has gone through many revisions and changes since then to reach this final stage. Thank you to Priscilla Benterud for her honesty and efficiency during the editing process. It is my desire that this book will inspire readers to realize that God can take the discordance of life and turn it into beautiful music.

Tracy Krauss

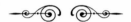

1 Samuel 16: 7b – For God sees not as man sees, for man looks at the outward appearance, but the Lord looks at the heart." (NASB)

FIRST MOVEMENT:
Overture

Chapter One

Smokey tendrils drifted in time to the soft strains of jazz music that filled the dimly lit lounge. Russ Graham surveyed the clusters of patrons at each small circular table, resting on the troupe of aging jazz musicians for a moment, before focusing on the amber liquid swirling in his own glass. It was not the kind of place he normally frequented, but business had brought him out to the island for a few days and there wasn't much else to do in the evening. Alone.

Earlier he'd noticed a sign in the hotel lobby advertising the Jazz ensemble. "Jack Burton Band" the sign read. He looked a little more closely at the aging troop and decided that Jack Burton must be the one wielding the saxophone and counting out the time. He was small and wiry, with thinning hair - probably in his early to mid sixties. Next, there was a burly, white haired, black man on the drums; a gangly, hawk nosed man bending over the piano; and a stocky man with longish gray hair and a mustache leaning on a big, bass violin.

Despite the band's aging appearance, the bluesy jazz that came from their instruments seemed to transcend all barriers of age and time. Russ closed his eyes for a moment and let the strains of music wash over him. How long had it been since he just let himself relax? Just let go and *be*. Too long. Much too long.

He quickly opened his eyes. Guilt and pride, his two constant companions, would not allow even this brief reprieve. He should probably just head back up to his room. He needed an early start tomorrow in order to finish up his business and head back to Winnipeg. Mark was in good hands at his mother's house, but he didn't like leaving him for too long. He took his responsibilities seriously, and he didn't like pawning his son off on others. Even his own mother.

Russ raised the tumbler to his lips and downed the rest of the fiery liquid. As if on cue, a pretty waitress was there to whisk the glass away and offer another. "Um ... I guess another wouldn't hurt," Russ said, glancing at his watch. It was only 9:30. He didn't drink much, as a rule, but one more was no big deal. Besides, who was here to see?

As the waitress retreated, Russ glanced around the room once again. What little light there was in the room cast an ethereal glow over the crowd. His gaze stopped at a young woman, sitting enraptured at a small table near the stage. Her hair, which was very short, appeared to be some shade of red, although it was difficult to tell in this light. Large hoop earrings hung at her ears, swaying in time to the music. She looked awfully young to be in a bar, but then again, there was also a sense of worldliness about her. She was a strange combination of girl and woman.

He was jolted back to reality by a resounding slap across the back. "Hey, bro! Fancy meeting you here!"

"What the ...? What are you two doing here?" Russ sputtered.

Ken Graham, Russ's older brother, stood next to him grinning, his wife Kathy hovering nearby. The contrast in appearance between the two brothers was as marked as their personalities. Ken was well over six feet tall, broad and well built, with sandy blonde hair and twinkling eyes. Although he was already thirty-seven, his boyish expression allowed him to pass for a much younger man. Russ, on the other hand, had a firm set to his chiseled features. His dark blue eyes held a deep intensity and his hair, which was dark and wavy, he wore in a neatly trimmed, conservative style. Shorter than his older brother, he still maintained a powerful, trim physique.

"Didn't I tell you me and Kath were coming out to Hecla for the weekend?" Ken asked as he plunked himself into the chair opposite Russ.

"No, I don't recall," Russ muttered.

"Must have forgot," Ken shrugged. "The company's having a sales convention. Wives are invited so Kathy came along." Hecla Island was a popular spot for business meetings with its scenic location just a two hour drive from the city of Winnipeg. Ken raised a hand and caught the eye of the oncoming waitress. "What about you? I didn't expect to see you here."

"My firm does their books, remember?" Russ answered. His scowl deepened as the waitress arrived with his scotch.

"What have we here?" Ken queried, raising his eyebrows as he looked from the glass to Russ.

"I'm not allowed to have a drink?" Russ asked.

"No, go ahead," Ken laughed. "It's just good to see you take off your priest's collar once in awhile."

Russ clamped his jaw tight. He wasn't about to react to his brother's jibes. "Where are the kids?" he directed at Kathy.

"Your mother's," Kathy sighed, as if that explained everything.

Russ frowned. "Oh. I guess three isn't too much for her to handle . . ."

"Relax," Ken said. "You've got nothing to worry about. At least your kid isn't a brat like some people's." He jerked his head in Kathy's direction.

"They're your kids, too, remember?" Kathy quipped. "Or have you forgotten already?"

"Whatever you say," Ken shrugged, taking a swig of the beer that had just arrived. He leaned in toward Russ. "Greg's not used to staying overnight without his mommy," he snorted.

"He's only five," Kathy sniffed, digging for a cigarette.

"She keeps babying the kid. No wonder he's such a brat," Ken continued.

"I hated to leave them, the way your mother was carrying on," Kathy explained, taking a long drag on her cigarette.

"Do you have to blow that right in my face?" Ken complained, waving at the smoke. "And just what did that mean anyway?"

"You know exactly what I mean," Kathy said, expelling another puff of smoke. "She's always trying to interfere with how we raise our children." Ken grunted, dismissing the comment. "No, I mean it! She's always pushing all that religious garbage at them. I've had it with them coming home and asking me if I'm going to heaven or hell. It's scaring them."

"A little fire and brimstone never hurt anybody," Ken defended. "Look at me. I turned out okay."

"Fine example," Russ noted dryly.

3

"Oh, right, " Ken snorted. "Mr. Perfect talking."

"Is he always this sociable?" Russ asked Kathy, striving for lightness.

"Only on good days," Kathy laughed. There was no humor in the sound. She stubbed out her cigarette.

Ken tipped his beer back and guzzled the rest as if in some kind of competition. "Ah!" he breathed, followed by a loud burp. "What's a guy got to do to get another drink around here?" Kathy just rolled her eyes. "Hey, bro. Order us another round while I take my wife for a spin," Ken said. "How about it, Kath? Wanna dance?" He was already dragging her toward the dance floor.

Russ watched the pair with a combination of amusement and pity. Kathy was now laughing breathlessly up at Ken, obviously happy to be the recipient of some positive attention. It was a shame that it took liquor.

His attention was caught by another couple on the dance floor. It was the girl that Russ had noticed earlier, dancing with Jack Burton, the aging saxophone player. He'd laid aside his instrument while the rest of the troupe carried on. Mismatched as they were, they seemed to dance as one with energetic abandon. And despite what Russ considered to be her somewhat unbecoming attire – cut off jeans, a turtle neck sweater and hiking boots - there was something provocative about the way she moved with such grace and fluidity. In fact, she was so immersed in the dance, she seemed oblivious to any onlookers.

When the song ended, the young woman and her partner retreated to her table, laughing. The other band members took a break and joined them. The older men seemed very familiar with her. Especially the leader. He placed a possessive arm about her shoulders and was leaning in close to whisper in her ear. Something rose up suddenly within Russ's chest. Disapproval? Disgust? Envy, maybe?

He slammed back the rest of his scotch, wiping his mouth just as Ken and Kathy reappeared.

"Did you see that couple out there?" Kathy enthused. "Weren't they great? Just like out of a movie!"

"The old man certainly seems lively for his age," Russ offered with a shrug.

"I wasn't lookin' at the old man," Ken guffawed with a wink. "Mm-mm. Them's a great set of legs!"

"I didn't notice," Russ shrugged.

"Oh right," Ken laughed. "You can fool most of the people most of the time, but this is your bro, here, man. I know you've still got some red blood in there somewhere, no matter what you want people to believe."

"Whatever. She's not my type."

"She too skinny for you?" Ken asked.

"Just drop it," Russ responded tightly.

"Maybe it's been so long, you forgot how . . ."

"Shut up," Russ clipped.

"I know Miranda was a bitch, but —"

"I said, shut up." Russ rose from the table, his anger barely contained.

"Where you going?" Ken demanded.

"To my room. Goodnight." Russ turned sharply and headed for the exit. For a moment the three Scotch that he'd just downed went straight to his head. He slowed his pace enough to regain his bearings and then continued toward the door.

Directly in front of him, also nearing the exit, were the wiry old musician and the strange young woman. She had her arm slung casually around his shoulders, while his encircled her slim waist. Another wave of something he couldn't name flooded Russ's body as he watched them. He told himself it was loathing, but other parts of his anatomy whispered 'lust'. Probably just the Scotch. He wasn't used to drinking anymore.

Who cared, anyway? What wayward girls did with aging jazz musicians was really no concern of his. So why couldn't he get her image out of his head?

Chapter Two

Deanie yawned and stretched as she swung her legs over the side of the bed. She padded to the window, threw it open, and inhaled deeply of the fragrant autumn air. It was early September, and some of the trees had already taken on a twinge of color, yet the air was still very warm. It was going to be a beautiful day.

She smiled to herself. She hadn't felt this good in a long time. All her senses were alive this morning. Perhaps it was a sign of good things to come.

A snore came from one of the double beds. She looked over at the small man who lay tangled in the sheets and allowed a fond smile to cross her lips. How many mornings had she awakened like this? Different hotel rooms, different cities. Being the daughter of a vagabond musician was an unconventional upbringing, to be sure, but it was one that she wouldn't trade for the world.

"Wake up, sleepyhead," she said as she gently shook the man in the bed.

"Wha. . . What?" Jack Burton opened groggy eyes, finally focusing on his daughter.

"Go away, girl! You know I don't like mornings!" With a sound similar to a growl, he turned over and put his head under the pillow.

"Not so fast! I haven't seen you in six weeks, remember? I didn't come all the way out here just to watch you sleep."

"What time is it?" Jack's muffled voice came from under the pillow.

"9 A.M.," Deanie replied, glancing at the digital clock on the night stand.

"Really, Honey, couldn't you let your old man sleep for just another hour? You know I'm not much good for anything in the mornings. And I'm not as young as I used to be."

"Well. . ."

"You go on ahead. Do some exploring or something. I'll meet you for lunch." With a sigh, Jack settled back down into his pillow.

Deanie gave him a playful shake, but conceded. "I'll let you get away with it this time."

She thought she heard a mumbled, "Don't know what I ever did to that girl," coming from under the pillow. She just smiled.

Actually, she was surprised at how wide-awake she felt this morning considering she had driven out to Hecla last night after work. She hadn't seen Jack for most of the summer, what with his group traveling to so many summer festivals. It was a grueling pace for the aging foursome.

Deanie's own job as a waitress in a Winnipeg bar kept her from joining her father on the road, as she often liked to do. Serving drinks in a lounge was not a profession she would have chosen - given a choice. But she needed to make a living and the tips were good. She'd saved enough money over the course of the summer to pay for her tuition and books for the fall semester at the university.

She'd arrived last night after her father was already performing. It had been so good to see him again. And just as wonderful to hear him play. She loved her father's music, almost as much as she loved the man behind it. It was such an inseparable part of him. An extension of his spirit that allowed others a glimpse of the man within.

She was beginning to wonder if she was being too rigid in her decision to quit the music scene, herself. Oh well. There was no point in trying to figure her entire future out in one morning. Especially on such a beautiful morning! It was warm and sunny, even for September. What she really needed was to catch some more of those late summer rays before they gave way to the inevitable icy winds of a Manitoba winter.

She donned a pair of shorts and a halter top, catching a glimpse of herself in the full length mirror. She winced. Tall was okay, and most people would do anything to be so slim. But she did wish, on occasion, for a few more curves. You made due with the hand you got dealt, though. That's what Jack always said. She shoved her dark glasses onto her nose and strode out the door.

The deck wound around the hotel, a rambling two-story structure with a distinctly Icelandic flair. Some small private patios off the main floor suites were connected to a large common area that overlooked a small pond. Flowers still bloomed brightly along its edges and there were plenty of deck chairs.

There was a breeze blowing off the lake beyond, ruffling the leaves of the deciduous trees. Already, the brilliant gold and burnt reds of autumn had touched much of the foliage. Several people were out enjoying the morning. She noticed a dark, well built man stretched out on one of the loungers, reading. She also noticed an empty lounge chair beside him and headed in his direction. "Mind if I sit here?" she asked.

The man looked up. If she wasn't mistaken, he didn't seem pleased. "Suit yourself," came his crisp reply.

She bit back her own curt response. She felt like turning around, but pride wouldn't let her. Keeping her head high, she settled herself into the lounge chair. "Thanks. Beautiful day, isn't it?" she commented, overly bright. The man appeared to be ignoring her. "I said, beautiful day, isn't it?" she repeated.

"Hmm," was the man's noncommittal grunt. He didn't look up.

"I'm just here for the weekend," Deanie continued. "From Winnipeg." She wasn't sure why, but she felt determined to get a response. "Some weather we're having, eh?" She frowned. What was the guy's problem? He could at least be civil. Her own hot-temper was beginning to take over. He *would* speak more than a mumbled syllable, even if she had to irritate him into doing it.

"I think fall must be my favorite time of year. Don't you think so? The air is so fresh and clean. And being out here in the wilderness - it just makes you feel alive. Don't you agree?"

The man sat silently for a few more moments before lowering his papers with deliberateness. He lifted his sunglasses and his dark blue eyes bore straight through hers. "I'm not interested, so you might as well not waste your time, or mine."

If irritating him had been her objective, she certainly seemed to have succeeded. "Excuse me?" she asked, her voice rising ever so slightly. She sat upright in her lounger to look him squarely in the face.

"I don't want or need your services," was the blunt reply.

"WHAT?" Deanie's temper exploded as she catapulted from the chair, sending it onto its side. "What the hell? What kind of thing is that to say to a perfect stranger?"

"I saw you hanging all over your sixty year old 'boyfriend' last night. But don't worry. I won't tell him about today." He eyed her with open contempt.

"Sixty year old boyfriend?" Deanie echoed, her brow creasing. "What the. . ." Suddenly, the light of understanding dawned across her face. Her look of outrage was replaced by a slowly spreading grin. "You thought. . . ? Jack and I. . . ? Wow. That is too funny!"

Russ's frown only deepened. "Rather than laugh, you should be ashamed -"

Deanie cut him off. "Ashamed? Of what? Jack Burton is my father."

Warm color slowly suffused Russ's cheeks.

"Now, I think you're the one who should be ashamed for even thinking such a thing," Deanie said with a wide grin.

"I thought. . . I mean, I didn't think . . ." Russ fumbled for words. "I beg your pardon. I'm very sorry." He jumped to his feet and righted her lounge chair, waiting until she had seated herself before sitting down again himself.

"Forget it," Deanie said lightly. "Phew! I've been accused of a lot of things but. . ."

"I really am extremely sorry," Russ repeated. "I don't normally jump to conclusions without knowing all the facts."

"It doesn't matter," Deanie waved a dismissive hand. "Actually, it was pretty damn hilarious. Wait till I tell Jack. He'll get a charge out of it, too." Deanie began chuckling softly.

"It wasn't that funny," he said, the corners of his own mouth beginning to twitch.

"Sure it was. Especially when you realized. You should have seen yourself! I swear you looked like you could have just crawled under the nearest rock to hide!"

"I guess I really did put my foot in my mouth, didn't I ?" Russ grimaced. "Please accept my apology?"

"I told you I already did."

There was an awkward moment of silence. Deanie was trying to hide the smirk that was relentlessly pulling at the corners of her mouth. Finally Russ cleared his throat, "Well then, allow me to introduce myself properly. I'm Russ Graham." He reached over to extend a hand in a businesslike manner.

Deanie took his hand. She wasn't prepared for the warmth that shot straight up her arm and through her chest. He must have felt it, too, judging from the little intake of breath she heard upon contact. "Nice to meet you, Russ. I'm Deanie. Deanie Burton." Their eyes caught and held for a moment as they continued to shake hands in slow motion..

Russ cleared his throat and retrieved his hand. "Pleased to meet you," he said, his voice sounding gruff. He cleared his throat again, and picked up the discarded papers, shuffling them.

Deanie felt a rush of butterfly wings in her stomach. He was so good looking. And his eyes . . . She felt a sudden wave of inadequacy. Why hadn't she worn something more flattering? Sexier? Normally, she didn't care what other people thought of her. She was who she was. Sometimes she even enjoyed trying to shock people, or at least get their attention. But this morning she felt overly aware of any shortcomings in her physical makeup.

"Well, I suppose I'd better let you get back to your reading," she said, adjusting herself in the chair.

"That's okay," Russ said as he quickly lowered the papers. "It wasn't that interesting."

"Business?"

"Yeah. Our firm does the books for the resort," Russ replied. "I'm an accountant."

"I should have pegged you as an accountant right off the bat," Deanie said, scrutinizing him sideways out of the corner of her eye. "You look like an accountant."

"Hm. I'm not sure if that's a compliment or not," Russ laughed. "And what about you?"

"I'm a student, mostly. At the U of M. I'm going into social work, I guess," Deanie shrugged.

"Doesn't sound like you're sure," Russ noted.

"I really would like to help people," Deanie replied. "You know, people who are down and out and all that. It's just that sometimes I miss the music business, you know? It's pretty much been my whole life."

"So you think you might like to follow in your father's footsteps, so to speak?"

"Well, yes and no. It's actually kind of complicated, right now. My life, I mean." She looked down at her hands.

"Life can get that way sometimes, no matter how carefully you plan it," Russ reflected.

"Actually, that's probably most of my problem right there," Deanie laughed. "I don't often plan anything. I just kind of let life happen."

"Having a plan can be a good thing," Russ stated.

"Guess that's why you're an accountant. All those columns and numbers and stuff," Deanie teased. "You're probably good at it. Probably good at whatever you do."

Russ cleared his throat, and sat up a little straighter. "Well. Speaking of plans, I do have a meeting. It was nice meeting you, Miss Burton," he said, gathering his things and rising.

"Deanie will do, thanks. And likewise."

"Yes. Deanie." He hesitated momentarily, turned to leave, then stopped again and turned back toward Deanie's chair. His gaze seemed fixed on some point just above her head. "I'd like to make it up to you, if I could, for being so rude to you earlier."

"Forget it. I already accepted your apology."

"How about dinner tonight?" he blurted.

Deanie blinked. "I'd love to," she accepted. "I'll have all afternoon to spend with Jack and the guys, and then I'll be free all evening while they're playing at tonight's gig."

"Fine," Russ nodded. He stood for a moment, awkwardly. "Fine," he repeated. "Would seven be alright?"

"Seven would be great."

"I'll meet you in the lobby, then. At seven." Without further hesitation, Russ turned and strode toward the hotel entrance.

Deanie flipped her glasses up onto the top of her head and watched his retreating figure. She settled back into the lounger, a smile of satisfaction playing across her lips. It felt good to be back in the game.

Chapter Three

"Mark! Mark? Where'd you go?" The high pitched voice had just enough whine to make it really irritating. Mark Graham kept his mouth shut tight, hoping that his young cousin Greg would just give up and go away.

"There you are!" This time it was his grandmother. "Greg's been looking all over for you."

Mark quickly shut the photo album and stuffed it back into place on the shelf, hoping his grandmother wouldn't take too much notice. "Sorry. Guess I didn't hear you," he mumbled.

"Come outside with me," Greg pleaded. "I'm bored."

"I could turn on the sprinkler," his grandmother offered. "It's warm enough today, I think."

"Naw," Mark shrugged. "What's Sam doing?"

"She's helping me in the kitchen. We're going to bake cookies and a banana loaf."

"I wanna bake cookies!" Greg piped up.

"I thought you wanted Mark to go outside with you?"

"If Sam gets to bake cookies then I do too!" Greg turned tail and ran down the hallway, yelling at the top of his lungs and taunting his sister with the latest turn of events.

"I'm sorry, Mark," his grandmother apologized. "I know Greg is a lot younger than you and you get tired of playing with him."

"It's okay." Mark focused on his clasped hands.

13

"I see you were looking at the photo albums again," she noted.

There was no hiding from grandmothers. They had a sixth sense or something. "Yeah," Mark mumbled.

"Maybe I'll give you that picture someday. When you're old enough to look after it."

"I don't think my Dad would like it," Mark replied sullenly.

"I know. That's why I'll just keep it safe for awhile, okay? Now come on, you can help me with your cousins." Mark trailed after his grandmother as she continued to talk. "Your father phoned this morning from Hecla Island. You were outside so he said he'd call back later this afternoon."

"Oh. Okay. When's he coming home?"

"Well, that's just it, you see. He's going to stay another night at least. He knew you'd be having a good time with Samantha and Greg."

Mark frowned. As if.

"And," she continued. "That means you can all come to church with me tomorrow. Won't that be grand?"

Mark nodded stoically. He could suffer it out for the sake of his grandma. Besides, sometimes they got snacks at Sunday School.

❧

Russ arrived at the hotel coffee shop right on the dot of twelve. To his surprise, Ken was already waiting at a table. He didn't look so well.

"Hung over?" Russ asked with little sympathy as he sat down.

"My head's the size of a pumpkin," Ken groaned. He took a long swallow of the ice water that was in front of him.

"Serves you right. Where's Kathy?"

"Sick, I guess," Ken shrugged. "Again."

"Sick of you, maybe?" Russ teased.

They paused for a moment as the waitress came with menus. "I'll just have the special," Ken said. "And coffee. Lots of coffee."

Russ held up two fingers. "Might as well keep it simple." The waitress nodded before retrieving the menus and turning to leave.

"Nice ass," Ken commented, watching the twenty something girl swing away.

14

"Not something you should notice," Russ replied with a slight grin.

"I'm married, not blind," Ken snorted.

"Still . . ."

"You know, I just don't know how to handle her moods sometimes. I try to please her, but she still doesn't seem satisfied. I've held down this stinkin' job for what? Months now. We're making our payments. I hardly ever go to the racetrack anymore, let alone out with the guys for a beer."

"Sounds like you're really making a sacrifice," Russ noted with sarcasm.

"Hey! No smug comments. As I recall, you didn't do so well in your own marriage."

"I never said I did."

"Well, there's a whole lot more going on here than even you realize," Ken stated.

"Maybe she just wants you to show her some appreciation. Some affection. She needs to know you still love her. You do still love her, don't you?" Russ asked pointedly.

"What kind of an ignorant question is that? Of course I love her. And she knows it! She just wants me to fit into her perfect little box labeled 'ideal husband'."

"Quit deflecting the blame onto someone else," Russ said. "Take some responsibility for your own actions."

"There you go again," Ken blustered. "Mr. 'Take Responsibility'. Well that's not me. It's never been me. It doesn't matter what I do, I'll always be the black sheep. I might as well just concede."

Russ let out a gust of breath. "Whatever. I'm not your keeper."

"No? That's not the vibe I've been getting these past thirty five years or so."

"I never asked for the job," Russ reminded. "You're the one who always seems to get yourself into one predicament after another. And then calls me for help."

"Oh right. The favored son bails out the prodigal once again," Ken snorted. "The folks were sure quick to forget about your screw ups. But me? Not a chance. I can't do anything right."

"Quit whining."

"Why should I? Look at you. Mr. High and Mighty about to give me advice on marriage when your own wife couldn't stick around for more than six months."

"Quit bringing up my marriage, for Pete's sake!" Russ growled. "It's ancient history."

"No kidding. Poor sucker . . . " Ken grinned. "I mean her, not you."

"Would you shut up, already?" Russ shot back with a frown.

"Touchy," Ken shrugged. "You're obviously not getting enough sex. When's the last time you -"

"My personal life is none of your business," Russ cut in. "Besides, I am seeing someone. Sort of," he added.

"Oh?" Ken asked, leaning in for more. "Anyone I know?"

"No. Just someone from the office," Russ replied dismissively. "Quit changing the subject. We were talking about you, remember?"

"No we weren't."

"I give up." Russ threw up his hands, shaking his head.

"Good. Our food's here anyway."

Russ sighed, glad for the interruption.

"So, you heading back after lunch?" Ken asked, his mouth full of his clubhouse.

Russ frowned, making a noncommittal gesture with his shoulders as he chewed.

"No? I thought your business was all finished up after this morning."

Russ swallowed, taking his time as he took a sip of coffee. "I thought I might stay another night. Relax and unwind."

Ken almost choked on his sandwich. "You relax? Now that's a first! Must be some pretty hot babe to keep you here against your better judgment."

"Who said anything about a hot babe?" Russ demanded. "Why is everything about sex with you?"

Ken just shrugged. "I've known you too long to know that you just don't decide to 'relax and unwind'. Something else is going on and you never were very good at hiding stuff. So spill it, before I beat it out of you."

"As if you could," Russ laughed.

"You're a sly bugger, you are," Ken nodded. "But ole Kenny'll find out sooner or later."

"It's nothing," Russ replied with a dismissive wave. "I just made plans, that's all."

"Plans. . . ?" Ken raised an eye brow. "Now who's deflecting?" He waited expectantly, in no hurry at all.

"It's just dinner," Russ hedged.

"Dinner?"

"I met someone and we're going out for dinner," Russ stated.

"You met someone and you're going out for dinner. . . ?"

"Quit repeating everything I say!" Russ exclaimed.

Ken whistled. "You sly devil! Who is she?"

"Nobody you know."

Ken surveyed his brother closely. "I thought you just said you were seeing someone?"

"I said 'sort of'. Besides, it's just dinner," Russ replied with irritation.

"You are a real piece," Ken laughed. "I'm kind of proud of you."

Just then Deanie walked into the café. Russ's heart lurched, then sank into the pit of his stomach. Great. He hoped she wouldn't notice him, but realized it was a bit too much to ask when her eyes lit up upon scanning the room. She waved. Russ's returning gesture was barely perceptible. At least she didn't try to join them.

Ken's eyebrows shot up in surprise. "Her?" he asked incredulously. Russ's silence was answer enough. This time Ken let out a whoop, bringing a few glances from the other patrons. "I knew you were human after all. I *am* proud of you - real proud!"

"Don't make a big deal out of nothing," Russ frowned.

"No big deal? My no nonsense, 'not my type' brother is taking out a hot little number, and it's no big deal?"

"It's only dinner."

"So you keep telling me. I knew you had to have some red blood in those veins somewhere."

"Would you stop it already?" Russ rose from the table.

"Touchy, aren't we?" Ken pouted. "Hey. Where you going?"

Russ threw some bills down on the table. "I lost my appetite." He strode from the coffee shop without looking back.

Why did he let Ken get to him like that? It wasn't like he was doing

17

anything *wrong*. He was a single man going out for dinner with a pretty girl. Big deal.

On second thought, perhaps pretty wasn't exactly the correct term. She was certainly not beautiful in the conventional sense, and most certainly not the type of woman who would normally attract his attention, but there was something about her that he found compelling. She was tall, very slim and had a colorful tattoo on one ankle and another on her upper arm. In the bright morning sun, he'd also seen the true color of her hair - a fiery red, flashing copper highlights as the sun glinted off its closely cropped surface. He wondered if it was natural or if she had dyed it that way. He smiled. His dreams about her from last night came flooding back into his mind. There were plenty of other things he'd noticed about her, too. Maybe too much.

Russ shook his head, jolting himself back to reality. He was a disgusting pig. Maybe Ken was right. Celibacy was starting to warp his thinking. He needed to slow down. Even if Deanie Burton was not the type of girl he had originally thought, she was still definitely not the kind of woman he should be interested in. So why had he asked her out in the first place?

Chapter Four

"Girl, you and your daddy sure put on some fancy footwork last night," Toby Rantt exclaimed. The big drummer shook his white head, which stood out in stark contrast to the dark skin of his face and neck. He was a thick-chested man, whose heart was as big as the huge hands with which he so deftly handled the drumsticks. His was the steadying influence for the otherwise eccentric troupe and in many ways, he was like the father figure for all of them.

"Yep, just like the old days, eh Deanie ?" Jack agreed. "Bet you didn't know your old man still had it in him, eh?"

"Are you kidding?" Deanie laughed, giving her father an affectionate squeeze. "You can still out dance anybody!"

The ensemble were getting ready for their late afternoon rehearsal. The warm afternoon sun slanted in through the side door of the lounge, which had been left open a crack to let in some air. Dust particles danced through the beam of light, as if anticipating the music to come.

"I think we played better after she arrived, don't you agree?" Jack boasted. Assenting grunts came from around the room. "Yep, we put more soul into it," he stated emphatically.

"And just what does a white boy like you know about soul?" Toby teased. They all laughed. It was old, but friendly banter between comrades. The aging foursome had been together for such a long time that they were more like family than colleagues. They had been a team for as long as Deanie could remember, and she looked affectionately on all of them as "Uncle."

"Brent tells me you've been doing some jamming with them recently," Benny Walters drawled, leaning closely over the strings of his bass violin as he adjusted the tuning.

"Just a bit," Deanie replied casually. "Nothing serious. Just getting together with friends. The same as when I sing with you guys." Benny's son Brent was Deanie's best friend. He was actually more like a brother than anything else.

"What's this?" Jack piped up.

"I was just saying that I've been hanging with Brent a bit, lately. That's all," Deanie repeated with a slight shrug.

"Well now, as long as you're careful," Jack cautioned.

"Jack," Deanie rolled her eyes.

"What's the problem?" Benny asked, his voice sounding defensive. "The kids have always hung out together."

"Oh there's no problem," Jack interjected. "Not with Brent. It's more some of them other types he tends to hang with, though. You understand."

"Pretty heavy coming from a vagabond such as yourself," Benny snorted.

"You two stop arguing," Deanie scolded. "I'm a grown up girl, for goodness sake. I can take care of myself, thank you very much."

"Of course you can, Sweetheart," Jack began, " It's just -"

Deanie cut him off. "Just nothing! Now, I came here to hear some music. Are you guys going to rehearse or not? I can't stay here all night you know. I happen to have other plans for later."

"What kind of plans?" Jack asked.

"Well if you must know, I have a dinner date with a very attractive man," Deanie replied with a coy smile.

A chorus of male voices assaulted her almost in unison. "What man? Who? What's his name?"

"I must be the only grown woman I know that has to put up with not one, but four, old codgers trying to run her life," Deanie laughed.

"And lucky girl you are, too," was Jack's quick response. "Now quit skittering around the question. Who's this man?"

"Oh, no," Deanie shook her head, grinning. "All you'll get from me is that he is a very respectable accountant."

There were whistles from around the room. "Now you watch yourself," Jack warned, deadly serious. "Never judge a book by its cover, I always say. You can't always trust them respectable types."

Deanie shook her head in amusement at the look of concern on all four faces. "Come on, you guys, are we going to make some music, or not?"

❧

What had ever possessed him to ask that girl out, Russ mused for the tenth time that day. He should have just turned tail and run, especially after his lunch disaster with Ken. But then again, that was exactly one reason why he was still here. He couldn't let Ken think he'd caved after all. He had some pride left. . . he hoped. He'd tried to fill his afternoon, first by taking in a round of golf. That was a big mistake. He'd never lost so many balls in his life. Then he went on a little sight seeing tour, although it was hard to remember exactly what he saw. Now, he was in the process of dressing for his dinner date and was having trouble choosing a tie. He'd only brought two, but for some reason, neither one seemed right.

He just needed to get this dinner thing over with. She was definitely not his type, anyway. For one thing, she was much too young. He was thirty-five years old, for goodness sake. A divorcee with an eleven-year-old son. And she was. . . ? He must make a point of finding out how old she was, he thought, as he finally made his choice and began knotting the tie in place. She had said something about going to university, so at least she wasn't still in high school. Still, he was none the less uneasy about this evening. He felt like he was doing exactly what he had accused Jack Burton of the night before. Cradle robbing.

He glanced at his watch, remembering that he was supposed to phone Mark. He, at least, knew how to take care of his responsibilities.

"How's it going, Son?" Russ asked once he had Mark on the line. "Are you getting along with Samantha and Greg?"

"Yeah, I guess so. You know how Greg is sometimes."

"I know. But he is a lot younger than you."

"That's what Grandma says, too."

"She's managing all right with all three of you there?"

"I think so. Would you like to talk to her?"

"No, that's all right," Russ said quickly. The last thing he wanted was for his mother to start into a game of twenty questions. "I phoned to talk to you. To make sure you're all right."

"Of course I'm all right," Mark laughed. "Are you sure you're all right? You sound a little bit . . . funny."

"Oh? No, I'm fine. Just fine." There was a slight pause. "I went to an old, historic village this afternoon. The first settlers here came from Iceland. I think you would have enjoyed it. Maybe we'll come back together sometime."

"That'd be fun. What else did you do today?"

"Well, I golfed, I did some reading . . . not much."

"What about tonight?" Mark asked.

So much for worrying about his mother asking too many questions. "Oh, nothing too exciting. I'm just going out for dinner."

"With Uncle Ken and Aunt Kathy?"

"No."

"Who with?"

"Nobody that you know."

"Is it a girl?"

"Mark! What makes you think that?" Russ asked just a little too defensively.

"Well, is it?"

"As a matter of fact, it is," Russ replied.

"Grandma! Dad's got a date!" Mark yelled. Russ held the receiver away from his ear. "With a girl!"

Mark didn't know just how accurate the term 'girl' was, Russ groaned inwardly. "Now hold on," he cautioned, putting the receiver back to his ear. "Nobody said anything about a 'date'. We're just going out for dinner. And did you have to tell Grandma?"

"Why shouldn't I? Isn't she nice?" Mark asked.

Russ rolled his eyes, letting out a small pent up sigh. "Of course she's nice. Otherwise I wouldn't be going out with her."

"So it is a date!" Russ could hear the triumph in Mark's voice.

"Mark Graham! What's gotten into you? It's not like you to ask so many questions. Is Grandma putting you up to this?" Russ asked, knitting his brow.

"Well, only sort of. I mean, Grandma just wanted to know if it was business. But I think its kind of neat, too. I might like to get a mother someday."

There was an audible silence as Russ took in the impact of those words. Mark wanted a mother, even though his own mother had abandoned him. What was to say that another woman wouldn't do the same? Russ had been nurturing his mistrust of women for so long that it was hard to imagine a woman ever being part of their lives again. But clearly Mark felt a need for such a relationship. And what of his own needs? He'd been denying them for so long, that he'd almost fooled himself into thinking they didn't exist. But in the space of less than twenty-four hours, a strange redheaded girl-woman had brought all those thoughts and feelings to the surface again.

"Dad?" Mark's voice asked uncertainly. "You still there?"

"What? Oh, yes, of course," Russ blinked back to reality. "Listen. I'm going to have to get off the telephone now, Son."

"Okay. I think Grandma wants to talk to you for a minute first, though."

"No! I mean, not right now," he reiterated less forcefully. "I've really got to run. You just give my love to Grandma, and tell the other kids to be good for her. Take care. I love you, and I'll see you tomorrow."

"Okay, Dad. Love you, too. Bye."

Russ breathed a sigh of relief once he'd hung up the receiver. Thank goodness he'd managed to get off before his mother came on to interrogate him.

He really couldn't believe that he was all nerved up over a simple dinner date. It's not like he hadn't been out recently. He enjoyed the company of a woman on occasion, as long as things stayed under control. No unrealistic expectations, no demands, nobody gets hurt. That's the way he liked it. This was no different. Right?

He looked in the mirror once again, and scrutinized his appearance. He was wearing a dark suit, pale shirt, and nondescript tie. He frowned. It looked like he was dressed for a business meeting. But what did he expect? His entire wardrobe was made up of similar, sensible clothes. He wore conventional, respectable clothing because he was conventional and respectable. Maybe the suit would intimidate her enough that she wouldn't want to give him a second glance. That way, his problems would be over, and he wouldn't have to be rude by telling her he didn't want to have anything to do with her again. Besides, this whole evening was just a way of being polite for the mistake that he'd made earlier. It had absolutely no meaning for either of them.

With this determination in mind, Russ turned on his heel and headed for the door. It was precisely two minutes to seven, and he was never late. That was one thing she could count on.

Chapter Five

"Where is that purse?" Deanie grated to herself as she stumbled over some rumpled bedding that had made its way to the floor. She finished fastening her earring and pushed her heel down into her boot. No wonder she'd tripped. She didn't even have her boots on properly. Darn those guys in the band! They'd lost all track of time and now she was late.

She flipped the bedding up over the mattress and peered underneath. There it was! Hiding on her as if on purpose. She snatched the purse and flew out the door. She was only fifteen minutes late. Not bad at all.

❦

Russ glanced down at his watch once more, and tried to appear calm and collected as he waited in the hotel lobby. Maybe she just wasn't going to show, he told himself, almost relieved. He'd give her five more minutes, and that was it.

Just then the elevator doors came gliding open and Deanie rushed out. Russ's gaze swept over her lean form. The usual silver hoops jingled about her ears, catching the light. She wore a sleeveless black knit top, and a short brown leather skirt; a combination which left her midriff exposed. His glance went past her long expanse of legs to her feet to find. . . cowboy boots? Russ blinked, pasted on a smile and waited until she arrived in a flurry by his side.

25

"Sorry I'm so late," she apologized in a cheerful voice. "Kind of a bad habit, I'm afraid."

"Oh," Russ said, not sure how else to respond. Could he possibly compliment her on her appearance, he wondered? Instead he settled on, "Well, shall we?" He offered her his arm and they entered the dining room. Russ hoped the contrast in their appearance wouldn't attract too many stares. Deanie looked like she had just walked out of a country rock video.

Once seated, Russ ordered wine and then they busied themselves by scrutinizing the menu. After their order was taken, they were left to awkwardly nurse their glasses.

Russ cleared his throat, "How was your afternoon?"

"Just great," Deanie responded eagerly, letting out a pent up breath as if she'd been holding back. "I met up with Jack and the guys and we did some jamming. It was just like old times. We had a lot of fun, but we kind of lost track of time. That's partly why I was late. That and I lost my purse."

"Oh." There was more silence.

"Yeah. Jack says I'd lose my head if it wasn't attached, but then he's one to talk. I guess it's kind of genetic. Nobody ever accused a Burton of being organized."

"I see," Russ nodded.

"But the rest of the gang are good sports. They've been together long enough they know to never ask Jack to remember something important. Like one time when I was little and Jack was supposed to book the rooms and he forgot and we all ended up sleeping inside the van. Me, Jack — everybody. We put some of the instruments underneath under a tarp and Max kept watch all night for fear someone would steal something. They never asked Jack to book the rooms again."

Russ frowned, cocking his head to one side before looking at Deanie with questioning eyes. "Why do you call your father 'Jack'?"

"Actually, I never really thought about it that much," Deanie shrugged. "I've just always called him 'Jack'. Maybe he felt it put us on equal footing or something, I don't know."

"Hmm," Russ mused, thinking of his own son. He couldn't imagine Mark calling him 'Russ' instead of 'Dad'. It just didn't seem right.

"What is it?" Deanie asked.

"Oh, nothing," Russ said quickly, bringing himself back to the present. "So tell me. What was it like, being the daughter of 'thee' Jack Burton.?"

"I don't know," Deanie shrugged and smiled. "Normal for me, I guess."

"No paparazzi knocking down your door? Things like that?" Russ smiled back.

Deanie laughed. "Jack's hardly *that* famous, although he should have been. Some critics say he could have made it big in the States. Maybe New Orleans or even New York. Not bad for a farm boy from Manitoba. But I guess other musical trends moved into the spotlight. He's managed well enough, though. Mostly traveling the festival circuit and doing local clubs and stuff. He's managed to put bread on the table anyway, and he's cut quite a number of albums over his lifetime. You'd probably be surprised."

"No, I'm not surprised," Russ replied. "I think I remember seeing him on CBC once."

"That could be. I think that was quite a few years ago, but I'm not exactly sure. My father is a man with a passion for what he does. He loves his music probably more than anything in the world. Except me," Deanie added with a grin. "It was exciting to be a part of that. To witness someone giving their all, everyday, and loving it."

"But it must have been hard on you, too," Russ pointed out.

"I don't know, really. I never felt like I was getting gypped, if that's what you mean. It was pretty exciting for a kid to get to travel to different places and stay up late at night. But Jack always made sure I did my homework. I guess I must have had some pretty understanding teachers. Sometimes I'd stay with friends if the guys were going to be on the road for any length of time. Martha - that's Toby the drummer's wife - took me and Brent in quite a bit. But they did the majority of their traveling on weekends, so it wasn't that bad."

"Brent? Is that your brother?" Russ asked.

"Not exactly. I guess you could say he's more like a brother than anything else. He's Benny's son. Benny plays the base," Deanie explained.

"Ah, yes," Russ nodded, remembering the bass player with the mustache.

"Brent and I are pretty close. He did spend part of the time with his mother. His parents split, but we traveled together, whenever he was with his dad. We've been through a lot together, Brent and I."

"And your mother?"

"It's a very sad story, actually," Deanie responded, leaning forward. "Jack was a lot older than her when they married. She was a secretary and couldn't even carry a tune! But I guess their love for one another was more important than all the differences. She died when I was just two. An accident. I never really knew her at all, but Jack still talks about her all the time. He says I look like her. They loved one another very much."

"I guess that's important in a marriage," Russ commented dryly, raising an eyebrow. He picked up his wine glass and swished the liquid around, staring as it swirled in the glass.

"I think she must have been a very wonderful person. But thankfully I still have Jack. He's the best father anyone could have ever asked for," Deanie sighed. "But enough about me. I've done all the talking so far. What about you? What's your family like?" She sat up straighter and waited, inviting a response with her ready smile and bright eyes.

Russ let himself get drawn into their depths for a moment. A man could get lost if he wasn't careful. He focused on his wine glass again and drank the rest of its contents. "Pretty normal, I'm afraid," he said with a shrug, setting the glass on the table. "Certainly not as unorthodox as yours."

"Unorthodox. . ." Deanie repeated. "I like that word. I'll have to try it out on Jack. I'll bet you were one of those kids who had to stay in his own yard. Oh! And your mother baked cookies every weekend and you were never late for supper."

Russ just smiled. "Actually, my mother did bake cookies on occasion, and I was rarely late for 'supper', as you say."

"I'll just bet," Deanie teased. "Only 'rarely'?"

"My parents were quite strict, by today's standards," Russ added. "They had high expectations of my brother and me."

"Where are your parents?"

"My mother still lives in the city. My Dad died a few years ago. He'd only just retired when he had a heart attack."

"Oh, how sad!"

"Mmhm. But Mom's strong." He stared at his empty glass. "More wine?" he asked abruptly, reaching for the bottle.

Just then the waitress brought their food. Russ was glad for the interruption. He was not one who enjoyed divulging too much personal information. He'd have to watch his alcohol consumption if he intended on keeping it that way. In fact, he could already feel the wine going to his head. Or was that the effect of the woman sitting across the table?

They finished their meal in relative silence. Deanie seemed content to enjoy the food and Russ decided it was best to keep his own wayward thoughts to himself.

"That was delicious," Deanie groaned when she was finished, leaning back and patting her stomach.

"I noticed you seemed to be enjoying your meal," Russ commented with a grin.

"Don't let my looks fool you," Deanie laughed. "Jack says he'll never be able to retire as long as I'm still around consuming all his hard earned cash."

"So you still live at home?" Russ asked casually. *Good lord! She still lived with her father!* He glanced her way as he dabbed at the corners of his mouth with his napkin, then laid it on top of his plate.

"It's a good arrangement. We kind of look after one another, and since I'm going to school, I can't really afford a place of my own," she explained. "We've had the same apartment for years. Probably could have owned a house by now, with all the money we've spent on rent."

"True, I suppose."

"Of course you would. Own your own home, I mean," Deanie smiled and surveyed Russ with twinkling eyes. "A responsible man like you is bound to have some real estate."

"That's me. Responsible," Russ grimaced and let out a small depreciating chuckle. "You're beginning to sound like my brother."

"I get the feeling that isn't a good thing," Deanie noted.

Russ shrugged and tried to smile. "He's always reminding me how 'responsible' I am. How I take life too seriously."

"So, do you? Take life too seriously, I mean," Deanie asked, leaning forward on her elbows.

"Life is serious," Russ hedged. He took another drink of wine, not willing to meet her eyes.

"Hmm. I see what he means."

Russ shook his head and gave a slight laugh. "I guess I'm just more conventional than my brother. I like to think things through, where as he barrels straight ahead without a thought about the consequences."

"Sounds like a fun guy to me," Deanie said.

"Fun?" Russ gave a derisive snort. "Ken is the most irresponsible person I know. I've spent half my life getting him out of one scrape or another."

"Like?" Deanie probed.

Russ thought for a moment. A slight smile touched the corner of his lips.

"I see that look. No holding out on me now," Deanie laughed.

"Well," Russ began, "there was the time he jumped off the roof of the house onto the garage. He broke an arm and Dad had to replace parts of the roof. Of course, I got blamed."

"How come?"

"He said it was a dare."

"Was it?"

"Kind of, I guess," Russ smiled. "More like I told him he needed to retrieve the cigarettes he had stashed under the eaves. I thought they might spontaneously combust or something," he laughed.

"So why didn't you tell your parents?" Deanie asked.

"Not my style," Russ replied with a light grin. "Nobody likes a tattle tale."

"More like, you wanted in on the stash," Deanie offered with a raised brow.

"Maybe," Russ conceded.

"Okay. But that's kid stuff," Deanie continued. "Tell me something else. Something serious."

"Well, how about this," Russ replied. He leaned forward, too, meeting her eyes head on. "During High School Ken was dating these three girls simultaneously. It was up to me to keep his social calendar straight, so he didn't get killed, so to speak."

"Hm, that one's pretty low," Deanie said. "Although, I'd say, aiding and abetting is just about the same thing as being caught in the act, so. . ."

"Still no sympathy for my plight," Russ cut in with a grin. He was finally feeling relaxed in her presence. Or was it all nerved up? He held her gaze until his eyes slid lower to focus on her bow shaped mouth . . . her beautiful soft lips curved up in that playful, oh so soft way ...

"No sympathy what so ever," Deanie laughed, breaking the spell as she shifted her eyes away and took a sip of her wine. "Besides, if that's the best you can come up with, well, I'd say your brother is a real saint. You wouldn't believe some of the crap me and Brent have gotten ourselves into."

"I'll bet," Russ nodded. "Care to share?"

"I don't want to shock you," Deanie quipped and set her glass down.

"Maybe this responsible guy could use a shock to the system," Russ said.

"Oh? And what are you suggesting?" she asked, raising an eyebrow.

You really don't want to know, Russ thought. He captured her gaze once again and their eyes bantered for a few moments until Deanie's eyelashes fluttered downward. Oh God! What kind of game was he trying to play here?

He cleared his throat and sat back in his chair. "All teasing aside, Ken has real problems. He has trouble holding down a decent job, he's a compulsive gambler, and his marriage is constantly on the rocks."

"Sometimes people learn from their mistakes," Deanie offered. "I've had my fair share of trouble. But I think it helps build character."

"I suppose that is one way of looking at it."

"Jack always talks about how hard it was for him after my mother passed away, but I'm not sure that he and I would have been as close if she was still alive. Not that I wouldn't have loved to have a mother, but she probably would have ended up staying at home with me all the time while he was on the road, and who knows - they may have drifted apart. It happened to Brent that way. His Dad was on the road all the time, and pretty soon his folks got divorced and. . . but then again that probably wouldn't have happened with Jack and my mother. Even though they were complete opposites, they would have loved each other to the bitter end." Deanie stopped and looked at Russ. "Am I rambling? Just tell me to stop

31

if I am. I kind of get carried away at times and. . . are you laughing at me?"

Russ's eye brows rose in surprise. He *had* been watching her animated account with fascination, but hoped he hadn't been grinning like a schoolboy. "No, no. I'm not laughing in the least. Please go on."

She looked at him skeptically. "I know when I've been rambling. I can see it on your face. I can hardly be Jack Burton's daughter and not ramble just a little bit. Although I've been told I look like my mother, I'm more like Jack in personality. She was a quiet, steady type, whereas Jack's a bundle of nervous energy. Always on the go."

"Like you?"

"I guess. But getting back to Jack and my mother, I was just thinking how it seems so strange that opposites seem to attract like that. Don't you think?"

"I, uh, suppose." He focused on the candle flickering between them instead of her face.

"Now take me and you, for instance. We're pretty opposite, wouldn't you say?" She looked at him squarely, almost daring him to look away this time. When he didn't respond she continued. "And I don't mind saying that I find you attractive. Does that embarrass you? Because I don't mean for it to embarrass you. I'm just trying to be honest here. In fact, you're really quite sexy. For an accountant."

Russ sputtered his wine. He managed to cough into his napkin without choking.

"You see?" Deanie continued, "I can tell by your reaction that you're embarrassed. Why is that? People just don't speak honestly. Like a few minutes ago, I was sure you were, you know, like maybe coming on to me or something. Unless I was reading it wrong. But when I just come right out and say it, you almost choke to death."

"Um . . . I don't even know what to say," Russ responded, still dabbing his mouth.

"I wasn't telling you that I thought you were sexy because I'm expecting something to come out of it," she explained. "I just happened to be thinking it at the time, and didn't see any harm in telling you, that's all. So don't panic, or anything. I mean, really. This is the eighties. You'd think by now we could just let it all out."

32

"And it appears you're doing just that," Russ quipped.

"Well, Jack raised me to just tell it like it is. Really, when you think about it, it's about time there was some equality between the sexes. I mean, men say all kinds of things to women all the time and get away with it. And what about sleeping around? If a guy does it, no big deal. But a girl? She's a slut. It's not really fair. There should be the same rules for everyone, don't you think?" she stopped abruptly and looked at Russ. "Am I rambling again?"

Russ just raised an eyebrow.

"I was, wasn't I?"

"It's okay," Russ replied. "Kind of lightened the mood. It was getting pretty heavy there for a minute," he laughed.

Deanie nodded with a smirk. "Sorry. You're probably thinking, 'What kind of nut case is she anyway?' Right?"

"Not exactly," Russ smiled. "It's probably best that you don't know what I was thinking."

Their eyes caught and held - again. Just when he thought things were getting back to light conversation, one word, one look, and they were right back to the sexually charged atmosphere that threatened to squeeze the life right out of him. The air in the restaurant was heavy with it.

"I'll get the bill," Russ said, his voice a low rumble.

There was no need for conversation as Russ paid the waiter. Body language said it all. Loud and clear.

He put his hand on the small of Deanie's back as he guided her toward the exit. It burned like a brand. Once out on the deck, he was able to breath again, taking in the freshness of the night air as it wafted off the nearby lake. The strains of a slow jazz tune drifted out into the coolness of the night from an open side door.

"Now what?" Deanie asked, her lips turning up slightly at the corners. She reached for his hand, which was still along the small of her back and used it to turn a slow pirouette until they were facing one another. Russ's eyes were still darkly intense as he focused on her. He wondered if he was going to kiss her on the spot. "Let's dance," she giggled. "You're way too tense. Besides, this is a good one."

"I don't really dance much," Russ faltered, blinking back to reality.

"Don't be silly. It'll help you relax and it's easy," Deanie said. "You just put your hands here and here and sway to the music. Like this."

The seductive melody, combined with the close proximity of her body, effectively chased any notion of relaxing far from Russ's mind. His arms moved to enclose Deanie's slim waist even tighter as her arms crept up around his neck.

Russ inhaled deeply of her scent. It had been a long time since he'd felt this urge to protect and care for someone. Sure, he was able to express the paternal side of those feelings, but this was different. His mind jerked abruptly. Paternal side? He stopped swaying and held Deanie away by the shoulders. "How old are you?" he demanded. When she didn't answer right away he repeated the question, as if to a child. "I said, how old are you?"

"Does it matter?" Deanie asked, stepping back, her brow furrowed.

His arms dropped to his sides. "It matters to me," he said flatly.

"Twenty one," Deanie replied.

Russ groaned. "It's as bad as I thought." He turned and took a few decisive steps away from her.

"And just what is that supposed to mean?" she clipped, folding her arms.

"You're practically still a baby."

"I can almost bet you weren't thinking that a minute ago," Deanie countered.

"I don't know what I was thinking. I need to get back to reality," he said, running a hand through his closely cropped hair.

"Reality is what people feel," Deanie stated. "Age is irrelevant."

"How would you know?" He looked at her squarely. "You're only twenty one."

"Just how old are you, then, if it's so important?" Deanie asked, coming closer and running her hands up and down his biceps. She didn't look him in the eye, but focused her eyes on the rhythmic movement of his chest as he breathed.

"A lot older than you, that's for sure." Russ could feel himself melting, any resolve he may have left, seeping out with each stroke of her hand along the fabric of his jacket.

"Now you're the one not answering my question," she said, a hint of seduction in her voice.

"Thirty five," Russ enunciated each syllable.

"Oh my! You really are over the hill," Deanie said, her mouth coming dangerously close to his as she leaned toward him on tip toe.

"Too old to be acting like an adolescent." Any further protest was silenced as their lips came together. Neither one was prepared for the intensity of passion that seemed to instantly ignite.

Russ pulled away first, breathing heavily. He broke free from her embrace and turned, taking a step away for safety's sake, running his hand through his hair. "Nope," was all that came out of his mouth.

"Let me tell you something," Deanie said, coming up behind him. "Jack was forty years old when he married my mother, and she was only twenty-four. But they didn't let a number stand in the way of what they felt for each other. And that's all age is, Russ. A number. It has nothing to do with how mature you are, or what kind of a person you are, or what you can offer someone."

Russ was staring out over the rippling water of the lake. The dark silhouette of Black Island loomed in the distance. Deanie moved to stand beside him. "What are you really afraid of?" she asked gently.

"Right now I'm mostly afraid of myself," he admitted.

"Then let me help you stop being afraid," Deanie whispered, placing her hands on the muscles of his chest as she leaned into him.

Russ looked down into Deanie's large, luminous eyes, and saw mirrored there his own awakened desire. For a fleeting second he was tempted to throw caution to the wind. But only for a second. The old Russ wouldn't allow it. He shook his head. "You don't seem to understand," he said soberly. "A relationship between us would have absolutely nowhere to go."

"How do you know?"

"Because I'm older and wiser."

She didn't laugh at his vain attempt at a joke. "Okay. So who said anything about a relationship? This is the eighties, Russ. Did you miss the sexual revolution, or something?"

He looked at her, hard. "Is that it, then? This is only about sex?"

"No," she responded. "Well, maybe." She threw up her hands. "I don't know! Geez! Usually that's the girl's line of defense. You're getting me all confused."

"You and me, both," he quipped. He let out a gust of air and rubbed the back of his neck.

"There's something going on here, Russ," Deanie said. "And it scares the hell out of me, too. And no, it's not just about the sex. There's more. Some kind of chemistry, or something. Don't you feel it?"

"I feel it, alright," Russ nodded gruffly. He did. But what was its name? Attraction? Curiosity? Lust, maybe? "I'm not one to go on feelings alone. I won't make the same mistake again."

"Mistake?" Deanie raised her eyebrows, obviously hurt. "Thanks."

"I didn't mean it that way," Russ shook his head

"No? Then what did you mean?"

Russ looked up at the night sky for a moment, taking in a prolonged breath. He expelled it and turned to look at Deanie. "I was married once. A long time ago."

Deanie blinked. "Okay. And . . .?"

"But now I'm not. End of story." He turned away and gazed across the lake.

"How long were you married?" she asked.

Russ just laughed, an unpleasant sound. "Not very long, thank goodness. It's been over long enough that it shouldn't matter any more."

"But it does," she said quietly.

A slight breeze rustled through the trees sending whispered messages among the leaves. It ruffled Russ's hair, making him look younger and more vulnerable.

"You want to talk about it?" Deanie asked. She reached out and touched his sleeve.

"Not really."

"Come on, then. Let's sit down over there and just watch the water." She guided him to a deck chair and they sat silently for a few minutes, taking it in. A harvest moon hung low over the silhouetted forms of the trees, casting an orange trail across the rippling water of the lake. The rhythmic sound of waves gently lapping against the shore provided a background for the melancholy song of a loon.

Deanie shivered.

"Are you cold?" Russ asked. "Here, take my jacket." Without waiting for her consent, he slipped his suit jacket over her shoulders.

"Thanks," Deanie said. She snuggled into the warmth of the jacket, letting the heat that lingered from Russ's body seep into her own as his scent enveloped her.

"I have a son," Russ offered, still gazing straight ahead. "He's eleven."

Deanie took this information in. "He live with you?"

Russ nodded. "His mother abandoned us when he was just a baby." He wasn't sure why he was telling her this. Now, when he'd said he didn't want to talk about it. But somehow it seemed important that she know. That she understand why a relationship would be a mistake.

There was silence for a moment.

"Guess that's why you're kind of bitter about it," Deanie mused.

"You think?" Russ asked, allowing a twisted grimace to cross his features.

"You need to let it go."

Russ let out a deep gust of air. "It's hard. The whole marriage was a mistake right from the beginning. It barely lasted a year. Then Miranda took off and left when Mark was only four months old. What kind of a mother would do that?"

"I'm. . . I don't know," Deanie responded, for once at a loss for words.

"Mark's never even met his mother," Russ continued. "She's never bothered to contact him. Not even a card on his birthday."

"Oh. I'm sorry," She reached over to lay a sympathetic hand on Russ's arm.

In the emotion charged atmosphere, the heat of her hand seemed to seer right through Russ's sleeve. The weight of it was as heavy as a stone. He was filled with a swirling mixture of anger and bitterness that the memories of his past had brought to the surface. He felt renewed mistrust and disillusionment with womankind in general, not at all helped by the new and unnamed feelings that this woman had ignited within him. He stood abruptly and took a deep, steadying breath in an attempt to regain his composure.

"There's nothing to be sorry about anymore. I made a mistake, and I've learned to live with the consequences," he finally said.

"Have you?"" Deanie asked.

"Yes."

"It seems to me you're being awfully hard on yourself. Everybody makes mistakes."

"Not me," Russ laughed. The sound was harsh and self depreciating. "Good old Russ Graham. Always steady. Always dependable. Always in control. Then once - just once! I let my guard down and wham! My whole life turned upside down."

"Come on, you're not the first person to get divorced," Deanie reasoned.

"It's more than that. The whole thing was just such a bitter disappointment to my parents. They were good Christian people. Now, if it had been Ken, they wouldn't even be shocked." He shook his head and finished with a touch of bitter irony, "But I had never let them down before. It hit pretty hard."

"Sounds to me like your pride is hurting more than anything," Deanie observed.

He snorted. "Thanks."

"Sorry," she apologized. "That was rude. The old 'say the first thing that comes into your head' syndrome again."

"Don't worry about it," Russ replied, his voice curt. "I shouldn't have unloaded on you like that."

Deanie surveyed him closely. "You gonna be okay?" she placed her hand on his arm again. This time it made his skin crawl.

"Of course," he laughed, moving away so that her hand lost contact. "Always." The concern on her face was irritating. He turned away.

"Good," Deanie responded flatly. She waited. There was nothing more. "So, what now?"

Russ just shrugged.

"I guess that's it then," Deanie said.

"I guess."

"You're just going to shut me out. Just like that," she stated.

Russ considered her words for a moment. He *was* shutting her out. He could feel it just as if it were a tangible thing. Like a shade was being drawn, blocking out the sun. Good. It was for the best. "I'm not sure what else you expected," he responded coolly.

Deanie sighed and then threw up her hands. "Thanks for dinner."

"You're welcome."

Deanie slid the jacket from her shoulders and handed it to Russ. He took it without saying anything. She blinked, obviously fighting back the tears that threatened and spun on her heel. Russ watched her retreating figure. Head held high she marched toward the entrance, her cowboy boots clicking loudly on the wooden terrace. Each reverberation sent a jolt right through his gut. Good. Let her think he didn't care. It was much safer that way.

Chapter Six

"Hey, hon. You all right?" Toby asked, scrutinizing Deanie's face. The jazz ensemble was gathered at their usual front table, taking a break, and Deanie had just joined them.

"Fine," she said, smiling brightly. Toby didn't buy it for a minute.

"Your date not pan out so well?" he asked.

"Sh!" She looked around to make sure her father hadn't heard. He and Benny were engaged in an animated conversation. Max was up at the bar getting a drink. "I don't want Jack to hear. He's way over protective as it is."

"You know what they say," Toby shrugged. "Don't nothin' chase the blues like singin' the blues. How 'bout it? You sounded so pretty this afternoon. These folks deserve a treat."

"The owners won't mind?"

"Are you kidding? It'll up their business if anything. And it'll make your dad so proud."

"Okay," Deanie smiled. "First two in the next set. You pick."

❧

Russ scanned the lounge. It was time to take his perceived responsibilities in hand and check on his older brother. At least that way, he wouldn't be able to focus on his own confused feelings.

It didn't take long to spot Ken. He was sitting with a colleague, talking loudly above the general din. "Hi, bro," Ken waved. "Have a seat."

Russ did just that. Ken didn't appear to be too inebriated. . . yet. He didn't see Kathy anywhere, though. Maybe she was up in their room. So much for their romantic weekend get away.

"Oh, by the way, this is my brother," Ken said to the other man.

Russ shook his hand and introduced himself, then turned back to Ken. "Where's Kathy?"

"Around here somewhere," Ken shrugged. "Hey, weren't you on a date or something?"

Russ ignored him and signaled for the waitress.

Suddenly a husky female voice reached out to him across the room. There she was on stage. As slim and graceful as she had been not long ago in his arms. And the voice. Never had he heard such a beautiful sound. So full of raw emotion and power.

Warmth tingled through Russ's body as a dull ache formed in the pit of his stomach.

"Guess your date had another gig," Ken observed, leering slightly. "Not bad. . . "

Russ swallowed half of the amber liquid in one gulp, taking a moment for the fire in his throat to disperse as he swirled the remaining contents around in the glass. Slow down, he cautioned, before taking another, slower sip. The song ended to resounding applause and the group launched into another livelier tune. Russ couldn't take another one. He slammed the remaining contents and rose to leave.

"Leaving so soon?" Ken asked.

"Yep. Early day tomorrow. Gotta get back to town," Russ replied.

Ken just shrugged.

Russ couldn't get out of there fast enough. He made a bee line for the side exit and expelled a pent up breath once back out in the openness of the night air. For some reason, his feet led him back to a now familiar deck chair. He sat down in it, daring the music to try and tantalize his memory.

Instead, unhappy thoughts of his previous marriage rose up to taunt him. Women were nothing but trouble. They were put on this earth to torment unsuspecting men. He was glad he'd listened to his sensible side and turned her away. Getting emotionally involved only led to heart ache.

He had been just twenty-three when he first met Miranda. A hard working honor student holding down a part time job at a gas station. The pride and joy of his parents. It was an image he'd worked hard to cultivate, falling as he did in the shadow of his rebel rousing older brother.

One day, he and a couple of his buddies were sitting in a booth at a small café - one of the haunts of the college set. There was this one particular waitress. She'd caught the eye of more than one of the younger male patrons, but had never paid any particular attention to him or any of his buddies before. However, this particular day, she seemed to make a point of singling him out. She purposely leaned over a little farther than necessary as she passed him his coke, and gave him more than one inviting glance as she went about her work.

It was obvious she was hot for him. So his buddies said. They dared him to ask her out. To his surprise, she accepted without any hesitation. Later that evening, he picked her up at the small apartment she was sharing with some girlfriends, and took her to a drive in movie.

He had been brought up in a home where high moral standards and Biblical principles were strictly adhered to. Included in that list was the command to 'save' one's self for marriage. To say that he was inexperienced would have been an understatement. But there, in the back seat of a car, at a sleazy drive in movie, he made love to a woman for the first time in his life.

He didn't see Miranda again. At least not right away. In fact, he avoided the cafe where she worked like the plague. The truth was, he was overwhelmingly ashamed of himself. He knew he'd done something wrong; broken a commandment or something. But mostly he was ashamed at his own response to the experience. Sometimes he caught himself reliving the whole thing, wishing for a repeat.

Then, just before school was about to begin again that fall, Miranda showed up on his parent's doorstep. She was pregnant and needed money for an abortion.

Abortion. The word itself still stabbed like a knife. Like a blow square in the gut. God must be punishing him for his sins. He wasn't ready for fatherhood, but the thought of the child - his child - being executed, was more than he could stand. No. He would do the right thing.

He remembered the day like it was yesterday. He had grabbed Miranda by the arm, marched her right into his parent's living room, and there, before his totally unprepared parents, he'd announced that Miranda was pregnant and they were getting married.

His parents never came right out and said it, but he knew, from the grim look in his father's eyes, and the pained look on his mother's face. He'd hurt them deeply. His one misdemeanor had affected them more than all of Ken's antics put together. He knew that his mother spent many hours in fervent prayer for her wayward son. He had vowed early on that he would never put his parents through the kind of disappointment and disgrace that his older brother had. Yeah, right. With one smooth move he'd unraveled all of the trust and respect he'd worked so hard for. And even though it had all happened years ago, he still had trouble letting go of the guilt.

The marriage had been difficult right from the start. He put in extra hours at the gas station while still keeping up his studies. It was tough. Really tough. Then Mark was born, just before Christmas – a six pound eight ounce son who looked just like him. Good thing, too. He'd heard some nasty rumors about Miranda's penchant for sleeping around, but one look into the tiny infant's eyes and there was no doubt about where he came from. Finishing his schooling almost seemed like an impossibility at times, though. But he'd doggedly continued. Russ Graham was not a quitter. Then, just as he was preparing to write his last set of exams. the final blow.

He'd found the note propped on the nightstand:

"I never wanted this life. I'm not ready to be a mother and I don't love you. Please take care of him and I won't bother you again. Have a good life. Miranda."

'Have a good life?' What did that mean, anyway? Thanks a lot, God. I think I've paid enough, already. Fortunately, his mother stepped in, and he was able to complete his exams and graduate. But once he'd made it over that hurdle, he never looked back. He found himself a good job, bought his own house, and determined to take care of his own responsibilities.

It was funny, looking back on it now. Russ couldn't imagine life without Mark. But the early days had been a struggle. He'd worked hard to build a life for himself and his son. They were traveling down the path that he had carefully charted. But now, suddenly, his mind was in turmoil. All because of some red haired girl-woman.

She was nothing like Miranda. And he was no longer the inexperienced idealist. That was a different era and he a different man. He should just take whatever she was willing to offer, no strings attached. What difference would it make? It wasn't like he'd become a monk since getting divorced. But this was different somehow. Scary and unpredictable. Something he just couldn't put his finger on.

He closed his eyes, letting the music – her voice – sooth his raw emotions like a balm. When it stopped he allowed the reverberations still lingering in his brain to continue to work their magic. He would make love to her, he realized, if she were here with him now. He wouldn't be able to stop himself. He wouldn't *want* to stop himself.

Suddenly his eyes flew open, sensing her presence. It was as if the very thoughts that had been swirling around his fevered mind had summoned her.

"Hi," she offered, her voice barely above a whisper.

"Hi."

"You're still here."

"Yep."

Their eyes locked, as had happened so many times already in such a short space of time. He rose slowly and deliberately from the lounge chair. This time he initiated the kiss, long and slow, taking Deanie's breath completely away. When they finally parted, his eyes sought hers with a question. One that needed no words. Her own answer was just as evident. He kissed her again, gently, and then took her smaller hand in his and led her toward the building.

Chapter Seven

The green of the grass was in startling contrast with the brilliant colors of the deciduous trees. Mingled among this vibrant palette was the darker shade of the conifers. A spectacular view of the lake spread out before her as Deanie struck out along the sandy white beach. The water was as still as glass. Not a cloud was reflected on its surface. She stood for a moment taking in the panorama, then released a satisfied sigh. She couldn't believe it had really happened. The thought of their love making, long into the night, sent a new wash of warmth and desire through her body. It was like heaven. She didn't remember the sensations being so intense, the passion so quick to surface – or even the grass so green! Maybe it was love.

She'd snuck back to her own room sometime in the wee hours, leaving Russ sound asleep under one sheet. She'd left him a note, propped on the nightstand that read, "See you later. D." She didn't want to leave, but knew her father would have something to say if she didn't make her presence known somehow. She managed to make enough 'waking up' noise and carry on the usual morning banter with Jack that she was sure he'd fall for it. He seemed content to continue sleeping now as she went for an early morning walk.

❦

Russ opened his eyes the moment Deanie slipped from the room. Part of him wanted to grab her and make love to her again, but another part – the real Russ, knew he should let her go. Now that he'd gotten the initial desire out of his system, thoughts of just what he was getting himself into crowded into his already confusion fogged brain.

That he desired her, he could not deny. He was shocked at how easily he had given in to the natural instincts that had been warring within him since the moment he'd seen her. She seemed to have a strange power over him that sucked the very self-control and reason right out of him. How did she manage it? She was no raving beauty. And she was much too young. And her upbringing! They were, for all intents and purposes, completely mismatched. And yet. . .

Animal lust was nothing to base a relationship on, Russ sternly chided himself. There had to be more than that. There had to be mutual respect. Common goals. Mark needed a mother, not an older sister. And trust? Russ admitted that he had a somewhat tainted view of the trustworthiness of women in general, but Deanie Burton seemed the least likely candidate to allay those suspicions. After all, what did he really know about her? A one night stand was not the best gauge with which to judge a person's character. Besides that, why was his mind even going in that direction? Who said anything about a lasting relationship? No strings. Remember?

So now what? Just lay here and wait for morning? Wait for her to come back to him or get up and find her? Meet her for breakfast maybe? He frowned. Ken might be there. And Kathy. The last thing he wanted was to be seen with her in a public place. Not after last night. He stopped, his own thoughts jolting in their tracks. If he was afraid to acknowledge their relationship in front of his family, even after last night, there was a real problem. Never mind Ken, what would Mark think? His mother?

No, this needed more careful consideration. A plan. He flung the sheet off his still naked body and sat up, flinging his legs to the side and onto the floor. Was it his imagination, or could he still smell her presence, lingering on the sheets, hovering over the bed. A good shower was what he needed. Wash his mind clean as well as his body.

As he stood up to stretch he noticed it. A note. Propped on the nightstand. For a second a dark vortex of dejavue engulfed him. *She'd left him a note.*

He reached out to touch it, then stopped. What it said didn't really matter. He already knew what he needed to do. It had come with sudden clarity. Any future dealings with Deanie Burton were ridiculous and futile. There was no hope of a future with a woman like her. They just didn't fit and to think otherwise was foolish. Why, he couldn't even stand the thought of being seen with her in public. What kind of a relationship was that? And he wasn't about to go sneaking around to various hotels around the city. No, he was better off not even reading it. What he needed was to pack up and get the hell out of there – fast. Before he changed his mind.

❧

Deanie arrived back at her room, refreshed and invigorated. And anxious to see Russ again. The prospects made her tingle.

"And don't you just look like the cat that swallowed the canary," Jack chirped, coming out of the bathroom, fresh from the shower.

Deanie just smiled even wider. "You're up bright and early."

"Toby wants to get back to town as early as possible. And he's driving."

"Oh. You're leaving already?" Deanie asked, not wanting to sound too anxious. With her Dad out of the way, she and Russ could be together all afternoon if they wanted.

"You were awfully late last night," Jack commented gruffly, looking his daughter in the eye before combing his few hairs into place. "Or was it early?" he added, eyeing her reflection in the mirror.

"Um, what do you mean?" she asked. "I came home."

"Hmph." He set the comb down. "You can't fool your old dad, you know."

"You knew I was out on a date," she hedged. "We just lost track of time."

"I'll bet," Jack grunted.

"Jack," Deanie rolled her eyes. "I'm not a baby anymore."

"I know," Jack huffed and sat down beside her on the bed. "But you're still my little girl. And it's hard for me to think of you with. . .well, you know. With a man."

47

"Jack," Deanie protested again.

"I know, I know!" Jack sputtered, flinging his hands in the air and rising. "The accountant, I suppose?"

"Um, let's not talk about it," Deanie said. "Now, do you want me to help you get packed?"

"What's your hurry?"

"You said Toby wanted to get going," she reminded.

"I suppose. Well, help me if you must," he blustered. "I know you're just trying to get rid of me. I wasn't born yesterday, you know."

"Don't be so silly," Deanie laughed. "You know you forget half your stuff when I'm not around to help you. Besides, I drove all the way out here and I might want to see a few sights before I have to drive all the way back to town."

"Sights?" Jack asked. "Now why didn't I think of that? I could stick around and ride back to town with you. The boys can handle all the equipment without me."

"Jack!" Deanie protested.

"Ah ha! I knew it," Jack winked. "Thought you were fooling your old dad, but I caught you. Don't worry, my dear, I won't spoil your time with this new beau. Just make sure he treats you right. And bring him around some time to meet me. Not like the last one."

"Don't worry, I will," Deanie smiled.

It was all she could do to see Jack and the rest of the troupe off. She kept thinking she'd caught a glimpse of Russ's dark head as she helped them pack up the van outside near the deck. She felt sure she'd run into him some time this morning. The resort wasn't that big.

Once they were gone, she scooted to the nearest telephone in the hotel lobby and dialed the number for his room. Her heart fluttered in anticipation as she waited. No answer. Maybe he was in the shower. She could surprise him by just going up.

Into the elevator. Press the button. Waiting. . . Swoosh! The door opened and she practically bolted for the corridor that led to *him*. Suddenly she stopped in her tracks. Her eyes darted to the room number once again, just to be sure. The door was ajar. Housekeeping was already vacuuming and making up the bed.

"Um . . . excuse me?" Deanie asked, peering into the room. "Do you know what time he – I mean, Mr. Graham left?"

The cleaning woman frowned and then shut off her vacuum.

"Has he checked out already?" Deanie repeated.

The larger woman just shrugged. "I guess. I just clean rooms."

"Thanks," Deanie shouted behind her, running for the elevator once again.

"Excuse me," Deanie said, arriving at the front counter. "Has a Mr. Russ Graham checked out already?"

The man behind the desk surveyed his records. "Yes. Very early this morning, I'm afraid. Is everything alright?"

Was everything alright? Deanie blinked, considering the question for a moment. "Um, yeah. Thanks." She turned, a horrible sick feeling growing in the pit of her stomach. He'd checked out. Early this morning. Without even telling her.

What had she expected, anyway? A tear fell and she brushed it away with vehemence. It wasn't like she was some kind of blushing virgin. So she'd slept with a guy. Big deal. She was the one who'd opened her big mouth about the 'sexual revolution' in the first place.

But this was different. She wasn't prepared for the absolute and total rejection. She sure knew how to pick them. Oh well. She'd get over it. She was tough. She had to be.

SECOND MOVEMENT:
Andante

Chapter Eight

Deanie emerged into the crisp autumn air and skipped down the stately stone steps, her breath sending a white puff into the atmosphere. It was cold for October. She crossed the University campus at a brisk pace, heading for the student parking lot and her beat up blue Chevette. A few leaves remained stubbornly intact along the tree lined walk, but for the most part, they crunched underneath her feet. A sign of colder days to come.

It was hard to believe she was already through half of this first semester. It had been a tough haul, so far. Especially these dreaded Friday afternoon classes. And if that wasn't enough, she was working double shifts at Georgio's. It wasn't a job she loved. Bar room waitresses had to put up with a lot from some of the customers. But the tips were good, the hours steady, and she knew full well that her father couldn't afford to put her through university on his own.

She reached her car and let herself in, shutting the door with a decisively tinny clunk. The Chevette had seen better days, but it beat taking the bus. Especially when she had to work late. There was one good thing about being so busy. At least she didn't have time to think about *him*. Actually that wasn't quite true. She had thought a lot about him in the past six weeks. Too much. She couldn't get him out of her head sometimes. . . the sound of his voice, the look in his eyes, the way they'd made love. . .

She swore sharply as she ran a red light. She needed to concentrate. But that man was making it awfully difficult. She could have looked him up once back in the city. But why humiliate herself further? He'd made it perfectly clear he wanted nothing more to do with her, the way he'd just up and took off. It still stung. Especially after all they'd shared in that one brief, heavenly night.

She gritted her teeth, accelerating just a bit too quickly through the next intersection. He just wasn't her type, anyway. He was a straight laced, stuffy accountant with baggage from the past. She, on the other hand, liked to have some fun. So good riddance. Yeah. That's right.

She released her foot from the gas as she neared the next light. Who was she trying to kid? She was an impetuous, disorganized, mess, that's what. An ex rock and roll junkie who was still trying to get herself together. Life sucked.

There was a good two hours before she had to be at work. She should really head home and try to get started on some of those assignments that seemed to be constantly looming. The thought was disheartening. What she really needed was some friendly companionship. There would be plenty of time for homework tomorrow. Decision made, she took the next exit.

Deanie swung her small car down the narrow street where her friend Brent Walters lived and parked her Chevette under one of the huge elm trees that lined the street. He and two members of his current rock band shared the older three-story house. The house and yard were not very well kept up, and sometimes the neighbors complained about the noise, but generally it was a great place for the group to rehearse. And a great place to get away for awhile. She hadn't spend much time with him lately, but if anybody could cheer her up, it was Brent.

Deanie knocked on the door, then poked her head inside. "Yoo-hoo!" she called. She stooped to pick up a huge gray cat that came gliding towards her. "Hi, Freddie," she cooed, scratching him behind the ear. The monstrous feline purred and bent his head for more. "Are you the only one home?"

As if in answer to her question, a voice boomed from somewhere in one of the back rooms. "Coming!"

The voice belonged to Chris Nambert, owner of the cat, and current drummer in Brent's rock group. The fact that he was a drummer brought back some painful memories. But Chris had turned out to be a loyal friend.

Nothing like Brad.

He appeared in the hallway just as Deanie released Freddie. "Hi," he said as he scooped the cat up and began stroking his slick gray coat. Chris was a giant of a man at least six foot seven and had to duck his head as he led the way into the living room turned rehearsal studio. For anyone first meeting him, he was an intimidating figure and he played the part of the Bohemian musician to a 'T'. He wore his curling blonde tresses well below his shoulders, lots of chunky chain jewelry, and he liked to show off his muscled tattoos by always wearing sleeveless T-shirts, even in winter. But once you got to know him, it was evident that he was a bigger pussycat than Freddie.

"Where's Brent?" Deanie asked as they entered the living room. Equipment, wires and speakers took up the entire space. She stepped over a cord, and peered at some music scrawled on a scrap of paper.

"He's off with his latest flame," a voice said from somewhere. A head popped up from behind a keyboard.

"Grant!" Deanie exclaimed, her hand on her heart. "You scared me! I didn't see you there!"

"Just patching up some wires," Grant drawled. "You're looking good, as usual."

"Sure, sure. All talk, no action," Deanie quipped.

"You want action? You've come to the right source, baby," Grant winked, still working on the wires.

"Whatever," Deanie laughed. "I've got your type figured out."

Grant was the keyboard player in Brent's band, and fancied himself a real ladies' man. He was of average height and build, with longish curling brown hair and small wire rimmed glasses. He really wasn't anything spectacular to look at, if you really took the time to inspect him, but he did have a certain easy going charm, and did in fact, seem to attract his share of the women. But Deanie knew she was in no danger. She had long since made that point clear. It was just a game they played.

"So what new woman are we talking about here?" Deanie asked, running her fingers over the keyboard.

"Huh?" Chris asked, frowning.

"Brent. New flame. You guys said he was seeing some one. Duh!"

53

Deanie teased, throwing up her hands.

"Oh, that," Chris shrugged.

"You don't know?" Grant asked. "I thought Brent told you everything. Geez, maybe he didn't want you to get jealous."

"Come off it," Deanie said, giving him a swat. "You know Brent and I are practically like brother and sister. I guess I just haven't been around much lately."

"Remember when he cut his hand, working on his car?" Grant asked.

"Yeah, I talked to him on the phone after that."

"Well, it appears he took a shine to the little nurse who looked after him in the emergency room," Grant finished the story with a grin. "I couldn't have done better myself."

"Oh, please," Deanie rolled her eyes. "Your ego is the size of this room."

"He's late for rehearsals half the time," Chris offered. "And he used to give *us* shit for being late."

"Oh, he gives us all kinds of excuses," Grant continued, "but we know exactly what he's been up to."

"I can't believe it," Deanie smiled. "I mean, its great, but its not like Brent to let anything come before his music."

"Maybe he's bit the big one this time," Grant suggested with a shrug.

"Poor sucker," Chris added. "I'm grabbing a beer," he announced, heading toward the kitchen. "Anyone else want one?"

"Sure," Grant responded. "How about you, Dee?"

"Nah," she shook her head. "Not tonight."

Just then they heard a motorcycle pull up in front. Deanie peered out the window to see who it was. Len Colby was the only member of Brent's group that had been with him in the 'old days'. He played the bass guitar like nobody else she knew. Kind of with the same intensity as her dad. But apart from his music, Len was a very reserved person. He always looked the same - hair tied back in a haphazard ponytail, rumpled jeans and T-shirt, slightly stooped and thin. He was also the only member of the present group that chose to live on his own.

Len slouched into the room, nodding a greeting toward everyone in general, before opening his guitar case and gently removing the instrument.

"So, Len. How's life?" Deanie asked.

He just shrugged, busy tuning the guitar. "The usual. You?"

"Okay. School's a drag," Deanie replied and yawned. "You know how it is."

"Hardly," Grant joined the conversation. "You forget you're hangin' with a bunch of drop outs. Present company excluded, of course," he added with a grin. Len kept tuning his bass, ignoring the jibe.

Chris returned a few moments later with two beer and handed one to Grant. "Beers in the fridge, Len, if you want one." He let out a loud belch. "Boss man just pulled up in back."

They all heard the back door slam, and in a minute, Brent Walters came bounding into the room. "Hey, Dee! Haven't seen much of you lately. Sorry I'm a bit late, guys." He tossed his jacket into a corner. "So, we ready or what?"

"How is the little lady?" Grant asked, eye brows raised.

Brent just made a dismissive sound and busied himself with his guitar. "I had to stay late after work, that's all."

"Whatever you say, Buddy," Chris said with a grin.

"Come on, you guys. I mean it," Brent laughed.

"So what's this I hear about a new woman in your life?" Deanie piped up.

"Don't believe a word these clowns say," Brent laughed, gesturing in their general direction

"I don't know. . ." Deanie shrugged, a playful grin in place. "It sounds kind of serious. I'm a wee bit hurt that you didn't mention it."

"Okay, what have you guys been telling her?" Brent asked in a warning tone.

"Nothing. Just that you've been out playing doctor a lot lately. Or should I say 'nurse'?" Grant teased.

"So come on Brent. Who is she?" Deanie persisted.

"Forget it," Brent sighed, shaking his head with a grin. "I'm not saying a word in front of this crowd. It's time to rehearse. No more questions."

Amid more guffaws and good-natured banter, they finished tuning their instruments before the jam session started in earnest. They began with the usual mix of rock and roll standards that they played in local bars and clubs. Although the group's sound wasn't exactly 'heavy metal', it definitely had a hard edge to it.

Deanie just closed her eyes and let the music transport her to a happier time. This was where she belonged. Where she felt safe and accepted. She could just be herself and not worry about trying to fit into someone else's mold.

Sometimes she wondered if she was making the right choices with her life. Music was such an integral part of her and Brent kept hounding her about joining their band. At times like this she was almost ready to say yes. Almost. She just wasn't sure if she was ready for it, though. Or strong enough. On the other hand, maybe she wasn't cut out for social work, either. She really wasn't a nine to five type of person. But she did like working with people and had an honest desire to help others and she certainly didn't want to end up working as a waitress for the rest of her life. She let out a sigh. She was a screw up, plain and simple. That's all there was to it.

At least she still had Brent. Brent was her one constant, non-judgmental supporter. Sure she had Jack, but fathers took things too personal sometimes. She fondly watched as Brent stopped to adjust his foot pedal, head bent low over his instrument, his hair curtaining his face. She and Brent had been through a lot together.

"That last one okay for you guys?" Brent asked.

"I think we should up the tempo during the bridge," Grant suggested.

"Easy for you to say," Chris mumbled.

"I kind of wanted to spend some time on the new material," Brent said.

"Sure, why not?" Grant agreed. "We know most of that old shit in our sleep, anyway."

"Okay. How about that ballad we tried the other day? The new one." Brent turned to Deanie, apologizing. "I haven't named it yet. Why don't you try it out with us?" he suggested, handing her a piece of scrawled music.

"This another ploy to get me to join you?" Deanie laughed.

"Whatever works," Brent grinned. "Seriously, though. I think it'll really suit your voice."

"Let's hear it first," Deanie suggested.

The group started playing, with Brent singing the lyrics. It was a hard-edged ballad and he sang it with feeling. Brent had probably written hundreds of songs in his life, but this one seemed deep. Personal. "Brent, that was absolutely beautiful," Deanie breathed when they had finished. "When did you write this?"

He shrugged noncommittally.

"About the time he started seeing his little nurse friend," Grant offered with a sly smile.

"Come on. Not this again!" Brent exclaimed, rolling his eyes. There was a touch of irritation in his voice "Would you guys get off my case?"

"It really was beautiful, Brent," Deanie repeated. "And if your friend inspires that kind of writing, then I'd say you've got a pretty good thing going."

"So? You wanna give it a try?" Brent asked hopefully.

"Why not." Deanie glanced at her watch. "But then I have to get going. I work tonight."

"We're playing a gig at Georgio's," Brent informed. "Tomorrow night."

"No kidding? Then I guess I'll see you there, too. I work all weekend."

"If it sounds good, maybe we'll get you to sing it," Brent grinned wickedly.

"Why do I get the feeling I'm being used?" Deanie laughed. Brent kept grinning and signaled for Chris to count out the time.

🌺

The digits on the paper began to dance and blur. Russ squeezed his eyes shut and pinched the bridge of his nose between his thumb and index finger. He'd stayed at work later than usual trying to finish up some paperwork. At least, that's what he told himself. Closer to the truth, if he cared to admit it, was the fact that he just didn't want to go home. Mark was spending the weekend at his friend's farm, and Russ quite simply dreaded the thought of returning to a big, empty house. Alone.

With a sigh, he turned back to the papers, determined to carry on with his work.

A head poked around the door to Russ's office. "Quitting time, my friend. You're the last soldier standing." It was Josh Fredrickson, a fellow employee.

"Just finishing up," Russ clipped.

"You've been working like a son-of-a-gun lately," Josh noted with an easy grin. "The rest of the troops are starting to complain. Putting us all to shame."

"Just trying to stay ahead of the game," Russ returned, not bothering to meet the other man's gaze. "You know how it is."

"Sure do," Josh replied. "It's why I stayed a bit late myself. I could have taken it home, but the wife doesn't care for me bringing the office home with me, so to speak. Weekends are family time, you know."

"Right," Russ commented, still not looking up. The small pencil in his hand started tapping out a rhythm on the paper in front of him

"How's your son doing these days?"

"Fine. Just fine." Russ set the pencil down and forced himself to look at the other man. "He's fine."

"That's good to hear. We'll have to have you two over some time. You and your boy."

"Um, yeah. That'd be great." Russ glanced down at the papers again, working his jaw.

"Well, I better get going. You better call it quits soon, too, buddy." Josh waved and disappeared.

Russ inhaled deeply through his nostrils and then let out a heavy sigh. Not that he didn't like Josh. But there was something about that guy that made him feel edgy. He was just too. . . positive.

He forced his gaze back to the ledger sheet and sat there for a few seconds. With an oath, he slammed the offending file folder shut and pushed back in his chair. He might as well go home and watch TV. With a sigh, Russ got up from his desk, found his coat and turned out the light on his way out the door.

Josh. The guy could be down right irritating at times. Always so upbeat. Always so optimistic. He was a successful accountant, much like Russ, himself, but he made no bones about the fact that his life did not revolve around his career. Family came first, he said. And faith.

As if he had all the answers! Russ's frown deepened, as he got into his car and revved up the engine. Who did Josh Fredrickson think he was? Russ had been brought up in the church. Been baptized and confirmed. His parents, especially his mother, had a strong faith and believed in the power of prayer. As far as his own faith went, he was a good person – for the most part. That must count for something. So who was Josh Fredrickson to come along and make like he had the answer that everyone else had missed?

The lights of the downtown core had transformed the prairie city from plain daytime attire to one of beckoning nightlife. A steady stream of traffic on Portage created a ribbon of white and red, as headlights and tail lights briefly crossed paths. Friday night. A time to unwind with colleagues in a local pub, meet friends for a pint and a game of pool, or exchange quiet intimacies with a lover in a dusky lounge. Every flashing neon sign called, "Life's weary travelers stop here!" God knows life had been more than wearisome lately.

Before his sensible muse could convince him otherwise, he pulled into the parking lot of one of the popular downtown bars and cut the engine. Mark wasn't home anyway, so what could it hurt to stop for a cold one? Some of his colleagues frequented this place, if he remembered correctly, so maybe he could join them. Be sociable for a change. He deserved it after the way he'd been pushing himself so hard.

Once inside, he stood near the door for a minute, scanning the room. There was a marked contrast between the crisp night air and the close atmosphere of the lounge. He didn't see anybody he recognized, so he headed up to the bar to sit on a stool and ordered a draught. No point in going for the hard stuff. He just needed a little pick me up. The bartender plunked the beaded glass in front of him and he took a long gulp from its bitter frothiness, before casually glancing around the room again. He stopped short when he got to the front corner table. Not again.

It was almost too coincidental to be funny. There she was. Just as he remembered her. But now she was wearing a small money apron and was carrying an empty tray. She must work here, he realized. Of all the places to choose to have a beer!

Now what was he supposed to do? Just up and leave? Run away like some kind of adolescent? Memories of their one night together crashed into his brain, swirling emotions wrenching his gut like he was going to puke. What an ass to just leave like that. To just exit the building without so much as an explanation or a parting 'farewell'. He was a brute, even in his own eyes and deserved any retribution he now suffered. But if he stayed he'd have to apologize. Explain. Something he wasn't sure he could do since it didn't make any sense, even to himself. Maybe she just wouldn't notice him.

No such luck. He knew the minute she spotted him and watched as she wound her way through the crowd, finally coming to a stop directly beside him.

"Russ," she stated the obvious. Her voice sounded curt. Angry, even. He couldn't blame her.

"Hello Deanie," he replied. She was unexplainably attractive. Beautiful even. He wondered if the heat he felt suddenly infusing his body was reflected in his face.

"What are you doing here?" she asked, her voice softening somewhat.

"What does it look like?" Russ answered, gesturing at his beer. The smile he tried for looked stupid, he knew. Fake.

"Oh." There was a moment of awkward silence.

"Yeah. I just stopped in for a beer on the way home," he offered. "Some of the guys at work recommended the place."

"Of course. Then you weren't. . . looking for me or anything," she stated, searching his eyes.

What might have been remorse washed over him. He couldn't hold her gaze. "It's good to see you, though."

"Right." She clipped, nostrils flaring. "Good to see you, too," she bit out. "I better get back to work now. Take care of yourself." She turned to leave.

"Wait," Russ swung on the barstool and grabbed her arm before she could leave. "I. . . I just wanted to say. . . I'm sorry." It sounded pretty lame, even to him. He let his hand drop from her arm.

"Thanks." Her eyes narrowed and she swung away, leaving him to watch her quickly retreating figure. His own jaw clenched as he took in a steadying breath. With one fluid motion he downed the rest of his beer and rose to leave. What a pathetic fool he'd become. It was time to head

60

home, to the safety of his own domain.

Chapter Nine

It was all Deanie could do to maneuver her body through the required motions for the rest of the night. The nerve of that man! To come into *her* bar and act like nothing had happened between them. At least it should help get him out of her system, the unfeeling bastard.

She was stowing the last of some empty beer bottles into the recycling when someone came up behind her and poked her in the ribs. "Ah!" she screamed and almost dropped a bottle. "Brent!" she chided, trying for a kick. "Don't do that! I could have ripped your head off! I've had enough slime balls trying to make a pass at me for one night."

"Sorry," Brent held his hands up in defense. "Promise not to hurt me?"

Deanie gave him a playful swat. "What are you doing here?" She untied the tiny money apron that she wore and tossed it on to a shelf.

"I knew you were off soon, so I thought I'd come by and see if you wanted to go out for a coffee."

She was extremely tired, but the expectant look on his face made her agree. "Sure. I just have to get my coat."

They drove separate vehicles to their favorite all night truck stop along the Perimeter. Once inside, they slid into one of the vinyl covered booths and ordered coffee.

"You got a cigarette?" Deanie asked, rummaging in her purse.

"Nope. Trying to quit."

"Really?" Deanie asked, eyes wide. "Good for you! What brought that on?"

"It was time," Brent shrugged. "It's been twelve days, four hours, and six minutes now. Approximately," he added with a grin.

"It wouldn't have anything to do with a certain new friend, now would it?"

"Those guys have big mouths," Brent mumbled.

"Why so embarrassed? It's me, remember?"

"Yeah, I know. Sorry," Brent grinned. "Probably just because I want a cigarette."

"You and me both."

"Hey, I thought you quit," Brent narrowed his eyes.

"I did," Deanie stated matter of factly.

"So what are you doing trying to bum a cigarette?"

"I just feel like one, okay?" Deanie defended herself. "It's not like I'm going to start smoking again."

"Yeah, right. I've heard that line before."

Deanie ignored him and sauntered over to the cigarette machine. She returned with a package of her old brand, and lit one with relish.

"I'm serious about you joining the band, Dee," Brent said, leaning into the smoke that curled up from Deanie's cigarette. "All the guys are in favor of it. And after tonight's rehearsal, there's no question. We could really use you. You bring a certain. . . energy that we're lacking right now."

"Thanks, Brent. But I've told you already, I'm too busy at the moment."

"Right! With a bunch of classes that you hate."

"That's not fair, and you know it," Deanie replied. "I want to make something out of my life."

"And you think I don't?" Brent asked. Deanie wasn't sure if he were teasing or not. He usually wasn't this touchy.

"Hey, what's gotten into you? I didn't come here to argue with you, you know. I can do that at home with Jack."

"Sorry. How is he, anyway?"

"Okay, I guess. He's starting to slow down a lot, though. Sometimes I worry about him"

"He's no spring chicken, you have to remember. He and Dad are getting up there."

"True."

"So, if you don't want to quit school, then quit work. Georgio doesn't pay you enough anyway."

"Just stop it okay? If I want back in, you'll be the first to know. Great plan, by the way," she added sarcastically. "What would I do without a job? I still have to eat, you know."

"Right. And are you eating properly? Taking your vitamins?" He grinned.

"Yes, mother," Deanie rolled her eyes. "What's with you?"

"Just trying to distract you for a second." He leaned forward without warning and grabbed the cigarettes out of her hand.

"Hey! I thought you said you were quitting!" She made an attempt to retrieve the cigarettes, but he kept them effectively out of her reach until he'd lit one up.

"So did you, right?" He cocked an eyebrow, then blew the smoke in her direction.

Deanie laughed. "We're a pretty weak pair, huh?"

Brent sobered somewhat. "You could say that."

Deanie looked at her friend for a moment. "Is there something that you wanted to talk to me about? I mean, something in particular?"

"What makes you ask that?" Brent asked, trying to be casual as he removed some ashes from the tip of his cigarette by rolling it gently along the rim of the ash tray.

"I don't know. Maybe I've just been around you enough to know when there's something on your mind."

"Well. . ."

"Is it this new girlfriend? What's she like? And why are you acting so secretive about her?"

"Now who's being mother hen?" Brent teased. When he saw the genuine concern on Deanie's face, he immediately sobered. He let out a long breath. "She's great, Dee. You'd love her."

"So what is the problem, then?"

"Well, I don't know really, It's just —"

"Wait, wait, wait!" Deanie cut in. "Start at the beginning. I want to hear it all. How did you meet her, where is she from, and all that. Everything!"

64

"Let's see," Brent cocked his head to one side. "Well, I met her at the hospital. You know, after I cut my hand?"

"Yeah, I got that much from the guys. Said she was the emerge nurse, or something."

"Right. She was really nice, you know? Took the extra time for me when everyone else was rushing around. So, just up out of the blue, I asked her out for a coffee sometime. I never figured she's accept, her being the type she is."

"And what type would that be?"

"Oh, I don't know. Just kind of clean. Wholesome."

"Wholesome?" Deanie repeated skeptically.

Brent flushed. "I know. It sounds stupid. But anyway, I never figured she'd accept an invitation from a guy like me."

"Why not? You're the sweetest guy around," Deanie stated.

"True, but how was she to know that?" Brent laughed. "But anyway, she said she was off work in half an hour and suggested we meet for coffee then."

"So you did. Boom. Just like that."

"Right."

"And you've been seeing her ever since," Deanie nudged.

"Yes."

"Okay. Um, I don't see the problem," Deanie shook her head. "You like her, she likes you. . ."

"Well, its not exactly the way you think." Brent looked uncomfortably down at the smoke wafting from his cigarette.

"Brent! Just what are you trying to get at? I've known you long enough to know when you're trying to hide something."

"Well, its not quite the way everyone - the guys - think it is. I mean, she is a really super person. Different. But our relationship isn't. . . physical, you know?"

"So what you're trying to say is, she's a nice person but she's ugly," Deanie said, stubbing out her smoke.

"No!" Brent shook his head vigorously. "No. That's not it at all! She's beautiful."

"Okay. . . ?"

"Holly is like no one I've ever met before."

"Sounds like you're in over your head," Deanie commented.

"Maybe. And that's what scares me, I guess."

"Why? What are you scared of?"

"Myself. That I might blow it with her."

"You? Come on!" Deanie laughed.

"No, I mean it, Dee. I've never felt this way about someone before. And it scares the hell out of me."

"Does she know? How you feel, I mean?"

"That's the really bizarre part," Brent frowned. "Like I said, there's nothing physical between us. I mean *nothing*," he emphasized. "So how could she know? I've never even kissed her."

"Wow. That's not the impression I got from the guys this afternoon," Deanie mused.

"Exactly. I'm getting really tired of all their shit. Holly's not that kind of woman."

"Come on, Brent," Deanie scoffed, rolling her eyes. "What is she? A throw back to the Victorian era? That almost sounded archaic."

"Now don't you start. Holly is a really special woman and I'm not going to spoil it. She's got really high morals."

"So if you're not between the sheets like the guys think, what exactly are you doing with her all the time?"

"We talk. We go places," Brent shrugged, and reached for the pack of smokes again.

"You're doing it again," Deanie warned. "Trying to hide something from me. And what are you doing now? Chain smoking?"

Brent observed the half open pack in his hands for a minute, then closed them and set them with finality on the table. "You wouldn't believe me if I told you."

Deanie folded her arms. "Try me."

Brent opened his mouth to speak, then shook his head. "Naw. You'd never believe it."

"Come on," Deanie coaxed.

"You'll laugh."

"I'm not going to laugh!"

"Yes you will."

"Brent!"

"All right then," Brent said, taking a deep breath. "We talk about spiritual things a lot. Like the Bible mostly. And I even went to church once."

"What?" Deanie blurted. Whatever she'd been expecting, it wasn't this.

"I told you you'd laugh!" Brent scowled.

"I'm not laughing! Do you see me laughing?" she squeaked.

"Well, I knew you wouldn't believe me," Brent said, warming up to the topic now that it was out in the open. "It was kind of neat, though. Not what I expected. When she first asked me if I'd like to go I thought, 'No way!' I had visions of white haired old ladies taking a snooze. But man, was I wrong."

Deanie scrutinized her friend out of the corner of her eye. "My Brent? Set foot in a church?"

"What's wrong with that?" Brent defended. "I'm telling you, this place was rockin'. You should see it. Whole band up at the front - guitars, drums, the works. Music's not bad either. Reminded me of what our dads used to play."

"Sounds pretty whacked out to me," Deanie shook her head. "Sure it isn't some kind of weird cult or something?"

"Well, I must admit, I was a little freaked out while the one dude was praying. He was so intense! I kept my eyes open cause I thought something might swoop down from the ceiling."

Deanie giggled.

"There might be something to it, though," Brent continued. "The people there are all really nice and seem pretty happy. Maybe it really does make a difference."

"Careful," Deanie cautioned. "Don't go freakin' out on me and get religious."

"Holly says it's not 'religion' but a 'relationship'." Brent offered sheepishly, looking down at his mug.

Deanie's frown deepened. "Well, just be careful that's all."

"All the time," Brent quipped. "You know me." They sat in contemplative silence for a moment.

"Brent," Deanie finally spoke up. "Can I tell you something? It's kind of something that's been on my mind a lot lately, but I haven't discussed it with anybody."

"Of course, Dee. You know that."

"Well, its just. . . I've been having some trouble in the romance department myself lately."

"What kind of trouble? Some guy bothering you?"

"Well, no, not exactly." She sighed, then took the plunge. "It's just that I thought I was over it. This guy, I mean. We met out at Hecla on the Labor Day weekend when I went out to see Jack and the guys play."

"Okay . . ." Brent nodded. "And?"

Deanie shrugged, "Well, you know. We kind of had a little fling, sort of. No big deal. I mean - I don't know! It obviously meant nothing to him, cause he just took off the next morning. I know I should just forget about it, but I haven't been able to get him out of my head. I mean, its been weeks. Almost two months! I thought I was over it."

"But you're not," Brent stated.

Deanie shook her head. "No. Well, I mean, yes! I thought I was until I saw him again tonight."

"You saw him tonight?" Brent repeated.

"Mmhm. He came to Georgio's for a beer. It was bound to happen. Winnipeg's not *that* big," Deanie sighed. "I just wasn't prepared, that's all. To see him again. He made me feel like garbage. Like trash. He never even said good-bye." She forcefully brushed at a tear that threatened to spill over and sniffed.

Brent grabbed a napkin out of the dispenser and handed it to her. "That's bullshit and you know it," he stated. "Don't let some ass hole drag you down like that. I'd kick the shit out of him right now, if it'd make you feel any better."

"No thanks," Deanie smiled weakly. "Besides, he's not really like that. He warned me, I think. So it's my own fault."

"You should know better than to put too much onto a one night stand," Brent advised. "He probably had no idea that it meant anything to you. Men are like that. I know, I am one."

"I know you're right," Deanie sighed. "It's just that when I saw him again, it was like all the emotions I've been fighting for so long came right back. I thought maybe he'd come looking for me or something. I'm pathetic."

"You're too hard on yourself," Brent said and grinned. "We're both a real couple of cases, aren't we?"

"That we are," Deanie agreed. "Thanks. I feel better already."

"No sweat. What are friends for?"

"Yeah, well thanks for being such a good one."

Brent grinned and slapped the table top. "Come on kid. Time to go home. I'm exhausted."

"Me too." Deanie agreed. And she meant it.

Chapter Ten

The next day dawned crisp and bright. Russ awoke at his usual six AM. He considered staying in bed a little longer, since Mark wasn't around anyway, but decided against it. He pulled on a clean pair of sweats and light windbreaker and headed out into the cool, late October morning for his usual Saturday jog in the park. What better way to exorcise the painfully embarrassing images from last night?

Russ and Mark lived in a newer, upper middle class section of the city. Most of the houses on the wide crescent were two stories high with attached double garages in front and well kept lawns. Russ's home was no exception, with gray siding, white trim and the standard basketball hoop over the garage doors. It was situated near good schools, shopping facilities, and a large open park for recreation. Everything the upwardly mobile family could ask for.

Russ set a more demanding pace for himself than usual. It was going to be a long day. Too much time for thinking. Once he finished the chores around his own place, he should probably go over to his mother's. She always had odd jobs that needed to be done and he hadn't been the most attentive son, lately. He'd been kind of avoiding her, to be truthful. She was always so full of questions about his personal life. And without Mark around to deflect her attention, it might be more than he bargained for. But duty called. He couldn't avoid her forever.

❧

"Russ! How wonderful," Dorothy Graham gushed as she greeted her son at the door. She was not a big woman, although pleasantly plump now that she had reached a 'certain' age. She wore her hair in the typical 'roller set' style. Lumpy, Mark called it. "You must have been reading my mind. I was just thinking to myself that I must call one of you boys over to put the storm windows back on the house before winter."

Russ kissed her cheek and entered the small foyer. "No problem. Sorry I haven't been over sooner. It's been really hectic at work."

"Where's Mark?" Dorothy asked. "I just baked some cookies. He always loves my cookies."

"He's staying with a friend for the weekend," Russ explained. "The Harris's."

"All weekend?" Dorothy asked, her brow furrowing with concern.

"Yeah. He and Tommy Harris are good buds. Tom's grandfather lives out on a farm by Steinbeck. They love to get out there and ride horses and stuff. Help look after the animals. It's good for him."

"No doubt," Dorothy nodded. "But still . . . does Mark know anything about horses? Can he ride?"

"Mother, you worry way too much," Russ laughed. "He'll be fine. He's a kid. Besides, with winter coming, he might not get another chance until spring. Now, let's get at those windows."

Russ spent several hours putting up the windows, fixing a leaky faucet, and patching some rickety boards on the back fence. He came in from outside to the smell of roasting chicken. Ah! His favorite!

"It smells great, Mom," Russ called from the bathroom sink, as he washed his hands.

"I called your brother earlier to invite them over, too," Dorothy said. "He said he might drop by later with the children, but Kathy wasn't feeling well again. I'm worried about her. She's been sick a lot, lately." Dorothy was busy at the kitchen sink rinsing some vegetables.

"Has she been to see a doctor?" Russ asked as he entered the kitchen. He lifted a lid from one of the pots and took a sniff.

"I'm not really sure," Dorothy replied. "I'm almost afraid to ask. They seem so sensitive these days. Maybe you could ask Ken for me when he comes over. He won't think that *you're* prying. You two are so close."

Hm. If she only knew. Russ smiled, however, and put a reassuring arm around his mother's shoulder. "Sure, if it'll make you feel better."

"Someday you'll understand," Dorothy said. "When Mark gets a bit older. It's hard to stand by and let your precious ones make mistakes when you could save them all the heartache. Especially when you know the 'One' who can help." Her eyes met Russ's for a second with the same intense dark blue that his possessed. He looked away.

"Yes, well, I'm sure that's very true," he said lightly, distracting himself with a carrot stick.

Dorothy dried her hands with deliberateness, then turned to her son. "Is there something troubling you, dear?"

"No," Russ denied. "What makes you say that?"

"A mother's instincts, perhaps?" Dorothy said thoughtfully. "You just haven't been yourself lately. You've been rather. . . moody."

"Really?" Russ feigned surprise. "Sorry. Things have been awfully hectic at work these days."

"So you said," Dorothy noted.

"Mother," Russ gave her a patronizing pat. "You really do worry too much. I'm fine. Really."

"Well, the Lord knows," she quipped. "Even if you won't tell me."

Russ rolled his eyes and sighed. "Yes, Mother, I know. You taught me that."

"But do you *know*, Russ? Not just with your head. Do you really know it in your heart?"

Russ clamped his jaw tight for a moment. "Any other jobs?" he asked, changing the subject.

Dorothy sighed. "Not for today. Ken and the children should be here any minute. Then we'll have a nice family supper together."

As if on cue, the doorbell sounded, and Ken came bounding in, herding his two children in front of him.

"Where's Mark?" seven year old Samantha demanded. Her blonde head peered around the room. She was small for her age, but she was very observant and her mannerisms were often exceptionally grown up for her years.

"He's out at his friend's farm for the weekend," Russ replied.

"Too bad," Samantha said, frowning. "I was hoping to have someone to play with besides him." She gave her brother a disgusted nod.

"Samantha stinks like poo-poo!" Greg yelled, swinging at his sister's leg with his small fist. He hit Russ's thigh instead.

"Hey! Hold on there, buckshot!" Russ laughed, sidestepping another blow.

"Greg!" Ken barked. He grabbed the boy roughly by the arm. "You'll be out in the car in a second!"

"But Dad," Greg started to whine.

"Shut up!" Ken growled and gave him a cuff across his curly brown head. The boy started to cry in earnest and ran for the shelter of his Grandmother's apron.

"There, there," Dorothy cooed. "You children come with Granny. I've got a surprise for you in the kitchen. I made cookies!" She led the children toward the kitchen, trying her best at happy chatter, while Greg continued to sob loudly into her skirt.

"That was a little over the top, don't you think?" Russ observed, his brows a stern line.

"He's a sissy. And a brat," Ken stated, and plunked himself down on the living room sofa.

Russ had to admit that Greg did act a little spoiled at times, but he still felt led to defend his young nephew. "Violence isn't the answer."

"I don't need your advice on how to raise my kid. He needs some toughening up."

"That was getting a bit rough, though. You're a lot stronger than he is."

"What do you know about it?" Ken snorted. "Your kid's always perfect."

"Maybe because he's had some *proper* discipline," Russ countered.

"Hey!" Ken defended. "It's not easy to discipline the kid when his mother just babies him up afterwards. He's got no respect for me whatsoever. She keeps coddling him behind my back."

"I hear she's been sick a lot lately," Russ mused, observing his older brother closely.

"Sick? She's been sick all right," Ken snorted with disgust.

"Has she been to see a doctor?" Russ asked.

"Maybe," Ken replied, his voice cooling.

"I was just asking," Russ shrugged.

"I suppose mother put you up to it?" Ken asked, raising a brow.

"She's just concerned. For you both. We all are."

"Forget it," Ken sighed. "There's nothing you could do about it anyway."

"If you're sure."

Dorothy interrupted the conversation by calling them to the table. "Besides, it's none of your damn business," Ken said under his breath as they made their way to the dining room.

Russ ignored the comment and took his usual spot at the table.

"Russ, why don't you pray?" Dorothy suggested. A brief scowl crossed his features. "It reminds me so much of when your dear father used to pray at meal times," she added.

How could he refuse? Guilt was one of her best tactics. "Sure. Ah . . . bless this food and the hands that have prepared it. Amen." He looked up and noted that his mother still had her eyes shut.

"And thank you, Lord, for this family," Dorothy continued. "I pray that your hand of guidance and protection would be upon every one. Amen."

Roast chicken and all the fixings went around the table and the group dug in heartily. Small talk dominated, much to Russ's relief, and after the meal, the 'boys' helped their mother with the dishes as the children went to play. There was a sudden screech from the basement where Dorothy kept the toys and games, followed by general shouting.

"Oh my!" Dorothy exclaimed, pausing with her hands in the sink. "Do you think they're okay?"

"I'll handle it," Ken said gruffly, slamming down his tea towel and stalking from the kitchen.

"Did you find anything out about Kathy?" Dorothy asked the moment Ken was out of ear shot.

"No," Russ stated. "Ken didn't want to talk about it."

"I just hope everything is alright over there," Dorothy stewed.

"Maybe you're making more out of it than there is," Russ suggested. "They're adults. They'll figure it out."

"Hmph," Dorothy snorted. "Still . . ."

"Mother," Russ gave her a withering look. "Relax. Really."

Dorothy sniffed. "Well, you boys don't make it easy. Neither one of you."

Russ let out a puff of air and continued drying the next dish.

"And what about you?" she queried. "Are you seeing anyone these days? Whatever happened to that Rita woman you were seeing?"

"Nothing," Russ replied lightly.

"What does that mean, exactly?" she pried. "Nothing?"

"Just what it's supposed to mean," Russ countered, irritation in his voice. "Nothing. We still work together if that's what you mean. But we haven't been 'out' lately."

"The Lord never intended us to be alone, Russ. You know that," Dorothy clucked.

Russ set his towel down with deliberateness and looked directly at his mother. "And what am I supposed to do about that, Mother? Just pick up the first woman that comes along?"

"No, of course, not," Dorothy exclaimed. "But I just can't understand how such a fine, good looking man like my son can't seem to find a suitable wife. Mark needs a mother."

"So now we're talking about Mark?" Russ countered.

"And you," Dorothy responded, sniffing. She turned back to the sink and resumed scrubbing the dishes in the sudsy water. "You both could use a woman in your lives and you know it. And you're not getting any younger."

Russ threw up his hands and laughed outright - a sarcastic bark. "You pull every trick out of the bag, don't you? Now you're resorting to the age factor. God, Mother! Lay off, already."

"Don't swear," Dorothy clipped. "You know I don't like it when you use the Lord's name."

"I didn't use the Lord's name," Russ rolled his eyes. "I said 'God'."

"It's the same thing," Dorothy said. "It's disrespectful to the Almighty. Something you might want to think about a little more often."

"Now what is *that* supposed to mean?" Russ railed.

"When was the last time you've been to church?" Dorothy demanded. "Mark should be going to Sunday school."

"Oh for pities sake!"

"Hey, what's all the fuss about in here?" Ken asked, coming into the room and leaning on the kitchen counter. "You two sound worse than the kids."

"I was just telling Russ that it's time he let the past be and find himself another wife," Dorothy explained, her breathing quick and her voice rising.

"Cool it, Mother," Russ growled under his breath. "You're starting to hyper ventilate."

"Don't get smart with me," Dorothy shot back. "I'm still your mother!"

Ken laughed. "Don't get your panties in a knot, Mum. Russ still knows how to play the field, isn't that right, bro?"

"You should learn to shut your mouth," Russ countered, his voice low.

"What does he mean, Russ?" Dorothy asked, frowning.

"Absolutely nothing," Russ responded, stalking toward the exit. He pushed past Ken, who was grinning widely.

"You're not leaving already, are you?" Dorothy scampered after him. "I thought we might play a game of cards later."

"Sorry. Not tonight," Russ clipped, pushing his arms into his jacket by the front door.

"In an awful big hurry," Ken said with feigned innocence, still grinning. "Was it something I said?"

Russ ignored his older brother. "Thanks for supper." He leaned forward to plant a kiss on his mother's cheek. "Ken," he acknowledged with a nod. "Say bye to the kids."

Once outside he could breath again. Ken hadn't really said anything. Just being his usual, obnoxious self. He shouldn't let his older brother's remarks get under his skin like that. He was always spouting off. But maybe this time it had hit a little too close to home.

And what was all that crap about Kathy? As if it was his job to keep tabs on his brother's wife. The last few years had taken their toll on Kathy, he knew, both mentally and physically. Not that she had ever been a raving beauty, a factor which had probably worked in her favor at first, since she was so very different from Ken's usual type. She had been young and inexperienced when she'd met Ken. To her he had seemed like a knight in shining armor coming to whisk her away from a dull existence. As if. She'd learned a thing or two since.

No wonder he didn't like visiting too often. His mother just wouldn't let go – of any of it. Somehow she managed to turn every conversation into a guilt trip about religion. That or her not too subtle hints about his love life. And although he was the younger of her sons by nearly two years, somehow he'd been thrust into the role of Mr. Fix It. He had, in effect, become his brother's keeper. He was sick of it. He couldn't figure out the mess he'd made of his own life, let alone try to fix someone else's.

As if of its own accord, Russ found his vehicle heading down Portage. Georgio's neon sign flashed tauntingly at him, daring him to enter. A smile crossed his face as he thought about his mother's reaction if he showed up one day with Deanie by his side. How ironic would that be? She said he needed a wife . . .

Screw it. Screw them all. If he wanted to see her again, he damn well would. He pulled sharply into the parking lot, extracting a staccato of honks from the vehicle directly behind.

Russ entered the dim interior for the second time in two consecutive nights. He spotted Deanie almost immediately and his stomach lurched up into his throat. Damn, she was beautiful. Even in this dim light and wearing nondescript jeans and a stupid little money apron. Mark wasn't home. He'd take her back to his place after work. Show her where he lived. Make love to her in front of the fireplace . . .

His thought was to catch her eye. Smile. Somehow communicate that he was sorry and wanted to make it up to her. First he'd order a beer, so as not to look so out of place. Then he'd saunter toward her, casually. See if she could take a break so they could go somewhere and talk. He placed his order at the bar and rehearsed the scenario in his mind as he took a sip before turning around. She was right behind him.

"Back again, I see," she clipped.

"Um, yeah," he nodded.

"This your new favorite hang out, or what?" she asked.

"Maybe," he shrugged. "Or maybe I'm meeting someone." He tried for a smile and hoped it didn't look as unsure as he felt.

"Really," she stated dryly.

"Yep," he nodded. "I think I found her." He held her gaze, hopeful that she wouldn't just slap him or something.

Instead she sighed wearily. "Wow. That's original. Look, I'm not sure I'm up for any more games, Russ. Last time hurt too much."

"Yeah. . . about that. . . " he looked down at his beer and hesitated before continuing. "Is there somewhere we can talk? Privately?"

"I'm working, if you hadn't noticed," Deanie said, gesturing at the surroundings in general.

"Don't you get a break or something?" Russ asked. "Even for a couple of minutes? I'd like to. . . explain."

"Explain?" Deanie repeated sarcastically.

"Okay, apologize," he amended.

She consulted her watch. "Since you put it that way, I'll just go tell Georgio I'm taking my break early. But I only get ten minutes."

Russ nodded. "Thanks." Their eyes held for a moment until Deanie turned to leave. Russ caught her hand. "I am sorry, you know. I don't want you to think that night at Hecla didn't mean anything to me. It did."

She didn't say anything, but turned away quickly. Russ was sure he saw tears sparkling in her eyes. It made his own heart ache to think he'd hurt her. He obviously hadn't been thinking straight that morning. The morning he had up and left. Probably still wasn't. She seemed to have that effect on him. He wasn't exactly sure where he was going with any of this, either. All he knew was, now that they'd run into each other again, he had a need to keep on seeing her. It was like an obsession.

He watched as she talked to Georgio. He seemed angry, but waved a dismissive hand as if to let her go. She turned, a slight smile on her lips, but before she got more than two steps, a long haired, rough looking man grabbed her hand and started dragging her toward the stage. Russ's first instinct was to bolt to her rescue. Then he saw the laughter on her lips; the teasing way she resisted. He thought he saw her look his way and mouth an apology, but he couldn't be sure. Now there were three others surrounding her, blocking his view.

A dark knot of jealousy formed in his stomach. He took a gulp of his beer. It fizzed in his gut like cold water hitting a hot stone. They were on the little stage now. Hoisting her up among them. She placed her hand casually on the dark one's shoulder and then directed a playful swat at the bare armed giant with the curling blonde tresses. Russ thought he might be sick.

"Hey! We're back for another set." It was the dark haired man Deanie had been flirting with a moment ago. "Hope y'all don't mind, but Georgio's own Deanie Burton is going to join us for a couple of songs. Isn't that right, Georgio?" He pointed at the balding man behind the bar who just waved his consent. "Come on, let's hear it!" he encouraged and the audience cheered as Deanie waved demurely, tambourine in hand. With that he stepped back, counted out the time and the group launched into a rocking version of Steppenwolf's classic, 'Born to Be Wild.'

Russ normally didn't mind the song. He liked classic rock for the most part, but somehow this particular version seemed to grate on his nerves. Deanie seemed to be enjoying it, though, he noted with a scowl. She seemed awfully familiar with the group. He wondered just how familiar. The song came to a crashing end, amid whoops and cheers. Somehow, he found another beer sitting in front of him. He took a long swig.

The group leader was talking again. "This next one is an original. And it's my pleasure to have my friend Deanie sing it for us."

The song started out slowly, the melody in a haunting minor key. Deanie's voice caressed each phrase, her voice low, sultry and full of raw emotion. She was staring right at him as she sang, as if it was for his ears only. Russ was stunned. Mesmerized. Transported back to Hecla Island, when he had heard her sing for the first time, her voice drifting across the still night air.

But this song was not for his ears only. It was for a room full of whistling drunks whose eyes were undressing her right there up on the stage. For four long haired men with tattoos and guitars. Men who seemed to know her intimately. When the song ended, amid a burst of applause, she jumped down from the platform and headed straight for where he was sitting, nursing his third beer.

"Sorry about that," she smiled, sitting up to the bar herself. "The guys wouldn't take no for an answer. But maybe you could stick around and we could talk when I'm finished work."

He opened his mouth to answer. To say 'Okay' to her suggestion. To say he'd wait forever if he had to. To say how beautiful the song was and how beautiful she was. . . But then the image of those men. . . those long haired baboons teasing her and laughing with her and touching her crowded everything else from his mind. "You sing with a rock group?" He made it sound more like a question than a statement.

"I don't, really. We're just good friends."

"I can see that." His reply was laced with sarcasm.

"What is that supposed to mean?" Deanie asked, frowning.

"Have you slept with all of them, too?" He knew that it was rude. Petty, even. But the jealousy was churning inside of him and the alcohol had loosened his tongue. He was ready for the slap, though, and he caught Deanie's hand in mid air with a vice-like grip.

"Let go! You're hurting me," she hissed, trying not to draw attention to the situation.

Russ dropped Deanie's hand, still surveying her pale, stricken features.

"So much for your apology," she fumed.

"No manhandling my girls," a heavily accented man stood behind Deanie, hands on hips. "Or I call the cops."

This was not going at all the way he'd planned. Without a word, he swung off the stool and strode toward the exit. He could hear Georgio directing a string of angry expletives at Deanie, but he let the bump of the outside door cut them off in mid sentence.

The cold night air hit Russ in the face like the slap he hadn't received. He had never humiliated himself quite like that in public before. Miss Burton had some strange effect on him. That was it, then. Three strikes, you're out. He fumbled with his car keys, trying to unlock the driver's seat door. Suddenly a firm hand descended on his shoulder. Russ swung around and was face to chest with a giant. Looking slowly upwards, he recognized the drummer. Close behind him stood the other members of the rock group.

The dark haired leader spoke up. "You have a problem with that waitress we should talk about?"

"Nothing that's any of your business," Russ replied calmly. Inwardly he was calculating his chances against the burly blonde giant. Not too good, he was afraid, although he was in pretty good shape. But if the others joined in. . .

"We won't stand for anybody bothering her, you understand?"

"Perfectly," Russ said. "Now if you'll excuse me – " He didn't get a chance to finish the sentence. With one forceful blow to the abdomen, the wind was completely and thoroughly knocked out of him. He tried to look up from his doubled over position and saw the huge blonde man smiling wickedly, rubbing his knuckles as if preparing for more.

"I assure you –" Russ gasped, straightening.

"No, I assure *you*," the leader cut in, "if we ever catch you bothering her again, things will be a lot worse. Understand? Consider yourself warned."

The men turned without a backward glance, and strutted back toward the building. They needn't worry, Russ mused as he slumped into his car. The exhibition ride was over, and he was definitely getting off.

Chapter Eleven

Winter descended on the city of Winnipeg with a vengeance. It was early December, and as Deanie woke and looked out her bedroom window, the entire world was covered with a thick, white blanket. Icy gusts of wind whipped the snow into drifts that piled up against buildings and other barriers. There had been snowfall before now, but it had usually melted within the day. The entire autumn had been especially warm, but now it looked as if winter was here to stay. It would definitely be a white Christmas in Winnipeg.

Deanie sighed heavily. She usually welcomed the first evidence that winter was really here. It gave her a warm, cozy feeling to be inside while the frosty elements had their way out of doors. But today, the icy cold fingers of the winter wind seemed to penetrate right into the recesses of her being. She felt as if her heart was frozen as solid as the ice that now lined the gutters. It would take only one sharp tap to break it into splintered pieces.

Tests had confirmed what she'd known in her heart for weeks. In fact, the real revelation had come the very night she'd last seen Russ. Georgio had reamed her out, blaming the whole episode with Russ on her.

"What the hell kind of place you think I'm running here?" he'd spouted. "Bad enough that you're parading up on stage instead of doing your work, but next you bring your personal business into my bar! No boyfriends if they keep you from your work!"

"He's not my boyfriend," she'd defended.

"Well, I pay you good money to be nice to customers, not hit them."

"But -"

"No buts," Georgio had wagged his finger. When he wagged his finger, you knew he meant business. "And I'm taking time off your timesheet for all that fooling around on stage. I paid them to perform, not you."

"But it was my break -" It was no use. He had already turned his back and was trundling away. With resignation she went to clear some empties off the counter. That's when she'd cut herself on a broken bottle.

Turning on her heel, she'd made a bee line to the bathroom. She wasn't normally squeamish around blood, but for some reason she could barely keep her hand steady under the stream of cold tap water. Fumbling with a piece of paper towel, she'd formed a makeshift bandage, then leaned against the counter as a wave of dizzying nausea swept over her. She was suddenly overcome. With urgency, she'd bolted for one of the cubicles, just making it in time before she vomited.

Stress, she told herself. Nerves. Lack of sleep. But something inside of her knew. This was more than any of those things. So much more. She knew the feeling.

And now here she was. A continuous interruption to her cycle and yesterday's medical tests confirmed the fact. She was pregnant. Again.

So far she had been able to hide any physical evidence of her pregnancy. It was definitely one of the advantages of her slim build. However, she couldn't help but raise Jack's suspicions with her frequent bouts of 'flu' in the mornings. She knew she was going to have to break the news soon. She just wasn't sure how.

Thank goodness she was almost through with her semester exams. The last month had been a real nightmare. What with her morning sickness, she had missed more than half her early morning classes. And she was so exhausted by the end of each day that she literally fell into bed each night.

She hadn't heard Jack come home last night, and now peeked into his room to see if he was there. He lay sprawled half in and half out of his covers, amid an array of rumpled clothing and papers. She smiled. At least she still had Jack.

She tiptoed into the room and sat on the edge of his bed. "Jack! Wake up," she whispered loudly, giving him a slight shake.

"Wha. . . !" Jack sat bolt upright, panting.

"Hey! Slow down," Deanie laughed. "I just need a lift to school."

"What?" Jack scowled, rubbing his already tousled hair. "You woke me up for that? Take your own car." He flopped back down onto his pillow, clutching for the blankets.

"I can't, remember? It blew a gasket," Deanie explained patiently, shaking her father. "Brent figures he should have it fixed today, and he'll bring it by later. But in the meantime, I need a ride. Now!"

"Take the bus," Jack mumbled from under his pillow.

"It's too late," Deanie continued. "Besides, I'm not sure which of the buses will be running today, anyway. They said on the radio that some streets were blocked with snow."

"And you expect me to go out in that?" Jack asked, removing the pillow, and squinting up at her.

"But you have to! I've got one of my finals today," Deanie pleaded. She flipped the covers entirely off Jack's sprawling body and poked him hard in the ribs.

"Ow! Blast it!" Jack burst out. He avoided another poke by scrambling from the bed. "I should give you a darn good spanking for that!" He muttered his way to the bathroom and slammed the door. Deanie just laughed.

Half an hour later, Jack's beat up station wagon maneuvered its way out onto the icy streets. They passed several cars abandoned along the sides of the road. "How did I ever let you talk me into this?" he wondered and let loose with an especially colorful string of expletives.

"Jack? There's something I've been meaning to tell you," Deanie began tentatively. "I mean, I can't keep it a secret much longer."

"Go ahead. I'm listening," Jack responded, keeping his attention fully focused on the task at hand.

There was a momentary pause. "I'm pregnant," she finally blurted.

"What?" Jack croaked. The car fishtailed on the icy street, but he managed to right the situation. "Dang it, girl. That's not funny. Not when the streets are a death trap and I'm trying to concentrate."

"It wasn't supposed to be funny," Deanie retorted.

Jack frowned, hesitating. "What did you say?"

84

"You heard me," Deanie stated.

"No, I don't think I did. Say it again."

"I'm pregnant."

He nodded. "That's what I thought you said."

"Sorry," she said flatly, looking out the window.

"Sorry? Well, you picked a fine time to spring it on me!" Jack puffed, gripping the steering wheel with both hands. "I could have killed us both back there!"

"Sorry."

"I suppose you figured I couldn't give you a whoopin' if I was otherwise occupied."

"As if you've ever given me a whoopin'," Deanie countered, eyeing her father with amusement.

"I could you know," he said. "Never too late to start."

Deanie sighed heavily. "I'm just so sorry, Jack." She looked sideways at the grim set of her father's mouth as he continued to drive along the snow filled streets.

"Quit saying you're sorry. I know you're sorry, but that don't fix things, now, do it?"

"I've let you down again." She looked away, watching the whiteness of the world as it passed by.

"Now, now," Jack soothed, giving her hand a quick pat. "We'll figure something out." He continued driving, slowly, remaining uncharacteristically silent for several minutes as he maneuvered down the street.

"Jack?" Deanie ventured.

"Hmm?" he mumbled.

"You're pretty quiet," Deanie noted. "Say something."

"I guess for once you've caught your old man speechless," he shrugged.

"Sorry."

"I told you to quit sayin' that," he instructed.

"Sorry."

They drove quietly for another space before Jack spoke again. "So who, if I may be so bold to ask, is the lucky father of my grandchild?"

"You don't know him," Deanie said, shaking her head.

Jack grunted. "Hmph. I haven't noticed you going out with any new fellas lately. You been sneakin' around on your old man?"

"No. Not really," Deanie replied.

"Good gravy, girl!" Jack exclaimed. "Are you gonna tell me who this mystery man is or do I need to take you over my knee to get it outta ya?"

"I already told you, you don't know him," Deanie bit back.

"Maybe not today. But I intend to, by gum! You're my only child. All I've got left in this world, and I think I have a right to meet the man who's been sportin' with you. I'm bound to meet him one of these days, anyway."

"It's a little more complicated than that."

"Complicated? What do you mean by that?"

"He doesn't know."

"What? Why not?"

"Because I don't want him to."

"He better not be another one of those —"

"Calm down," Deanie reassured her father. "He's nothing like Brad."

"Because I swear if another son of a bee lays a hand on you like that last one did, I'll. . . I'll. . . well, you just be sure your old man won't stand for any funny business!"

"I promise you he is very respectable," Deanie said firmly.

"Well, now, that's a bit of a paradox if you ask me, considering the condition he's got you in."

"It's not like I didn't have anything to do with it," Deanie reminded wryly.

"Did he drop you once he found out? Why, I'll teach him a thing or two about responsibility. I'll –"

"Jack! I already told you that he doesn't know," Deanie reminded. "And he's not going to, either. I don't need his charity, or anything else."

"Do you think that's really very fair?" Jack mused, furrowing his brow. "I surely know that I would want to be told about it if I had a child out there somewhere. Not that I ever would have, you understand. None besides you, I mean. I've always been faithful to your dear mother's memory. You know that."

"I know," Deanie said with affection. "But that's different. I just don't want to tell him."

"Why not?"

"It's complicated."

"So you keep telling me," Jack grunted. "So, how far along are ya?"

"A few months."

"So I take it that you haven't seen him in a while."

"You could say that. I hardly knew him, really. It was just one of those stupid things. A mistake that should never have happened."

"I thought you knew about taking precautions," Jack said with a frown.

"Jack! I do. Just – just never mind. It's too late now, anyway." Deanie turned to look out the window.

"How far along did you say you were?" Jack asked, the wheels in his brain obviously turning, as he continued to maneuver the car along the treacherous streets.

"Oh, three and a half months, I guess."

"Three and a half. . . " Jack mused. "That'd be about the first of September. We wouldn't be talking about that time out at Hecla, now would we? The time you didn't come home?"

Deanie opened her mouth in stunned silence for a moment. "Jack! How did you remember all that?" she demanded.

"An accountant, wasn't it? If I remember correctly?" He glanced her way with a gleam in his eye.

"Wow," Deanie stated. "You are incredible."

"Don't think your old pop isn't watching out for you," Jack nodded. "You think I'm getting senile or something. But I know what's what."

"Well, whatever. In any case, he's no longer in the picture. It'll be just us three."

"You never said what happened," Jack persisted. "Maybe you two can patch things up."

"There was never anything to patch up, Jack," Deanie said, exasperated. "It was a stupid mistake and that's it. Okay?"

"Well, don't you think he has a right to know, at least?"

"No!" Deanie belted. "I'm never telling him and that's all there is to it. I'll get out and walk the rest of the way if you don't stop."

"Suit yourself," Jack shrugged. "But 'never' is a mighty strong word.

Seems to me, now that you're in the family way, you ought to let him know. It's only right."

"Jack, please!" Deanie pleaded. "I seriously don't want him to know about it. Ever." She choked on the last word, and quickly turned to look out the window again.

"There, there," Jack soothed. "Just let it out, girl. Nothing wrong with a few tears, I always say. Cleanses the soul. Don't you worry one bit. These things often have a way of working themselves out. But you don't need to worry about me. I won't be telling anyone, if you don't want me to. Your belly will be making its own announcement soon enough. I think I might like the idea of being a grandpa, anyway." Deanie could tell by the gravelly catch in her father's voice that he was trying to be strong for her sake.

"Jack, what would I ever do without you?" Deanie asked.

"Now that's a question," Jack replied gruffly. "Seems to me you go and do as you damn well please with or without me as it is."

Deanie gave her father a quick kiss on the cheek. She could always count on Jack.

❧

"I love it when school's closed," Mark declared. "I wish it would storm more often."

Russ looked up from his desk. Mark was standing tentatively in the doorway of the den. "Come on in, son," Russ invited.

"You're not too busy?" Mark asked as he slipped into the room and sat in a chair opposite his father.

Russ had opted to stay at home for the day, since Mark had no where to go and the roads were terrible. Besides, he always had lots of work to catch up on, even at home. "I think I can spare a few minutes."

"I think it stopped snowing," Mark said. "Wanna come outside and build a snowman?"

Russ surveyed his son's hopeful face. Why not? The paperwork wasn't going anywhere. "Sure. Let's do it."

Father and son donned their warmest winter boots, mitts, jackets and hats and headed out into the great outdoors.

"This snow's a little too fresh for a snowman. Not sticky enough," Russ explained, surveying the yard. "But maybe we could pile it up and make a fort."

"Okay!" Mark agreed enthusiastically.

They spent quite awhile in the back yard with their shovels, piling up banks of snow into a semi-square fortress.

"We could stock pile snowballs and have a snowball fight," Mark suggested.

"Maybe," Russ nodded. "Rita might be coming over later, though, depending on the roads."

Mark was silent.

"What's wrong? Don't you like Rita?" Russ asked.

Mark shrugged. "I don't know. I guess so."

They worked for a few more minutes, intent on stabilizing one of the walls.

"You gonna marry her?" Mark asked.

"I think it's a little early for that," Russ laughed, slightly taken aback.

Mark didn't say anything.

Russ observed his son closely. "I thought you wanted a mother."

"Well. . . maybe," Mark shrugged. "But it has to be the right kind of mother."

"Oh, so you get to do the choosing now, do you?" Russ teased.

Mark thought about that for a minute. "Well, Rita's okay. I mean, she's nice and everything. Just kind of boring. She seems awfully old."

Russ laughed out right. "Old? She's the same age as your old man! So what's the problem?"

"She's just not any fun. She seems worried about messing her clothes and stuff."

"That was just at Grandma's when the other kids were there," Russ reminded. "She's not used to lots of noise and kids underfoot." He surveyed his son's stoic expression. "Maybe we need to do something fun together, just the three of us. How about it? What if we took Rita bowling or something?"

"I suppose," Mark shrugged.

They both went back to work, shoveling and patting, shoveling and patting. He had taken up with Rita Holmes again as much for Mark's sake as his own. At least that's what he told himself. Admitting that he needed some way to get the red-haired vixen out of his mind would be to admit his own utter weakness. And he was tired of chastising himself over a one night stand. It was over and done with and he was moving on. Besides, Mark needed some female influence, and sometimes Russ's own mother was a little too overbearing. Especially when it came to the religion thing.

But Rita was the perfect candidate. Raised as a Catholic, but now an agnostic, she understood people's need for a spiritual crutch but wasn't too verbal in expressing her own views, especially to his mother. Best not to make anyone uncomfortable, she said. His view exactly!

Rita had worked at Russ's accounting firm for two years, now. An accountant herself, she knew what it was like to want stability in her career and in a relationship. No steamy mishaps for them. When the time was right they would move to that next level in their relationship and not before. Funny how he didn't really care about it with Rita anyway. Not that he didn't find her attractive. She was pretty and well groomed with an average figure, and she liked to stay in shape, too, which was another thing they had in common. But he was almost dreading the sex thing. For now he was quite content to keep things on low. It was helping him get stabilized. Stay focused…

Yeah right. On the surface, anyway. He might be able to fool the rest of them, but there was no fooling himself.

❦

Deanie emerged from the university campus several hours after her father dropped her off. Her head felt light and her eyes were aching. She's made it through the exam, but how she'd faired was another thing altogether. She squinted into the brightness of the sparkling, snowy world. It looked as though the weather was clearing somewhat. The snowplows would be out in full force now, trying to unplug the streets. She decided to walk the eight blocks to Brent's house, to see if her car was ready. The fresh air was just what she needed to clear her brain.

Trudging through the snow was harder work than she had imagined.

She was glad when she finally reached Brent's front door. Brent himself answered her knock and heartily beckoned her in. "You're just in time for hot chocolate," he beamed.

Deanie raised a doubtful eyebrow. "Hot chocolate? Now doesn't that sound cozy. Somehow, I just never imagined you guys sitting around sipping on hot chocolate."

Brent laughed, "That is quite the picture. Actually, the other guys aren't here. But. . . there is someone else that I would like you to meet."

"Ah," Deanie nodded knowingly and motioned for Brent to lead the way.

Sitting at the kitchen table was a petite woman with shoulder length blond hair and a pretty round face.

"Deanie, this is Holly Trenton," Brent said, shifting his weight from side to side, "and Holly, this is Deanie."

"I'm so glad to finally meet you," Holly exclaimed, standing up and shaking Deanie's hand. "Brent talks about you all the time."

Deanie smiled back. There was something very warm and genuine about the other woman. "Thanks. Brent has mentioned you, too. You're a nurse, right?" She took a sip of the steaming hot chocolate that Brent had just poured for her. "Mm. This is just what I needed. I just wrote my last exam and I feel really fried. I could really use a cigarette, too, but I'm trying to stay off them."

"Sure, sure," Brent teased. "Heard that line before."

"So Brent tells me that you two grew up together," Holly said.

"Our friendship goes back a long way," Deanie agreed.

"She's more like my sister than anything else," Brent laughed. He put his spoon, hot from the scalding liquid in his cup, against Deanie's bare forearm. She jumped, then gave him a not so soft punch in the arm. "See what I mean? She even hits me."

"Whatever," Deanie laughed. "You deserve it."

"So tell me about it," Holly suggested. "This sibling thing you've got going."

Deanie and Brent both looked at each other and shrugged. Their bond was palpable. "We were on the road a lot, I guess," Deanie spoke first. "And our dad's were busy with their music . . ."

"Which is why we got busy with our music, isn't that right, Dee?" Brent interjected. "We started our first band when we were little more than kids."

"Yeah," Deanie laughed. "Probably not that great, but we thought we were awesome. We called ourselves the DeeBee's. Get it? The DeeBee's. How lame is that?"

"Hey, I thought it was pretty clever," Brent defended with a chuckle.

"Yeah, because you're the one who made it up," Deanie retorted. "We did get better, though, eh? Even played a few high school dances."

Brent shook his head, smiling. "Those were the days."

"Then what?" Holly asked. "Why'd the band break up?"

"Oh, you know," Brent said with a shrug. "Things get crazy. People change." He took a sip of hot chocolate. The laughter had suddenly subsided.

Deanie cleared her throat. "Yeah. Well, anyway, I'd better drink up. You got some milk or something that I can use to cool this down? I don't want to be late for work again. You did manage to get my car going?"

"Yep. It's right out back. You can't possibly hurry, though, with the roads the way they are. You'd better call Georgio and tell him you'll be late. He can't expect you to make it on time under these conditions," Brent advised.

"Good idea. I'll just borrow your phone," Deanie agreed.

A few moments later, Deanie came back to the table. Her face was completely crestfallen.

"What's wrong? What happened?" Brent asked.

"Georgio said not to bother coming at all. I'm fired." Deanie relayed dully.

"What? He can't do that!" Brent exclaimed.

"Oh yeah? He just did."

"That's crazy," Brent blustered. "You can't control the weather."

"He's just been waiting for some kind of excuse to get rid of me," Deanie sighed.

"Probably better off. You don't need that jerk anyway," Brent declared.

"Maybe not, but I do need to eat. Now what am I going to do?" Deanie wailed.

"Like I've been telling you all along, come and join us. The band needs you," Brent said.

"Brent! Be realistic," Deanie cried. "You know yourself that you need another job besides the band. It's your hobby. It doesn't pay the bills." She put her head in her hands. "I am just such a screw up!"

"Maybe I should go now," Holly said quietly. "You two look like you could use some time alone."

"No, its okay," Brent said quickly, standing up.

"Really," Holly insisted. "It was really wonderful to meet you, Deanie. And I hope things work out for you with your job and everything. I'll be praying for you."

Deanie looked up in surprise. She saw that the other woman really meant what she'd said. "Thanks," she said simply. "I'm not sure anyone's ever done that before."

Brent saw Holly to the door and then came back and sat down directly across from Deanie. "Okay, spill it," he demanded.

"What do you mean?" Deanie hedged.

"I know it's not like you to get all teary over a jerk like Georgio. You hated that job anyway and this is your chance to break free. Something else is going on with you lately."

"I've really blown it this time," Deanie said, shaking her head. "I really need that job, even if Georgio is a jerk. And I don't think I'll be able to go back to school next semester. My marks are too low and how could I afford it now without a job?"

"We'll think of something," Brent reassured. "It's not like Georgio's is the only place on earth to work. Something better will come along. Just wait and see."

"You're probably right. This news is going to freak Jack, though. Not like he hasn't had enough excitement for one day." Deanie sighed. "I'm just so tired these days."

"So, get some rest. And in the mean time, you won't have any more excuses for not joining the band. We've got lots of gigs coming up for the Christmas season," Brent reasoned. "You can make a few bucks there."

"You really don't get it, do you?" Deanie looked squarely at her friend and shook her head again.

"What do you mean?"

"I can't join the band now," Deanie stated.

"Of course you can. You said yourself you were just too busy -"

Deanie cut him off. "Brent, I'm pregnant. Okay? I can't join the band because I'm pregnant."

Brent's mouth dropped open for a moment.

"I can see you're speechless," Deanie noted with a wry smile. "Now do you see?"

"Being pregnant doesn't mean you can't sing," Brent said, frowning. "Does it?"

Deanie laughed. "Of course not! But you wouldn't want my swollen belly up on stage with you, now would you? What would that do for your image?"

"Who cares? I'm not that much of a bigot," Brent shot back.

"But what about the rest of the guys? You're not a one-man show. How do you think they'd feel about it? It'd cramp their style, not to mention putting up with hormonal outbursts and all that other great stuff. Think they'd feel like catering to the 'fat one's' needs all the time?" Deanie asked, a sarcastic tinge to her voice.

"This isn't the Middle Ages. I thought you of all people would want to stand up for yourself," Brent said, shaking his head.

Deanie sighed. "Frankly, Brent, I can't think straight these days. I don't know what I want. All I know is what I don't want, and that is parading around on stage with my gut sticking out a mile."

Brent whistled and sat back in his chair. "Phew! I can't believe it. Does that make me like, an uncle?"

"Honorary," Deanie stated. She thought for a moment, then admitted, "It feels good to finally tell. I've been keeping it a secret so long its been killing me. I told Jack this morning."

"How'd he take it?" Brent asked.

"Okay, I guess. I kind of sprung it on him suddenly, when he really didn't have a chance to prepare himself." Deanie laughed. She looked at Brent for a moment and then continued soberly, "And thanks for not asking."

"Not asking what?"

"Who the father is, you dumb -"

94

"Well, to be honest I was kind of wondering. I mean you haven't been seeing anyone that I know of . . ." Brent stopped and held up his hands. "But that is completely your business. If you want me to know, you can tell me."

"Thanks." More silence.

"Does he know?" Brent piped up.

"Who?"

"The father!"

"Not you, too!" Deanie wailed. "Now you're sounding just like Jack! Well, thanks, but I've already heard this lecture from him."

"Don't you think he has a right to know? I'd want to know if I had a kid. Besides, he could help you out, you know, financially," Brent reasoned.

"That's it! I'm outta here!" Deanie jumped to her feet. "The last thing I want is charity. Besides, he has nothing but contempt for me already and this would just prove him right."

"Hey, wait a minute," Brent detained her by grabbing her arm. "I'm sorry. You do what you think you have to and I'll back you, one hundred percent. You know that."

Deanie let out a frustrated sigh. "Thanks. I guess."

"Now sit down. There's no point rushing off mad," Brent said.

Deanie plunked her body back down into the kitchen chair.

"So what's your plan?" Brent asked.

"Plan? Obviously I don't have a plan," Deanie retorted. "Haven't you been listening?"

"Are you keeping it?" Brent asked.

"Of course I'm keeping it!" Deanie shot back, glaring.

Brent threw up his hands. "Hey, just asking. It is your call, and I said I'd back you, no matter what."

"Am I keeping it," Deanie repeated, half under her breath.

"Sorry," Brent apologized again. "Dumb question, apparently."

"Apparently," Deanie repeated sarcastically. They sat for a few moments, contemplative.

"So are you going to tell me, or not?" Brent finally asked.

Deanie eyed him, allowing a small grin to touch her lips. "I thought you said it was my business."

"It is, it is," Brent quickly retracted.

Deanie took a deep breath and then let the air out slowly. "Remember the guy I was telling you about a while back? The one from Hecla?"

Brent nodded.

"It's him."

"No shit," Brent mused.

"No shit."

"Hm," Brent shrugged. "And you're not going to tell him?"

"Brent," Deanie warned.

"Okay, okay!"

Deanie sighed. "Maybe it wouldn't have been so bad if I hadn't run into him again, you know? Maybe I would have told him. But he made it perfectly clear what he thought of me those two times he came to the bar."

"Two times?" Brent asked.

"Yeah," Deanie replied. "Remember I told you about it that one night after it happened? When you first told me about Holly?" Brent nodded. "He showed up again the next night. The night you got me to sing with you guys. At first I thought he was there to make it up to me. To apologize. At least, that's what he said. But then he got all mad, like he thought I was sleeping around or something."

"Jealous," Brent mused. "Maybe that's a good sign."

Deanie let out a harsh laugh. "I doubt it. He's an unfeeling ass. I sure know how to pick them."

Brent frowned. "Wait a minute . . . Are we talking about a guy with dark, short hair? The one you were fighting with at the counter?"

"Yeah, that's him."

"Oh shit!"

"What?" Deanie asked, eyeing her friend.

"We kind of roughed him up a bit, out in the parking lot," Brent admitted, looking up at Deanie through his lashes in a sheepish way.

"You did what?!" Deanie squeaked.

"Nothing much," Brent assured. "Well, Chris kind of just gave him a little warning."

"Brent! You didn't!"

"Well, no, *I* didn't, Chris just -"

"Brent!" Deanie wailed again. She let out an exasperated breath.

"Honestly, Deanie. We didn't really hurt the guy. Just a friendly warning not to bother you again."

"Forget it," Deanie said. "It doesn't matter anyway. I won't be seeing him again."

"I'm really sorry."

"I said forget it," Deanie instructed. "And I still need to find a job. Who wants to hire a pregnant person?"

"Well, maybe you should do like Holly said."

"What?"

"You know. Pray," Brent avoided her eyes and looked at the wall.

"Really. That's your answer?" Deanie asked, raising her brows skeptically.

"You know, you shouldn't knock something until you've tried it," Brent defended. "Holly says -"

"Come off it, Brent," Deanie interrupted. "Do you really believe in all this 'God' stuff? You probably think we've all got guardian angels hovering over us, too. Well, where was my angel a few months ago? Or a few years ago with Brad? Huh? Tell me that?"

"I never said I had all the answers, or that I even understand it. I just said it was worth a shot. You shouldn't knock something until you try it," Brent mumbled.

"And I suppose you have?" Deanie asked, cocking her head to one side, daring him to deny it.

"What?"

"Tried it. Praying, you idiot!" Deanie exclaimed. She threw up her hands.

"Well," Brent hesitated. "Not exactly, but I've been thinking about it a lot. About spiritual things. There's something to it, Dee, I think. I'm not sure what it is, but there is something. Something inside. . . here -" he stabbed at his chest, "that kind of scares me sometimes."

"And Holly is 'helping' you find the answers?" Deanie asked, then shook her head in disgust. "I thought she was nice, not some kind of lunatic taking my best friend for a ride."

"Don't start bad mouthing Holly," Brent warned.

"Why? You care more about her than about me?" Deanie asked. She stopped and clamped her mouth shut. The remark sounded catty, even to her own ears. "Sorry. I didn't mean that."

"I should hope not," Brent retorted. "You know that I love you - that I always will, but not in that way. Don't make me choose between you and Holly."

"I'm sorry, Brent. You're right. That was really rotten of me to say. Forget it, all right? I'd never make you choose between me and anybody, and you know it. I'm just upset - and tired. I'm sorry that I chased her off this afternoon, too."

"That's all right. I think she had to go to work soon, anyway."

"And she doesn't mind? About your rock and roll fantasies?" Deanie asked

"What do you mean, mind?" Brent frowned. "You make it sound as if I'm doing something illegal."

"Just that I didn't think her religious type would approve of your choice in music - or company," Deanie shrugged. "Besides, we both know you haven't been a saint."

"You've got her all wrong, Dee. She is anything but judgmental. Besides, I'm getting a little tired of the party scene anyway. It's all the same."

"I never thought I'd hear you say that. Just a few minutes ago you were going on and on about your music. Brent! Music is your life!"

"I didn't say anything about my music. Music is still my life," Brent stated. "It's just, maybe I can use my music - my talents - for something else. Something better."

"Looks like we both need to do some praying," Deanie sighed with a smile. "You sound just about as mixed up as I do."

"Could be," Brent nodded. "Could very well be."

Chapter Twelve

The Christmas season came with its usual flurry of activity. Shopping, concerts, parties. Russ was not looking forward to his staff party. This year he would be a 'couple' – not something he relished. It was one thing to socialize with Rita in private, but in public, at their work place no less, was quite another.

He dropped Mark off at his mother's house for the night and drove the twenty blocks or so to pick up Rita. She lived in an upscale condo near the river. She came promptly to the door when he rang the bell. "Hi. You want to come in for a minute?" she asked after opening the door. "I'm not quite ready."

He raised his brows in surprise. Rita wasn't the type of person to be late for anything. "Okay," Russ shrugged and looked at his watch. "I guess the party doesn't start for awhile yet." He stepped inside and shed his coat, throwing it over the waiting rack. The interior of Rita's home was tasteful, understated and classy. Like the woman herself.

"Can I get you a drink?" Rita asked, leading the way into the living room. She switched on a side lamp before turning to Russ expectantly.

"Well. . . how long are you going to be?" he asked, looking around.

"We don't want to show up too early," Rita laughed. "These functions can get so dull." She smiled. "So? What'll you have?"

Russ blinked, slightly unsure how to respond. Was she trying to be provocative? "Uh. . . a scotch on the rocks, I guess, if you've got it."

"Coming right up." Rita sauntered to the liquor cabinet and proceeded to mix their drinks. She came back moments later and handed Russ a tumbler, amber liquid swirling among large chunks of ice. "Let's sit down, shall we?"

Russ did just that and watched as Rita settled onto the sofa beside him, just inches away. This was a side of Rita he'd never seen before. Maybe he'd been reading her wrong. He cleared his throat and took a swallow of his drink.

"So I was thinking," Rita said as a slight smile played on her lips. "After we make an appearance at the party, we could come back here for awhile. Unless you want to go to your place. Mark's looked after, right?"

"He's at my mother's," Russ informed, nodding.

"Good," Rita said and placed her hand on his knee. "Unless you want to show up late for the party. . . " So. Tonight was the night. He should feel more excited about that.

Somehow she'd moved the drink from Russ's hand to the coffee table and was leaning in for a kiss. Sure, they had kissed before. Fleeting touches at the door as they said good night. But this was no feather light meeting of lips. Rita obviously wanted more. Was ready to move to the next level, as she put it.

Russ managed to extract himself from her embrace and stood up. "I think we should head to the party now," he said.

Rita frowned briefly, but then replaced the look with one of acquiescence. She unfolded herself from the depths of the sofa and stood also. "Okay. Later then. I just have to head up to my room for a minute. I wouldn't want to wear my diaphragm out for the evening."

Russ blinked in surprise and watched her retreating figure. So she had this planned all along. He wasn't sure how he felt about that. He went to the front door and retrieved his overcoat, then waited.

Rita returned several minutes later, her mask of aloof professionalism back in place. Everything was back to normal. As if.

The staff party was held at a downtown hotel. Several agencies from their building had gone together and rented one of the conference rooms. There was finger food, drinks for a price and a DJ who'd been hired for the occasion. At least he didn't have to worry about live entertainment, Russ mused blackly. That hadn't boded so well for him in recent months.

Although many of the staff knew he and Rita were seeing each other, they had never actually been out together socially with other colleagues. They always kept their dealings strictly professional at the office. So it was a bit uncomfortable to have Rita always at his elbow. He couldn't have a decent conversation with her hanging about!

"Um. . . excuse me a minute," Russ said, gesturing with his glass toward another colleague across the room. "I just need to go and talk to Ron for a minute. Be right back."

With a sense of relief, Russ wound his way to where Ron, one of the junior executives, was talking to someone else. He arrived with a ready smile as the other man turned. Great. Ron was conversing with Josh Fredrickson. Just the person he *didn't* feel like talking to tonight. "Hi, Ron. Josh," Russ greeted, pasting on his best smile. "How are you this evening?"

"Fine," Ron said. "Good to see you and Rita could make it."

"Uh, yeah."

"I didn't actually know you two were together," Josh admitted. "That's what I get for keeping my own nose to the grindstone, I guess. " He laughed. "So, you all ready for Christmas?"

"As ready as I need to be," Russ responded with a nod. "Mark's getting kind of big for the Santa thing and we always go to my mother's for Christmas dinner."

"My kids are crazy for Christmas," Josh laughed. "My wife, too. We've had the tree up for weeks."

"That so?" Russ said, trying to sound interested.

"Of course, one of the reasons I love Christmas is it's a great opportunity to share the gospel," Josh went on. "People don't mind hearing about peace and good will at Christmas time and of course, it is Jesus' birth."

"Um, my wife's waving me over," Ron interrupted. "I'll see you guys around." He turned and beat a hasty retreat.

"I'm surprised you're here," Russ noted after Ron left.

"Oh? Why's that?" Josh asked.

"I don't know," Russ shrugged. "I just figured you wouldn't like this kind of thing. All the drinking and such."

"Just because I'm a Christian, doesn't mean I don't like to have fun," Josh laughed. "And besides, I can have a good time without drinking."

Russ nodded. "Yeah. I'm not much of a drinker myself." He looked down at the half full glass of amber liquid. "Well, not as a rule, anyway."

"People have this idea that Christians think they're better than other people or something," Josh continued. "Or that they're afraid to get out in the real world. But that's not what Jesus did. He hung out with tax collectors and prostitutes all the time. We're supposed to be salt and light. It's pretty hard to do that if you stay home in a bubble."

"I suppose."

"Are you a man of faith?" Josh asked, eyeing Russ with candid openness.

"I was brought up in the church, if that's what you mean," Russ answered tentatively. "And I do believe in God."

"Even the devil believes," Josh countered. He was still smiling.

"Yeah, right. . ." Russ looked around for a way of escape. It was going to be a long evening.

❧

"Grandma? Why did my mother leave us?" Mark asked, yawning widely and snuggling closer into Dorothy's side. They were sitting together on the couch downstairs, looking at old photo albums. An activity only allowed when his father wasn't present.

"She was young," Dorothy offered. "Too young to get married, I guess."

"Dad was young, too," Mark observed.

"Yes," Dorothy nodded. "But your mother was . . . she was a free spirit, I guess. She just needed to leave. Had other plans for her life."

"Didn't she love us?" Mark asked.

"Of course she loved you!" Dorothy exclaimed and gave the boy a squeeze. "What's not to love? Now that's enough for tonight, I think," she said, struggling to rise from the depths of the soft sofa. "Time for bed."

"I thought we were going to watch a Christmas special on TV." Mark yawned again.

"Nothing's on this late," Dorothy replied. "Besides, you wanted to look at pictures."

"Grandma?"

"Yes, Mark?"

"Do you like Rita?" he asked. His brow, which looked so much like his father's, was furrowed in thought.

"Yes," Dorothy replied, considering. "She seems like a nice enough lady. Do you?"

"I don't know," Mark shrugged. "I haven't decided yet."

"Wouldn't you like to have a mother?" Dorothy asked.

"Yeah. Sometimes." Mark hesitated. "But sometimes I worry she'll just run away. Like my other mother did."

"Oh, my dear boy!" Dorothy exclaimed and squeezed him to her bosom. "Don't be so silly. Nobody's ever going to do that to you, again. Now, up to bed you go."

❧

Thankfully, Rita had too much to drink by the end of the night and forgot about her earlier designs on Russ's time. Actually, he'd made sure of it. He just kept refilling her glass and she just kept consuming it. By the time the last few partiers were ready to leave, Russ put her in a cab and sent her on her way. He'd had a few himself and needed to take his own cab home. It was a good excuse. This time. But not one he could keep on using.

He was just going to have to make up his mind. Either he and Rita moved on in their relationship or they called it off all together. But after tonight there was no stalling on that front. Rita had made that perfectly clear.

Russ fluffed his pillow and settled back into the comfort of his own bed. Alone. Maybe some good bedroom Olympics was what he needed to get that other woman out of his brain for good. He thought about the prospects for a minute and smiled, then shook himself and turned over with an oath. The woman in his fantasy had the wrong color hair. Probably just the booze talking. It was clouding his brain...

Russ drifted off to sleep, visions of Deanie Burton dancing in his head.

103

Chapter Thirteen

"I do love Christmas," Deanie sighed, patting her belly.

"At least this year you have the excuse of eating for two," Brent observed with a grin.

"Brent!" Holly chastised. "That's terrible!"

"What?" Brent asked, all innocence. "You should see the way this kid eats. I know you wouldn't think so to look at her, but she can really pack it away!"

"Shut up," Deanie laughed and fired an after dinner mint in his general direction. "Nobody asked you. Aren't you supposed to be doing dishes or something?"

"Later," Brent dismissed. He popped the mint into his mouth. "Think I need to move to the couch and let my stomach settle for a while first."

"Nope," Benny Walters said as he rose from his seat with a satisfied grunt. "We'll get it done and out of the way and *then* relax. Deanie, why don't you take Holly into the living room and let us men handle the clean up."

"I don't mind helping," Holly spoke up quickly. "Thank you so much for inviting me, by the way."

"Nonsense," Benny replied. "I won't have a special guest doing dishes."

"That's right. You two go on," Jack piped up. "We don't need no women hovering about the kitchen getting in the way."

Holly tried to protest. "Really, I -"

"No way," Benny insisted. "Brent, tell her."

"House rules," Brent shrugged with a grin. "Although we also have a rule that by the second visit you're no longer considered a guest."

"So you better take advantage while you can," Deanie interjected. "Besides, there's no arguing with those two." She gestured with her head toward Benny and Jack. "They can be equally stubborn when they want to be."

The two women left the clutter of the dining room table and headed for the sofa in the adjacent living room. Deanie was glad for the time alone with Holly. She liked the other girl, even if she was religious. Holly seemed so open and friendly. Deanie couldn't remember having a close female friend before, and even though she had only met with Holly a few times since their initial introduction, she felt an affinity for her.

"I'm really glad I came today. It was so nice of you to let me in on your family time," Holly said.

"Of course," Deanie replied. "Who ever heard of spending Christmas day alone? Besides, we're glad you came. It's usually just us. Me, Jack, Benny and Brent. I know for a fact Brent is extra happy you showed up."

"Um, yeah. Your dad seems like a lot of fun," Holly commented.

"Isn't he adorable? He's really been so good about the baby and everything." Deanie smiled at her friend.

"How's the job hunt coming?" Holly asked.

"Not too well," Deanie stated glumly. "Nobody is interested in hiring a single, pregnant woman with practically no skills."

"You know, I might know of something you'd be interested in," Holly said.

"Really? What?" Deanie asked, sitting up with interest.

"Well, I know of a street mission downtown. It's kind of a drop in center for street kids. My church helps fund it. They're looking for someone on a part time basis. It doesn't pay a lot. But it might be better than nothing."

"What kind of work is it?"

"Mostly just listening. A friendly, non judgmental ear. Keep the coffee pot warm, answer the phone, that kind of thing. Since you do have some training in social work, they might consider you, and it might be a good way to see if you really want to pursue that line of work."

"I'm not sure I'm the best person to be giving advice right at the moment." Deanie looked pointedly at her stomach. "Especially if it's a church thing. I don't know too much about that sort of thing, and I'm not exactly a saint."

"But that's the point exactly," Holly affirmed. "You can probably relate to these kids better than most. Just be a friend. The rest of the staff could handle any questions of a spiritual nature. The mission is mostly concerned with the immediate physical needs of these kids, anyway. It's pretty hard to preach the gospel of a loving and caring Savior to someone who is hungry and cold. Lots of these kids come right off the street. Drugs, prostitution, gangs. . . you name it. They need to know someone is out there who really cares about them, wherever they're at."

"So who would I contact?" Deanie asked, warming to the idea.

"The man who heads up the mission is Alec Turner. The kids really like him, but he doesn't put up with any nonsense from them. No drinking or drugs on the premises. You should give it a try. You've got nothing to lose, and I'll put in a good word for you."

"Hmm. It is something to consider. Thanks, Holly."

"I might even see you down there. I sometimes volunteer there myself," Holly explained.

"Holly, can I ask you something?" Deanie hesitated. "Something a little more personal?"

"Sure. What is it?"

"Well, I was wondering. The way you always talk about the 'Lord' and 'Jesus'. Like he was a real person, or something."

"He is."

"How can you be so sure?" Deanie asked. "Maybe it's just all this Christmas stuff that has me thinking. I mean, I've seen religious people before, but it seemed like almost a game to them. Or a way to take your money or suck you in, in some way. But it seems different with you. Real. Does that make sense?"

"I guess it's the difference between 'religion' and 'relationship'," Holly explained. "I don't have 'religion' so much as a 'relationship' with Jesus."

"I don't get it," Deanie shook her head. "I mean, that sounds pretty hokey to me. How can you have a relationship with God? I always thought

He was way up there in heaven or something. Doesn't He have enough problems just running the world?"

"There's no doubt that God *is* big," Holly explained. "He's everywhere and is all powerful and all knowing. He created the whole universe and set all the natural laws in motion. But He also created you - specifically - and wants to commune with you. But first you have to recognize that you need Him and really want to have Him take over your life."

"But how can you do that? Just somehow conjure it up in your mind or something?" Deanie frowned. "I don't think I have enough faith for that. I'm not good enough that He would want me, anyway."

"Deanie, the Bible says that we all need God. Romans 3:23 says all have sinned and fall short of His glory. Nobody is good enough. But the good news is, He isn't asking you to change first. He wants you just as you are. He'll do the work in you."

"How?" Deanie scrutinized the other woman. She really wanted to understand, but it just wasn't making any sense.

"The first step is admitting that you're a sinner, like I just said. You need to ask for His forgiveness. He wants to do that for you, if you'll only ask. Then simply ask Him to come into your life - to become Lord and Savior, and He will. It's a free gift. He wants to give it to you."

"Hmm," Deanie mused. "That's not the way I heard it before. I thought it was something you had to work at. Are you sure about this?"

"As sure as I am about anything," Holly nodded. "This is for real, Deanie. The Bible says our righteousness is like filthy rags to God. We could never be 'good enough' for Him. And somehow, that filthiness needs to be punished. He can't just ignore it, because He is pure and holy and just. Sin needs to be dealt with. But the miracle is, He sent His own son, Jesus, to pay that penalty for us. He took your sin and mine - the sin of the entire human race - onto Himself, and paid so that we wouldn't have to. All you need to do now is receive that payment as a gift."

"But if God is God, why couldn't He just zap everybody and make us good? Then nobody would have to die," Deanie reasoned.

"He doesn't want a bunch of puppets, Deanie. He's given us a free choice. He wants your love and devotion, and He wants to give you an abundant life, but He isn't going to force it on you."

"I still don't get it. It's too confusing," Deanie sighed. "What does Brent think of all this?"

"He's open," Holly said, "and hungry for the truth, as most people are. Jesus said, 'I am the way, the truth and the life, no one comes to the Father but by me.' You're welcome to join us in studying the Bible, if you'd like to."

"Brent might not appreciate it. Unless you need a chaperone," Deanie laughed.

"Oh." Holly looked down at her hands, color rising in her cheeks.

Deanie surveyed the other girl and smiled. "It's okay, you know. That you like each other, I mean. Brent's an awesome guy."

"I know," Holly agreed.

"And I think it's very commendable for you two to be studying the Bible and all, but I think we all know Brent is interested for more reasons than just seeking after the truth, if you know what I mean."

"Well. . . um, do you think?" Holly stammered, looking away.

"Hey, I didn't mean to embarrass you, Holly. I feel like we are getting to be pretty good friends, after all. And if I'm reading things right, I'd say you might feel the same way about him?"

"It's that obvious, huh?" Holly laughed. Her cheeks were a flaming pink.

"There's nothing to be ashamed of," Deanie reassured. "Although maybe that chaperone idea isn't such a bad one?"

"Did I hear my name?" Brent asked as he sauntered into the living room and perched on the arm of Holly's chair. He gave her a winning smile, which seemed to unnerve her all the more.

"We were just having some wonderful girl talk, weren't we Holly?" Deanie beamed.

"Oh, oh," Brent frowned. "Why does that scare me?"

"Who's for some Christmas carols?" Jack bellowed as he and Benny followed closely on Brent's heels. He was already taking his saxophone out of its case.

"Another Christmas tradition," Deanie informed with a laugh. "You can't live with a bunch of musicians and not expect any excuse for a jam session."

"Holly, since you're our guest, you get to pick the first song," Benny offered.

"Okay," Holly agreed. "How about Silent Night?"

"Wonderful choice," Jack enthused. "What key Walters?"

"C is fine," Benny said, adjusting his bass. Brent had also found a guitar and the three of them were tuning up.

"Welcome to a Walters-Burton Christmas," Deanie whispered to Holly. "The first of many, I hope."

"Thanks," the other girl beamed.

❧

"Thank you for your hospitality, Mrs. Graham," Rita said politely. "The turkey was lovely." She was standing inside the front door of Dorothy's home saying her good-byes.

"I'm glad you could join us," Dorothy responded, always the gracious hostess. "Come again."

"I'll walk you to your car," Russ offered. Rita had insisted on bringing her own vehicle since he and Mark had planned to arrive much earlier than she.

Once out by her car, Rita turned to Russ for the expected good night kiss. He provided it, somewhat mechanically, and took a step back as he opened her car door.

"Just a minute," she said.

"Yes?"

She surveyed Russ for a moment then sighed. "I suppose there's no coming over for a night cap?"

"There's Mark and the family," Russ hedged. "It is Christmas."

"When are you going to run out of excuses, Russ?" Rita demanded. "I'm beginning to think there's something you're not telling me."

"Like what?"

"Why don't you tell me?" she asked, giving him a pointed stare. "Healthy males don't usually balk at the prospects of sex."

"I'm not balking -"

She cut him off. "I'm not one to jump in and out of bed on a whim, but I'm not used to being rebuffed, either. Tell me what's going on."

Russ sighed. "I don't know what's going on. Maybe we just need more time . . ."

"More time?" she laughed. "Is it a medical problem?" she asked, raising an eyebrow.

"No! It's not a medical problem!" Russ blustered.

"Then what?" she demanded.

Russ let out a pent up breath and ran his fingers through his hair. "I like you, Rita. And I do find you attractive. Really I do."

"But?"

Russ shook his head. "There's no spark. I don't know. I can't quite explain it."

"How would you know there's no spark if you've never tried?" she countered, setting her mouth into a firm line.

"I'm sorry. I don't know what else to say," Russ shrugged.

"Maybe we should just call the whole thing off. Stop seeing each other all together," she suggested, eyeing him for his reaction.

"Maybe. I mean," he hesitated, surveying her with furrowed brow. "Is that what you want?"

"Actually," Rita replied airily. "I think the truth is you're still stuck on some other woman."

"Now, that's ridiculous -"

"Is it?" she interrupted, her glare icy ."I don't like being second fiddle, Russ. Make up your mind one way or another. I'll give you till New Year's Eve." With that Rita slid into her car and shut the door with a decisive click.

Russ watched her drive away. He felt nothing. Except, maybe, a little bit of relief. He strolled back up the sidewalk to the house, hands in his pockets. When he entered he wore a slight smile on his lips.

"She seems like a nice person," Dorothy offered, misreading his features. She was fixing the wreath that hung just inside the door.

"Hm? Oh. Yeah," Russ replied absently.

"Very sensible choice, I'd say," Dorothy went on. She stood back to survey her handiwork.

"I think we just broke up," Russ said off hand. He thought he heard a distinct 'Yeah!' coming from the living room. When he looked around the corner, he saw Mark, Samantha, Greg and Ken, all apparently absorbed in a Christmas special on television. Kathy was leafing through a magazine.

"What? You broke up? But why?" Dorothy asked, her brow furrowing with concern. "You seem so perfect for one another."

"Maybe that's just it," Russ shrugged. "Too perfect. You know, I have heard it said that opposites attract."

"But on Christmas day!" Dorothy clucked. "That is unfortunate."

"Forget it," Russ said, sauntering into the living room. "Hey, what's on TV?"

He hadn't felt this free in months.

Chapter Fourteen

Deanie sat at the downtown youth center, drinking another cup of strong, black coffee. Her application had been accepted on a temporary basis and it was now her new place of employment. The hours were unusual and the pay was not high, but the job itself provided some sense of satisfaction. Something that Deanie had been lacking of late.

"Kind of quiet, tonight," Thomas, one of her co-workers, commented. He was flipping through a sports magazine. He was not what Deanie had imagined as a typical Christian. None of them that worked there were, for that matter. Thomas wore small, round, wire rimmed glasses, his long brown hair was pulled back into a haphazard ponytail, and he had an earring in one ear. He'd fit in better with the band, she thought. So much for stereotypes. It was one thing that she really liked about working here. People didn't judge you on your appearance. They seemed genuinely interested in the person behind the exterior.

The center itself was located on a narrow side street right in the heart of the city. The building was a small, converted storefront, transformed on the inside with comfy couches, a large TV, pool table, foosball, some video arcade games, and lots of free coffee and pop. Sandwiches and other light food were also provided, as well as counseling services for those who wanted it. It was a place of warmth and friendship. A refuge for the alarming number of troubled kids who had somehow found themselves on the streets.

"I guess it's kind of cold for people to be out," Deanie responded, watching the two young males who were playing a game of pool. The only other patron was a girl, probably in her teens and wearing far too much makeup, who sat indolently watching TV.

"I don't know," Thomas mused. "We're often busier in January, as a rule. Once the season of good will is over, people tend to forget about all the needs that are still out there. That, and lots of people feel really let down once the party's over, so to speak."

"I suppose," Deanie nodded.

Suddenly a tinkling crash sounded outside.

Both Thomas and Deanie jumped from their seats - Deanie upsetting her coffee - and headed simultaneously for the door. The bitter coldness of the night pinched any exposed skin and Deanie hugged herself, shivering as they stepped out onto the sidewalk. There was a surreal calmness about the night, as she peered around for the source of the momentary, nerve shattering noise. The streetlights cast a bluish glow upon the white carpeted ground. Snow was falling gently, covering every surface, yet undisturbed by footprints. She spotted a small red car across the street. It looked as though it had slid into a lamp pole. The front fender was buckled in and the headlight smashed; the driver slumped over the steering wheel.

Thomas was already at the car, peering into the driver's door and calling out to the person within. "Ma'am? Are you all right, ma'am?" He turned to Deanie. "Come help me," he called. Deanie rushed to follow orders, slipping and sliding on the blanketed pavement. The woman was conscious, but seemed disoriented, mumbling incoherently.

"Maybe she hit her head," Deanie suggested as she came alongside and looked at the woman.

"Can you get out of the car?" Thomas asked. His voice was loud, as if he were talking to a deaf person. She mumbled something unintelligible. "Here, let's just undo your belt," he suggested, grunting as he bent into the car to unfasten her restraint. Between the two of them they managed to half drag the woman from the car and up onto her feet. She wobbled unsteadily.

"Oh, oh," Thomas frowned, quickly slipping an arm around her waist.

"Phew," Deanie wrinkled her nose. "I'd know that smell anywhere."

Thomas shook his head. "When are people gonna figure out that you shouldn't drink and drive? Come on, let's get her into the center."

The woman giggled, leaning heavily on both Thomas and Deanie as they supported her on either side.

"Looks like she's been in the bag," commented one of the boys, who had been watching from the doorway.

"Looks like it," Deanie agreed, scrunching her nose.

"She hurt?" asked the other boy.

"Don't know," Thomas answered. "We'll have to report this to the police, though."

The two boys looked at each other before beating a hasty retreat. The young woman who'd been watching TV had already taken her leave.

"Ma'am." Thomas was yelling again. "Do you have someone we can call?" The woman, who looked to be about thirty, squinted, trying to focus on Thomas's face. He sighed, turning to Deanie. "You go call the police. I'll see if I can get another number out of her. Oh! And then bring her a coffee, if you don't mind."

Deanie nodded mutely, rushing to do as Thomas had asked. Once the police had been notified, she brought a steaming styrofoam cup of coffee with a little sugar added. "Everything's going to be fine," Deanie said, not really sure if she believed it.

"What was I saying about a quiet evening?" Thomas asked, grinning.

❦

Russ pulled up in front of the youth center and put his vehicle in park with a jerk. He took a steadying breath before opening the door, slipping slightly on the fresh snow beneath his feet. He should have just ignored the call. Or said no. He was tired of being his brother's keeper. If Ken and Kathy were ever going to change, he'd probably have to quit coming to the rescue all the time. But the man on the other line said Kathy had been in an accident. What if it was serious? Duty called.

Russ stepped through the front door of the youth center, stomping the snow off his boots onto the mat. He stopped abruptly as his mind went completely blank. Why was he here again? All he could focus on was Deanie. And the fact that she was unmistakably pregnant.

He shook his head, taking an unsteady breath. "Kathy . . . Uh, someone called about Kathy?"

"Yes," Thomas replied. "But the ambulance has already taken her to the hospital. Health Sciences. You her husband?"

"Brother in law," Russ corrected with a sigh, running his hand through his hair. "Has her husband been contacted?"

"I'm not sure. The police took all her information, but yours was the number she gave me to call," Thomas replied.

"Of course," Russ grunted. "Can I just use your phone for a minute? Make sure Ken's been notified?"

"Be my guest," Thomas nodded.

Russ stole a glance at Deanie on his way to the phone. She hadn't looked at him since he entered. Kept her eyes on the floor. She looked genuinely stricken. No wonder.

He dialed Ken's home and waited. No answer. Ken was probably already at the hospital or on his way. With decisiveness Russ clicked the receiver back into place. "Well, thanks," he directed at Thomas. "I guess I'll head over there, then." He hesitated. "Um. . . how are you?" he asked. Stupid question. It was pretty obvious. She was pregnant. Probably one of her rock and roll boyfriends. He felt a mix of jealousy and deep sadness stabbing him in the chest. Making it hard to breathe.

"Can we talk for a minute?" Deanie asked, so quiet that he might not have heard if he hadn't been so aware of her presence. He turned slowly, planting his feet. "Thomas?" she spoke to the other man. "Would you mind? We just need a few minutes alone."

"Sure," Thomas replied, the unasked question in his eyes. "I'll just head to the back room. Call me if you need me."

Deanie waited until Thomas had disappeared. Russ hadn't moved an inch. She took a deep steadying breath. "Sorry I didn't tell you," she began. "Jack said I should, but -"

"Stop!" Russ stood stock still, forcing himself to breath. Icy fingers had begun to creep up his spine. "Tell me what." He already knew the answer.

"Isn't it obvious?" She gestured to her abdomen.

"Who's the father?" he asked, not really wanting to know. His head felt foggy, like he was awake but not, the way you feel sometimes when just waking from an especially graphic dream.

"Do you really have to ask?" Deanie blinked, the tears very close to the surface now.

Ice had turned to fire. Hot bile was churning and bubbling now in the pit of his stomach. His nostrils flared as he tried to inhale. "How do you know?" he asked, voice barely audible.

Deanie laughed outright this time, sarcasm lacing her response. "Geez, Russ. How do you think? Maybe the fact that I haven't had sex with anybody else in the last year?"

Russ knew he was about to faint if he didn't get to a chair. He stalked to the nearest couch and lowered himself into its depths. "Just a minute," he breathed, closing his eyes. Surely this couldn't be happening again? This same sadistic story line . . .

"I didn't get pregnant on purpose if that's what you think," Deanie offered, perching gingerly on the far edge of the couch.

"How do I know you're not lying?" Russ barely whispered.

"Bastard," Deanie shook her head. "Exactly why I wasn't going to tell you."

"Well?" Russ shot back, turning his head to look at her. "It's a reasonable question. You've got to admit."

Deanie stood, looking directly at Russ. "Go ahead and think whatever you want. I don't want anything from you, so you might as well just get the hell out right now."

Russ's mind was in a blur. She was pregnant. With his child. Could it really be true? "What are you going to do?" he asked quietly.

"Keep it, if that's what you mean."

"How are you going to support yourself?"

"I'll manage. I told you already, I don't want your charity," she said defensively.

"Um, excuse me?" It was Thomas. "Is everything alright?" he asked, sliding into the room.

"Um, yeah. Sure," Deanie nodded. "He was just leaving."

Russ frowned. "I never said that. I'm not through talking to you."

"Well, I'm through talking to you," Deanie informed. "Besides, aren't you needed at the hospital?"

Russ blinked, confusion clouding his brain for a moment. Kathy. He probably should make sure everything was okay. He rose from the couch with a heave and let out a gust of breath. "Right," he said. He looked at Deanie. "I'll call you."

"You don't have to," she stated, with a frown. "I told you -"

"I'll call you," he repeated more definitively. He held her gaze for a moment then glanced over at Thomas. "Good night." With that he strode to the front door, and stepped out into the darkness of the night. The cold hit him like a slap in the face. Just what he needed. Just what he deserved.

He slipped into the driver's seat of his car and shut the door. Like an automaton, he started the engine, letting it idle for a few minutes while he collected his thoughts, drumming his fingers on the steering wheel.

September till now . . . that would make her five months pregnant. That looked about right. Another cold shiver crept up his spine. What now? Maybe she was lying – maybe the baby wasn't his. He closed his eyes and took a deep breath. He knew it wasn't true. She wasn't even going to tell him. Didn't need his charity, she'd said.

But that's not the way he played, whether she liked it or not. He wasn't one to go around shirking his duties. The question was, how was he going to explain this to Mark? Never mind Mark, what about his mother? Ken and Kathy? His colleagues at work? At least with Miranda he'd had the inexperience of youth on his side. But now? He had no excuse. He had just set himself up for a very large dose of humiliation.

Russ shook his head. He had no idea what the next step would be, but if that child was indeed his, there was one thing for certain. Deanie Burton had not seen the last of him.

THIRD MOVEMENT:
Allegro

Chapter Fifteen

Russ approached the front door of the building and rang the bell several times, jamming his hands in his pockets and hunkering down inside his winter jacket as he waited for a response. There was a click and a gravelly male voice spoke over the intercom. "Yes?"

"Hello? Is this where I might find Deanie Burton?" Russ asked politely.

"Who wants to know?" came the gruff reply.

Russ frowned. The old man wasn't going to make it easy. He cleared his throat. "Ah, Russ Graham. I'm a. . . friend of your daughter."

"Are you an accountant?" the old man asked.

Russ hesitated. "Yes."

"Well, well," the old man's voice had changed. "Come on up, then. Second floor, third door to the left."

The door release buzzed, and Russ entered the apartment block. He took the stairs two at a time and turned left as instructed. He took one last steadying breath before raising his hand to knock, but before his knuckles could touch wood, Jack Burton was swinging the door wide. "Come in, come in," Jack blustered, ushering him in with his arms. The wiry musician looked just as Russ remembered. Kind of rumpled and unkempt in a Bohemian kind of way.

Russ stepped across the threshold and surveyed the general clutter. The combination kitchen and living room were sparsely furnished with odds and ends. Beige speckled curtains hung limply from a patio door leading out onto the balcony. Various photographs were clustered on any available surface, or simply tacked directly onto the yellowing walls along with old posters and calendars. Leaning in one corner was a battered guitar and a scratched black saxophone case. Newspapers and sheet music shared the floor with a few stray socks.

"Can I get you something?" Jack offered. "Coffee?"

"Um, no thanks," Russ declined.

"Sure? I'm having some myself. It's no trouble," Jack said. "Have a seat," He transferred a stack of papers from one of the kitchen chairs onto an already tottering pile on the table. Russ considered the cleanliness of the chair for a moment and then sat down gingerly on its edge. "What did you say your name was again?" Jack asked, squinting over the tops of his glasses at Russ as he filled the coffee maker with water.

"Russ Graham."

Jack nodded and cocked his head to one side. "The accountant."

Russ blinked, then nodded his own head. "I take it you and Deanie have. . . talked about me?"

"Nope," Jack denied, finishing his coffee preparations.

"Oh." Russ looked down at his hands.

Jack turned and leaned against the counter, folding his arms and surveying the younger man with deliberateness. "Nope. She never breathed a word," he reiterated.

"Um . . . okay." The way the old man was staring he couldn't make out if he knew something or not. "So. Deanie? Is she here?"

"Yep. Sleeping," Jack supplied, still scrutinizing Russ.

"Oh. I never thought of that," Russ frowned.

"She works late, you know," Jack explained. "Plus the fact that she needs her sleep these days." He kept staring. "But that's for her to tell you." He pushed off the counter. "I'll go wake her."

"Maybe I should just come back later," Russ suggested, beginning to rise from the chair.

"Sit!" Jack barked. Russ did. "Don't you be going anywhere. Now, I'll just be a minute. Stay put, you here?"

Russ drummed his fingers on the table. This was probably the dumbest idea he'd had yet. He hadn't really bargained on dealing with the father. He should have called first.

Russ's head jerked up as Deanie emerged from her bedroom. His heart jolted in his chest. She looked so young! She was wearing a bathrobe, and her hair was mussed from sleep. She yawned and blinked. Then her eyes flew wide open. "What . . .?" She turned on her father. "Jack! You promised!"

"Now, now! I promised not to tell and I never breathed a word to anyone," Jack defended. "He came here all by himself."

Deanie turned on Russ. "I thought you said you'd *call.*"

Russ shrugged. "I came in person instead."

Deanie folded her arms across her chest. "How did you find me, anyway?"

"It wasn't that difficult," Russ replied.

"Well, you can turn around and get the hell out," Deanie clipped, pointing at the door. "I said everything I needed to last night."

"Last night?" Jack interjected. "So you already know?" he looked at Russ with raised brows.

"Yes," Russ nodded, his tone controlled. "Although, I found out by accident. Apparently she wasn't going to tell me."

"I told her that wasn't a good idea," Jack blustered. "A man has a right to know, I said."

"Would both of you just shut up for one minute?" Deanie demanded, glaring

"Deanie," Russ broke in, standing, "I would appreciate a chance to talk to you. Privately." He looked meaningfully at Jack.

"I don't think so," Deanie responded, setting her lips in a firm line.

"Of course she's going to talk to you," Jack countered "I was just thinking that I needed to take a walk down to the corner store to get some cream for the coffee."

"Jack," Deanie said, pleading in her eyes.

"Now, now, my dear," Jack patted her arm before reaching for his coat. "This is for the best. You knew he was bound to find out, and the man needs to say his piece."

"I thought you were on my side," Deanie pouted.

"I am, but it's the only decent thing." Jack gave his daughter a swift hug, then saluted Russ on his way out the door.

Deanie waited until Jack had shut the door behind him, and then plopped down on the living room couch. "Well?" she asked. "What shall we talk about?"

"This isn't a joke," Russ chided.

"Believe me, I'm not laughing," Deanie cut back.

Russ sighed and sank back onto his kitchen chair.

"So? Why are you here?" Deanie asked, looking at the ceiling. "I thought I made it clear last night that I'm not expecting anything from you. You can just go about your life and I won't bother you for anything. I'm not like that."

"It's not that simple," Russ responded.

"Why not? It can be as simple as you choose to make it," Deanie clipped.

"I don't go around shirking my responsibilities," Russ countered. "I'm not like *that*."

Deanie just grunted.

Russ sighed heavily, running a hand through his hair. "I know you might think this sounds rude, but I need to know for sure. Is this child mine?"

"You're not winning any points, here, buddy," Deanie spat.

"I take it that's a yes?"

"Yes. Yes, yes, yes, yes, yes!" Deanie glared at Russ and he lowered his gaze. "How can you even ask? I already told you, I don't want your charity. I never even wanted you to know. So why would I go and lie about it now?"

Russ thought about it for a minute, and shook his head. "Sorry. I guess it's a little like dejavue."

Deanie blinked. "Oh. Your ex. I hadn't thought about that."

Russ laughed harshly. "Yeah. You'd think I'd have learned."

Deanie's features had softened slightly. "That wasn't your fault. And neither was this. Besides that, I'm not your ex."

Russ turned his head and surveyed her closely for a moment. "Somebody has to take responsibility."

"I am," Deanie informed. "Are you dense or what? I already told you, I'm not expecting anything from you. I know it's going to be tough. Life is not going to be easy for either of us – me or my baby. But I'm ready for it. I'm moving forward, Russ, and you should, too."

"It's not just your baby," Russ stated.

Deanie blinked, tears suddenly much too close to the surface. "You've already made it perfectly clear how you feel about that. I don't need sympathy or some self righteous sense of obligation."

Russ opened his mouth to speak, then closed it again. He *had* been acting self righteous. His lack of respect toward her was unpardonable. "I know it's probably too little too late," he ventured. "But I am sorry. For everything."

Deanie shrugged. "Whatever you say."

"I mean it. I was a self righteous ass and I treated you terribly."

A smile touched the corners of Deanie's mouth. "Agreed."

Russ allowed his own lips to twitch. "Rather quickly."

"So? Now what?" Deanie asked. "This doesn't change anything. I still don't want your charity."

"Who said anything about charity?" Russ asked. "I just know that I'm not going to walk away and ignore the fact that I have another child. I won't have a child of mine growing up in near poverty if I can do anything about it."

"Poverty?" she repeated. Deanie squeezed her eyes shut for a moment and then opened them again, blazing. "What was that you said a moment ago? Self righteous ASS, was it? Jack and I may not have much, but we have our dignity, and we have LOVE. Which is a whole lot more than you're capable of giving!"

Russ looked at the ceiling and expended a gust of air. "Okay. Sorry. I didn't mean it the way it sounded. I just mean, I want to be involved. I *need* to be involved. Surely you must understand that I am far better equipped, financially. . . and otherwise."

"What is that supposed to mean?" Deanie clipped. "Better equipped?"

"I mean, as in a stable income," Russ responded, trying to sound patient, "and as a parent."

"Hold on, just a minute," Deanie said, throwing her hands up. "The money thing I understand – not that I said I wanted any. But what's this about being a parent? If, and that's a big 'if', I was to accept some financial support from you, I did not agree to any other kind of parental anything."

"I don't think that's your decision to make," Russ quipped, his own ire rising. What was wrong with the woman? Couldn't she see sense? .

"Of course it's my decision!" Deanie shot back.

"Father's have just as much right these days," Russ informed.

Deanie fumed for a moment, considering the truth of his statement. "But why would you want that?" she finally asked. "Wouldn't that be. . . awkward? For your kid and everything?"

"I didn't say I wanted anything," Russ replied. "I'm just as confused as you are. All I'm saying is, somehow we're going to have to work this thing out."

Deanie let out a frustrated sigh. "I knew this was just going to get complicated."

"Listen. Why don't we talk about it some more later? How about over dinner at my place, tonight?"

"Dinner at your place?" Deanie screwed up her face. "Won't your son be there?"

"So? He doesn't have to know anything other than you're a friend. It'll give you a chance to see where I live. Meet your child's older brother . . ." They heard the rattling of keys outside the apartment door. Jack was returning from the store. "Please?" Russ added for good measure.

"Okay," Deanie finally acquiesced with a sigh.

"Be there at six."

❦

At 6:30 that evening, Deanie arrived at Russ's place - half an hour later than Russ had specified. It was a fact that gave her a small sense of satisfaction. Let him stew just a bit. She was duly impressed, however, by the neighborhood and Russ's house in particular. The guy must have a few bucks, she noted, as she slammed the driver's door of her car. Her shabby Chevette looked decidedly out of place in front of Russ's classic home. She straightened her shoulders, and held her head high as she ascended the steps and rang the bell.

124

Russ swung the front door open just seconds later. He must have been waiting, she realized again with satisfaction. He looked good - too good - in jeans and a sweater, and he smelled good, too. Like soap and after-shave. "Here I am," she stated.

"Yes," Russ replied. He seemed awkward. Nervous as they stood looking at one another in the entrance. Good. He cleared his throat. "Well, won't you come in?' he asked with formality, and ushered her into the warmth of the spacious foyer. Everything was clean and tidy, she noticed, as Russ took her jacket and hung it in the hall closet.

"I'll show you around," Russ said, as if conducting a tour. They entered the living room first. It was sparsely furnished and looked as if it was seldom used. A large bay window overlooked the front yard.

"Nice view," Deanie commented, nodding.

"Hm? Oh, yes," Russ replied, already leading the way into the formal dining room. Again, it was quite Spartan, except for a large oak dining set. "We don't use these rooms much," Russ explained, somewhat apologetically. He led the way past a main floor washroom and into the back half of the house. The combination kitchen and eating area, although spotlessly clean, had a much warmer feeling. Deanie noticed with amazement that there wasn't even one dirty mug in the sink. And the counters and appliances fairly gleamed under the panels of fluorescent light.

"Some housekeeper," Deanie commented under her breath.

"Pardon me?" Russ queried.

"Oh nothing," Deanie waved a hand. "I was just noticing how clean everything is."

"Oh." Russ looked around the room. "We have a cleaning lady who comes in once a week. But there's just the two of us," he explained.

"There's just the two of us, too," Deanie murmured.

"Dinner is almost ready," Russ informed. "You might as well sit in the family room until it is." He gestured to the adjoining, sunken family room. It was simply, yet tastefully decorated in shades of blue. A stone fireplace, with a large oak mantel and bookcases on either side took up one entire wall. A large leather sofa and chair were grouped to give maximum viewing access to the entertainment center, which housed the TV and stereo equipment. A low fire gave the room homey warmth.

Nothing was out of place save for the evening newspaper that resided on a corner table.

Deanie lowered herself into one of the chairs. He was well off, obviously. And he was being very civil, so far, not to mention the fact that he was so frustratingly good looking.

"Can I get you something while you wait?" Russ offered..

"No, I'm fine. I'll just sit here and enjoy the fire. Unless you need help with something?"

"No thank you. Just make yourself at home. Watch some TV if you want." Russ turned and went back to the kitchen. Deanie let out a pent up breath, and stared into the fire. She wasn't feeling nearly as brave as she was pretending to be. Russ, in his own environment, was totally intimidating.

Someone clearing his throat suddenly jerked her out of her contemplations. She looked up and was caught off guard by a small replica of Russ standing before her. "Hi," said the boy. "I'm Mark." He held out his hand in a formal greeting. How like his father!

"Hi there," Deanie greeted him, "My name is Deanie. Deanie Burton. I'm a. . . friend of your fathers." She smiled. From the proud set of his head, to his dark curls and deep blue eyes, he was very much his father's son.

"I know. Dad said you were coming," Mark said.

"Did he?" Deanie asked. "Did he . . . say anything else?"

"Not much," Mark frowned, obviously trying to remember. "Just that you were a lady friend, and that he wanted me to be on my best behavior. My dad never tells me much about his girlfriends."

"Does your dad have a lot of girlfriends?" Deanie asked, trying to sound nonchalant.

"No, not really," Mark shrugged. He looked around surreptitiously before continuing. "I didn't like the last one much," he confided.

"You've met Mark, I see," Russ said dryly from the doorway.

"Oh, yes," Deanie responded, catching her breath.

"Dinner is ready. I hope you don't mind if we eat in the kitchen."

"That would be just fine," Deanie said, standing.

Mark went ahead, and as Deanie brushed past Russ, he whispered, "Grilling my son, were you?" He was smiling wickedly.

126

Deanie gave him her best glare, and marched into the kitchen. She found her seat at the table before Russ could offer to help her. Laid out before them was a succulent roast of beef with all the trimmings. "My!" Deanie exclaimed. "This looks just delicious. I'll have to take some lessons."

"Can't you cook?" Mark asked

"Mark!" Russ cautioned sternly. The one word held a wealth of meaning, and Mark sat back demurely in his chair.

Deanie smiled at the boy. "Not as well as this, I don't think. Jack is always saying that I might starve to death without him around to feed me."

"Who's Jack?"

"Mark," Russ repeated the boy's name in warning.

"No, that's all right," Deanie assured Russ, then looked kindly at Mark. "Jack is my dad."

"Why do you call your own dad 'Jack'?" Mark asked, frowning.

"I don't know," Deanie responded. "But he's a great musician. You'd like him."

"Really? What kind of musician?" Mark asked.

"That's enough questions for the time being," Russ interjected before Deanie could respond. "Time to eat before everything gets cold." Russ reached for the platter of meat. "Miss Burton, would you care for some beef?"

"We should pray first," Mark suggested. "Grandma says its good for the digestion."

"Um, okay," Russ agreed. "You go ahead, son."

Mark recited a short prayer of thanks while the three of them bowed their heads. When Deanie opened her eyes, she wasn't exactly sure where to look, so settled on the tossed salad. "My friend Holly always says grace," she offered.

The food went around the table, and conversation turned to polite discussion about Mark's various interests. It seemed safer to focus on the boy. He shared briefly about school and his friends, then launched into an enthusiastic report on the latest rocks that he had added to his collection. "Dad says that maybe someday I can be an archeologist," Mark said with enthusiasm.

"That sounds interesting," Deanie replied. "And fun, too."

"Would you like to come up to my room and see my collection?" Mark asked hopefully. "I've got some really cool rocks that might even be fossils. And I even have a couple of arrowheads. Those are super cool."

"I should really help your dad clean up this mess," Deanie replied, looking over at Russ.

"Go ahead. This will just take me a minute to put everything in the dishwasher," Russ assured them.

Deanie followed Mark up the stairs to his bedroom. It was not what she would have expected from an eleven year olds room. For one thing, the bed was made, its navy plaid comforter neatly in place. Except for a model in progress and an open magazine on the bed, there seemed to be nothing out of order. Mark led her to a shelf lined with treasured memorabilia, and proceeded to explain how he had acquired each item. Deanie listened with one ear, as she surveyed the bulletin board hanging over the bed.

"This your dad?" she interrupted, pointing to a picture of a much younger man in a hockey uniform, posing with his stick poised for a slap shot.

"Yeah. That's when he played college hockey," Mark said proudly. "Before I was born."

Deanie smiled at Mark. "You look a lot like him."

"That's what everyone says," Mark shrugged.

"You're lucky. I guess he's a pretty good dad, huh?" Deanie asked.

"Yeah," Mark nodded. "But sometimes I wish . . ." He stopped abruptly, and turned away, busying himself with rearranging the items on the shelf.

Deanie's heart went out to this boy. He looked so much like his father, yet within him was the sensitive heart of a child who knew he had missed out on something, even though he'd never experienced it. "I never had a mother, either," she stated. "Is that what you were going to say?"

Mark turned and looked at her, eyes slightly wary, but hopeful. "You didn't?"

"Nope," Deanie smiled encouragingly. "I'm just like you. My mother died when I was a baby. So all I ever had was my dad. Just me and Jack."

"Why *do* you call your dad by his first name?" Mark asked, frowning.

"I don't know exactly. But it hasn't changed the fact that he's the best dad in the entire world," Deanie declared. "Well, except for yours, maybe." She ruffled Mark's hair.

"Is he old?"

"I guess to you he would seem pretty old," Deanie replied. "More like a grandpa."

"I don't have a grandpa, either," Mark stated.

"Well, maybe someday you can meet Jack. He's lots of fun. He loves kids. He'll make a terrific grandpa someday." Deanie stopped and blinked, realizing what she had just said. Jack *was* going to be a grandpa someday. Very soon. "Come on," she said abruptly. "Let's go see if your dad is done cleaning up."

Mark continued asking questions about Jack as they descended the stairs. "What kind of musician is he? Is he famous? Did he ever make a record?"

"He plays jazz music," Deanie informed. "And he's made lots of records, so I guess that makes him kind of famous."

"Jazz?" Mark screwed up his nose. "I'm not sure I like jazz. Is that like old people music?"

Deanie laughed. "No, it's not old people music! Jazz is anybody music – just like any other kind. I used to play in a band myself," she confided, a little more quietly as they reached the landing.

"What kind?"

"A rock band."

"Really?" Mark asked, eyes wide. He had lowered his own voice to barely above a whisper.

"Mmhm," Deanie nodded. "Maybe I'll tell you about it some time, but for now let's go see what your dad is doing."

Mark nodded. Deanie smiled inwardly. It was like they had suddenly formed a secret bond.

"There you are," Russ greeted them once they entered the kitchen. He pressed a button on the dishwasher and then hung a tea towel under the kitchen sink.

"Looks like you've got everything cleaned up," Deanie noted. She turned to Mark with a smile. "We timed that perfectly."

Mark smiled and nodded.

Russ consulted his watch. "You've got some homework to finish up if I'm not mistaken," he informed his son.

"Aw!" Mark grimaced.

"No buts about it, young man," Russ said firmly. "Besides that, Miss Burton and I have some things to discuss. So away you go."

Mark nodded, obviously knowing better than to protest further. "Nice meeting you," he mumbled and headed back up the stairs to his room.

"Let's move into the den," Russ suggested.

"Okay," Deanie shrugged. She followed him down the hall and entered what appeared to be an office as he ushered her inside. "Mark's a great kid," she offered as she sat in one of the plush chairs in front of Russ's desk.

"Thanks," Russ replied, sitting behind the desk.

Deanie frowned. It was a bit like a business meeting - Russ sitting behind his large oak desk and she sitting in front like a charity case come to ask for help. "Um, yeah. So? What's your big plan?"

"Putting our personal feelings aside, we just need to focus on the baby's welfare," Russ stated.

"I don't want your welfare," Deanie retorted.

Russ sighed. "Whatever. You know what I mean. I was thinking about setting up some kind of trust account that would pay you monthly benefits. I won't take no for an answer," he warned.

Deanie bit her lip. "I guess I'd be stupid to refuse . . ."

"Exactly," Russ nodded, satisfaction showing on his face.

"As long as you remember I didn't ask," Deanie said, her jaw jutting stubbornly.

"Duly noted."

She sighed. "What about the other? The visiting part?"

Russ tapped on the desk with his fingers, his brow furrowed in thought. "I haven't got that part figured out yet."

"You don't have to, you know," Deanie put in quickly. "Please. I don't want you to feel any sense of obligation."

"I'm sorry, but it's a little late for that," Russ quipped.

"Well," Deanie began. "Maybe we could meet sometimes. You know, when Mark's not around . . ."

"And just how long do you think that could last?" Russ retorted. "Once the child gets to be a certain age, he'll have questions."

"How do you know it's a 'he'?" Deanie asked. Russ surveyed her, exasperation written on his face. She knew she was acting childish, but she didn't like the smug way he was handling everything, as if it were some kind of business deal. Or charity case.

"You know what I meant. 'He or she' would have questions," Russ explained, overly patient. "And if we choose to tell 'her' that I'm her father, then she'll wonder why I don't care enough to acknowledge her openly. I know enough about abandonment issues with Mark. I'm not going to have another one go through it, too."

"Dad," Mark spoke from the doorway. Both Deanie and Russ jerked to look at him. He seemed small and confused.

"How long have you been standing there?" Russ demanded sharply.

"Only a minute," Mark said, his voice barely audible. He lowered his gaze and stared down at his feet.

There was deathly silence in the small room. Russ's jaw was working forcefully as he surveyed his son. Deanie looked from father to son and then concentrated on her own hands.

"Come and sit down, please, Son," Russ instructed, rubbing the back of his neck. Mark slid into the room and perched dutifully in the one remaining chair. "You see, Miss Burton and I, well, we. . ."

"Miss Burton is having a baby?" Mark supplied, looking up.

It took Russ a moment to find his voice. "Well you see, Son, sometimes men and women, well, they sometimes do things that aren't planned. And well. . ."

"Dad, I'm not a baby," Mark said, rolling his eyes. "I know all about the facts of life. You're the one who told me, remember?"

"Well, yes, but I just don't want you to get the wrong impression," Russ said, clearing his throat.

"Is it your baby?" Mark asked.

There was silence in the room again. Deanie held her breath, waiting for Russ's response. He licked his lips and inhaled deeply. "Yes, Son. Yes it is."

Deanie opened her lungs, allowing herself to expel the air that had been trapped inside. She felt the distinct marimba of butterflies in her stomach and a warm rim of tears collecting along her lower lids.

"You see, Mark," Russ fumbled on, "I don't want you to think that I condone casual relationships. Miss Burton. . .Deanie and I are planning to get married."

Deanie gasped. Mark's eyebrows shot up in surprise.

"Now just a -"

Russ cut off whatever Deanie had to say. "I wanted you to have a chance to meet her first, before I told you," he explained to Mark. "Everything is going to be arranged just as soon as possible."

Deanie tried again. "I think we actually -"

"So why don't you go see if you can find some ginger ale in the fridge and we'll have a little toast, hm?" Russ suggested, coming around the desk and ushering Mark toward the door. "We'll be right behind you."

"Okay," Mark agreed, looking back over his shoulder, first at Deanie and then at Russ. "Cool," he said, his face breaking into a grin.

"Cool?" Russ repeated, stopping short.

"Yeah. I get a brother or sister, a mother *and* a grandpa!"

"Oh," Russ frowned. "Well, go on!" he bustled Mark the rest of the way into the hall. "We just need one minute."

Deanie stood to her feet, her mouth aghast. "What in the world?"

Russ raised a finger to his lips to silence her and quietly shut the door of the den with a click. Then he took a deep breath and closed his eyes, leaning against the door.

"Are you crazy?" Deanie demanded. "How could you lie to your own son like that?"

"We needed a solution, I came up with a solution," Russ responded, rubbing the back of his neck, not meeting her haughty gaze.

"But you just lied to your son!" Deanie spouted.

"No I didn't," Russ denied. "Getting married isn't such a bad idea."

Deanie opened her mouth, but no words would come out. She raised her arms and then let them flop back to her sides as she fell back into the chair.

"What? Is marrying me so distasteful?" Russ asked, surveying her now.

"It's just dumb," Deanie spat. "Archaic. This is the Eighties, not the stone age."

"Now hold on," Russ said, pacing. "I realize you're in shock. We both are. I certainly had no intentions of suggesting such a thing."

"Then why did you?!"

"I don't know," Russ answered with a shake of his head. "It just - came out."

"Excellent!" Deanie mocked. "Just the way I'd always dreamed a proposal would be! Speaking of, you never actually even asked me."

Russ stopped pacing and looked squarely at Deanie. "Okay, then. Deanie Burton, will you marry me?" He waited expectantly.

"No!" she cried, sitting forward. "I will not marry you! Getting pregnant is not a good enough reason to marry someone. Marriage is supposed to be about love and respect and – oh, I don't know! All that other stuff you feel when you can't live without someone." She blinked rapidly, trying desperately to keep the tears that were now imminent from spilling over.

Russ considered her words for a moment and then sat down in the chair next to her. "I don't deny that I haven't shown you a whole lot of respect," he finally said. "And I'm not sure about love. But I know I've thought a lot about you in the last five months." He looked at her out of the corner of his eye.

"You have?" she asked, returning his gaze.

He nodded, holding her eyes for a moment before looking down. He suddenly looked vulnerable, not at all the no-nonsense business man from a few minutes ago.

"Oh." She digested that for a moment. He had been thinking about her.

He let out a nervous burst of laughter. "Yeah. That night, the second time I came around to see you at work? I had visions of making up for ditching you like that at Hecla."

"Why didn't you?" she asked.

He shook his head. "I'm not sure, exactly. It just kind of went sideways."

Deanie groaned. "I heard about that."

He frowned in confusion. "Huh?"

"Brent told me about it later. That the guys 'met' you in the parking lot."

"Oh that," Russ stated. He frowned. He suddenly didn't look so vulnerable. Maybe it hit a nerve. A male ego thing. He stood up and walked back behind the desk, looking at the wall.

"Um, anyway. Back to this marriage thing. It seems a bit drastic, don't you think?" Deanie asked.

"Maybe, but right now there's a kid waiting out in the kitchen with a bottle of ginger ale hoping to greet his new mother." He turned and looked at her.

Deanie sighed, but tried to keep her voice light. "So you're going to guilt me with your son?"

"If necessary," Russ replied, a slight smile on his lips. "Look, I know it's not the perfect solution, but I think it's the best one we've come up with so far. And if, say in a few months or so, we decide it was the wrong decision, we can always get a divorce and at least the baby will still have two legitimate parents."

Deanie grunted. "So you're already making plans to divorce me even before I say whether I'll marry you or not?" She tried to laugh. "You've got to be joking."

Russ caught and held her eyes with the intensity of his own blue ones. He stalked back to her chair and got down on one knee right in front of her. "I'm dead serious," he said, his voice sober. "Deanie Burton. Will you marry me?" He waited, his eyes never leaving hers.

Her voice caught in her throat. Suddenly all his twisted logic seemed inconsequential. For in that moment she knew she loved him. And because of that, there was only one answer. "Yes," she breathed. "I'll marry you."

Chapter Sixteen

The wedding was to take place at the courthouse. Nothing fancy, and no guests. Deanie wished that Jack could be there, but conceded that it would make it look even more like a shotgun wedding if he was. He would just have to wait to be surprised, like the rest of their relatives and friends. This way they could say they just eloped. It sounded romantic. As if.

Russ had been attentive in his own way. Not exactly gushing sentiments of undying love, or anything, but he'd been kind and they had actually spent three evenings together in the last week at his place. It wasn't exactly private, since Mark was there, but they'd watched TV, played a board game with Mark, and generally just hung out for a few hours. He had even given her a peck on the lips in parting, probably more for Mark's benefit than anything. It made sense that if she was going to be moving in shortly, Mark buy into the idea.

Deanie shivered involuntarily. What in the world was she getting herself into? She was a passionate person by nature and needed a partner that could reciprocate. She'd felt that passion with Russ. Once. But was she fooling herself into thinking she could ignite it again? A couple of times she'd caught him looking at her with the sort of intensity she remembered from their time at Hecla. It was momentary and only when he thought she didn't see, but hope had soared. It might just take some time for him to let his guard down.

They were in the car now, heading downtown to the courthouse. Mark was in the back seat, having been excused from school early. He was the only 'guest' allowed, if you could call him a guest. Since he was practically the instigator of the whole thing, it seemed only right that he be there. He'd had strict orders to keep his mouth shut and apparently had been successful so far. The pressure was starting to wear on him, though. Deanie could tell by the uncharacteristic way he was fidgeting. "When are you going to tell Grandma?" he asked.

"Soon enough," Russ replied, glancing at his son in the rear view mirror. "Promise you won't say anything until we come to pick you up tomorrow. Right?"

"Yes, I know," Mark nodded. He was quiet for a beat before the next question burst out of him. "What about my friends at school? Can I tell them on Monday?"

"I think we've been through this," Russ answered patiently. "I said once the wedding was over and done, then you could tell your friends. Since today is Friday, that would be Monday. Got it?"

"Yes, Dad," Mark replied. He cocked his head to one side. "Could I phone somebody before Monday?"

"Mark!" Russ laughed, exasperation rising.

"Or I guess I could wait till Monday."

Deanie smiled. At least someone was enthusiastic about the upcoming nuptials. They pulled onto a side street near the courthouse and Russ parallel parked the car. He opened his door and the wind almost took it right out of his hand. Not the most promising portent if the weather was any way to gauge the start of a new life together. He went around to the passenger side and opened both the front and rear doors, holding on tight to keep them from whipping the hinges. Mark scrambled out, while it took more effort for Deanie to hoist her bulky frame from the depths of the vehicle.

With his hand under her elbow, they scurried for the warmth and protection of the portentous building. It took a minute for Deanie to catch her breath once inside. Russ's arm had crept around her waist as he maneuvered her toward the elevators.

"Ready?" Russ asked, taking her hand in his as they waited.

She nodded her head, unable to speak. The reassurance of his hand in hers brought a lump to her throat.

"Probably not what you expected on your wedding day," he apologized. He looked at her, his blue eyes communicating what appeared to be true contrition.

"It's okay," she replied, trying to smile. "I guess I never really had any expectations. I'm not the kind of girl to sit around dreaming about the frilly white dress and all that. Besides, I don't think it would suit me at the moment." She looked down at her protruding abdomen.

Russ surveyed her rounded belly also, and lifted a brow. "True."

The elevator swished open, beckoning them to where the Justice of the Peace awaited.

❧

"So? What do you think?" Deanie asked Mark twenty minutes later as they swung away from the courthouse in his father's car. "Think I'll make okay mother material?"

Mark nodded. "Yep. It was kind of fast, though. I thought weddings had a lot more to them."

It was true. Russ felt kind of bad about that. Deanie probably would have wanted something a little more substantial, no matter what she said. It was a miracle he made it through as it is, though. Memories from that first disastrous round kept flashing inside his head like shots from a camera. He kept seeing Miranda standing there instead of Deanie and it made him want to turn and run. He had to keep reminding himself that although the circumstances were similar, Miranda and Deanie were nothing alike.

"You're quiet," Deanie noted, hazarding a glance at her new husband. "Regrets?"

He looked at her. "Not yet. You?" His answer was truthful. Despite everything, there was still something about her that drew her to him.

She shook her head. "No. Now what?"

"I guess we could go out for dinner now," Russ suggested. "If it's not too early."

"Can I come out for dinner, too?" Mark asked.

"Um, I was thinking maybe Deanie and I needed to go out alone," Russ stated. "Besides, Grandma is expecting you, remember?"

"I know, I know," Mark sighed. "A romantic dinner for two. You already told me."

Russ glanced over at Deanie and smiled. "That okay with you?" he asked. "Unless you'd rather go to my mother's house for dinner?"

Deanie laughed. "Not that I don't want to meet your mother, but. . ."

"The trick will be getting Mark into the house without raising her suspicions," Russ said. He turned slightly in the seat to look directly at Mark for a moment. "You promise you won't say anything until we come to pick you up?"

Mark nodded. "Promise."

Russ had plans for later, too. With Mark out of the way, they would go back to the house. Alone. For some reason he felt almost guilty about that. The fact that he wanted her, even when she was five months pregnant. But they were married now. Legit. He was only human, after all.

❧

"That was fantastic," Deanie breathed, leaning back against the cushioned chair. She rubbed her belly. "There is definitely no room for dessert, though."

"You seem to take the 'eating for two' quite literally," Russ mused, with a slight grin.

"Whatever." She threw her napkin at him playfully. "Unfortunately, I also need to make way too many trips to the bathroom. Excuse me. I'll be right back." She got up, with some difficulty, and headed for the restroom.

Russ watched her retreating figure and felt warm satisfaction on the inside akin to the paternal feelings he had for Mark. Despite his undeniable attraction to her, there was something more than just animal lust racing through his veins. There was a rush to envelop her, protect her. He was glad he married her, surreal as that thought still was.

The fact that he would suffer immeasurable humiliation the moment their relationship became known was also not far from his conscious mind. That was one aspect of their union he was not looking forward to. He sighed heavily. His emotions were such a mixed bag right now. If only they

138

could just disappear for about a year or two and come back later when enough time had lapsed so as not to draw any notice.

"Hello, Russ."

He looked up. Great. It was Rita. "Hi."

"You took the day off today," she noted.

As if he didn't know it. He tried to keep his face a mask of civility. "Yes. Some personal business."

She nodded. "I see."

"Well," he said brightly, "I guess I'll see you Monday." He glanced toward the restroom and then back to Rita. He raised his eyebrows and smiled, willing her to walk away.

"Is that your girlfriend?" Rita asked, cocking her head to one side. She smiled – a frozen, mask from a horror flick.

Russ blinked. "Uh . . ."

"I guess that explains a few things," Rita continued. "It certainly wasn't impotence."

"Rita -"

"No need to explain," she held up a hand. "Although I never would have pegged you as the two-timing sort."

"It's not like that."

"It's not yours? I wouldn't have thought you'd like used goods either."

Russ was about to spout a nasty re-joiner, but clamped his mouth shut instead, letting his insides percolate. Deanie was winding her way back to the table and Rita seemed bent upon waiting for her arrival. Russ rose from the table to greet Deanie. "Deanie, this is one of my colleagues from work. Rita, this is Deanie."

The two women nodded and Russ helped Deanie back into her seat, pushing in the chair. "I'm sorry," Rita said smoothly. "I didn't catch the last name?"

"Burton," Deanie offered as Russ simultaneously said, "Graham." Rita looked from one to the other, eyebrows raised, while Russ scowled. Deanie giggled. "My bad. I meant to say 'Graham'."

Rita blinked, obviously at a loss for words. Russ cleared his throat. "Yeah, that's right. I took the day off to get married. Deanie is my wife."

139

"Well," Rita stated. "Well," she said again, opening her mouth as if to say more and then shutting it.

"See you on Monday," Russ said pointedly, his mouth a straight line.

Rita nodded and quickly clicked her way back from whence she'd come.

"That must have been awfully embarrassing for you," Deanie offered, laying a sympathetic hand on his.

Russ looked down at their joined hands and scowled. Any thoughts of a romantic nature had vanished. Whatever he had hoped, there was no hiding the facts now.

Chapter Seventeen

S aturday. Today was the day they told their parents. Deanie stretched lazily and sat up in the bed. Russ had let her sleep in, but greeted her with a breakfast tray of fruit and cereal when she finally did wake up. He'd been out jogging already, he told her, and had finished reading the paper and done his chores. Whatever that meant.

Deanie set the tray aside and rolled out of bed. She inhaled deeply. The first morning in her new home. Her first night with her new husband.

Hmph. As if that had amounted to anything. Her fantasies about passionate lovemaking were put to rest when he simply rolled over. Probably too much stress after the way that woman had embarrassed him in the restaurant. Unless he found her pregnancy unattractive. . . Oh well. They had plenty of time for that. They had the rest of their lives.

"So?" Russ asked when she was ready to go. "Ready for the next heat?" He seemed fidgety. Nervous. Not a good sign, Deanie decided, especially since they were going to his mother's place first.

"I suppose so," Deanie grimaced. "Kind of like the Olympics. First your mother, then Jack. At least Jack already knows. Sort of."

"Well, no use putting it off. Might as well get it over with."

"What am I supposed to say?" Deanie asked. "What is *she* going to say?"

"Be damned if I know," Russ frowned.

"Thanks. I feel so much better, now," Deanie countered sarcastically.

141

"Don't worry about it," Russ reassured her. "No matter what she's thinking, my mother will take it in stride."

"Great. Now I'm something to 'take in stride'," Deanie muttered.

They had made their way to the garage and Russ was holding the car door open for her as she climbed in. "There's one thing, though," Russ said. "We'll have to pretend to be. . . you know. In love." He shut her door and went around to his own side.

No problem, Deanie thought. At least *she* wouldn't be pretending. She let out a sigh.

"I know that might be awkward, but we have to do our best," Russ continued. "For Mark's sake, as well as my mother's. I don't want to alarm her any more than necessary."

"She'll be plenty alarmed at the first sight of me," Deanie mumbled.

"Once the initial shock is over, she'll be fine," Russ assured. Deanie surveyed the tense jut of his jaw. He certainly didn't look as convinced as he was trying to sound. Great. Exactly what was she walking into? Please, God, make Russ's mother like me, she pleaded silently.

They made the rest of the trip in contemplative silence. As they neared the house, Russ swore, his brows coming down to almost hide his eyes.

"What is it?" Deanie asked.

Russ scowled. "Looks like my brother is here."

"We don't have to," Deanie offered. "You could come back and get Mark later. We can do it another time."

Russ pulled up in front of the house. "Mother has already seen the car. We can't leave now." He pointed to the movement in the front room curtains.

They sat for another moment, car idling, before he switched it off with finality. "Well, are you ready?"

Sudden fear washed over her. What if they hated her? What if they hated *him*? It was bad enough she kept making a mess of her own life, but now she was ruining someone else's as well. "Russ, I don't think I can do this," Deanie whispered.

Russ took her hand and with the other directed her chin so that she had to look directly at him. His eyes were so blue, so intense. She searched them for the comfort and assurance she so desperately needed and could almost see him willing himself to be strong. "It'll be okay. Mark's expecting us."

"But. . . it's not right to deceive your own mother like this," she fretted.

"We are not deceiving anyone," Russ reasoned. "We are legally married and I am here to introduce you to my mother."

"But you said we were going to pretend. You know. . ." she trailed off.

Russ frowned, his jaw moving. "That difficult, huh?" He sighed and released her hand.

"I didn't mean it that way," Deanie tried to explain. But Russ was already unbuckling his seatbelt.

"Come on. I can see the drapes moving again. She must be wondering what's going on."

Russ helped Deanie out of the car and up the walk. Dorothy Graham met them at the door. There was no turning back now.

"Hello, Mother," Russ said. The greeting sounded formal. Forced. And his smile was stiff, like he was greeting an acquaintance, not his own mother. "I brought someone I'd like you to meet."

"Wonderful," Dorothy exclaimed, turning to Deanie. "How lovely!"

Deanie tried to smile.

"Deanie, this is my mother, Dorothy Graham," Russ introduced. "And Mother, this is Deanie."

"So very good to meet you," Dorothy gushed as she squeezed Deanie's hand.. "May I take your coat?"

"Um, thanks." Deanie slowly removed the oversized winter garment, peeking out of the corner of her eye to catch Dorothy's reaction.

As expected, a look of shock and then consternation flashed across the older woman's face. With resolve, she quickly regained her composure and formed her mouth into a plastic smile. "Won't you come in?" she offered.

Dorothy led the way into the living room. Deanie was grateful for the warmth of Russ's hand on the small of her back, guiding her. She leaned into it's strength. A large, blonde man was lounging on the sofa watching some kind of sporting event on television. The brother, no doubt.

"Ken," Russ said, visibly bracing himself.

"Hm?" Ken looked up from the TV. "Oh, hi." His eyes brows rose in question as he noticed Deanie and he looked back at Russ.

"Ken, I'd like you to meet Deanie. Deanie, this is my brother, Ken Graham," Russ introduced stiffly.

Ken looked Deanie over from head to toe. "Hi." The one syllable held a wealth of meaning as a predatory grin spread across his face. Deanie felt uncharacteristic heat rising in her cheeks. If only there was a hole to crawl into about now.

Russ's reassuring arm continued to guide her to the loveseat, where he perched beside her, careful not to touch.

"I'll get refreshments," Dorothy blustered. "Do you drink coffee, Miss . . . um, Deanie?"

"Yes, thanks," Deanie nodded, smiling weakly at the older woman. Her eyes flickered away and she looked down at her hands.

Russ was obviously having his own issues. His jaw was working overtime. "So, how's Kathy doing?" he asked.

Ken grunted. "Fine. Treatment's going good, I think. Kids miss her, though. She'll be home next week." He surveyed Deanie as he continued. "Just brought the kids over before I head out to the center to visit her." He stopped, his eyes penetrating. "My wife's in a dry out center, in case you're wondering."

"Oh," Deanie mouthed the word and nodded.

"She knows," Russ added. "She works at the youth center downtown right by where it happened. She was at work that night."

Ken grunted. "That a fact. One upped me again."

Russ frowned. "What's that supposed to mean?"

Ken shrugged. "You always manage to find a way to air my dirty laundry before I get a chance to do it myself. Oh well. The story of my life."

Russ just rolled his eyes.

"Although," Ken continued, a wicked gleam in his eye. "You two look like you might have an interesting story to tell. Have you been holding out on me, little brother?"

Russ let out a pent up breath. "Here we go," he muttered.

"What was that?" Ken asked. "I didn't catch it." He grinned and cocked his head. "Now you look awfully familiar, Miss . . . what was it?"

"Deanie," she supplied.

"Right. Deanie," Ken nodded. "Have we met?"

"I don't think so," Deanie shook her head. Her hands were balled up in her lap, her nails almost cutting into her palms.

"Don't you have to get going?" Russ asked irritably.

"I'm in no hurry," Ken shrugged. "That coffee Ma's brewing smells kind of good. So what was your last name again?"

A sudden wave of nausea overtook Deanie and she stood abruptly to her feet. "Which way to the washroom?" she squeaked.

"This way." Russ bustled her down the hall toward the bathroom - just in time. Damn her queasy stomach.

If only she could stay in the safety of the bathroom forever. This was a bad idea. A really bad idea. There was a gentle knock at the door, and Russ's muffled voice was asking if she was all right. She splashed her face with cold water, took a deep breathe, and opened the door. He was standing in the hallway, leaning against the wall. As soon as he saw her he pushed off from the wall and gently grasped her by the arms, looking into her eyes with concern.

"You going to be okay?" he asked. He held her gaze while she nodded the affirmative.

She tried to breathe normally, but found her breath coming in shallow, uneven spurts. She lowered her gaze, afraid she'd be overcome by an all out bawling session.

"Hey, come here," Russ whispered, enveloping her in his strong embrace. "Sorry about my brother. I wouldn't have brought you if I'd known."

Deanie allowed herself to melt into the strength of his body, inhaling deeply of his scent while willing herself not to cry. She didn't want to let go. Didn't want to speak. Finally, Russ stepped back, unwrapping her arms from around his waist and holding her at arms length. "Come on. Time to get it over with."

"Whatever you say," Deanie sighed. "You're the genius who got us into this mess after all."

This time Russ took her hand in his and squeezed. Then he started down the hall, pulling her behind him. Dorothy was hovering between the living room and kitchen holding a tray laden with coffee and goodies.

145

"Well," Russ began, clearing his throat as they entered the room. "I'm sure you're . . . curious." He hesitated, the others waiting expectantly. "And it's probably obvious that Deanie is going to have a baby . . ." Deanie almost thought she heard a small whimper coming from Dorothy. When she looked, the other woman had set the tray down on the coffee table and was now perched beside Ken, her mouth in a taut line. "Actually, we're . . . " he placed his arm around Deanie's waist as if to add credence to his words, "We're already married."

Mrs. Graham's mouth dropped open. There was no mistaking the distraught gasp this time.

"Now, I know it seems sudden," Russ continued quickly, "but we've been seeing one another for quite some time -"

"That's pretty obvious," Ken cut in under his breath.

Russ frowned. "I know it looks bad. But we were planning to get married anyway, eventually. It just happened a little sooner, that's all."

"Not quite soon enough, I'd say," Ken snorted.

"Now that's enough out of you," Dorothy piped up, coming to their defense. With a gallant effort she squared her shoulders and took a deep breath, directing her gaze at Deanie. "Welcome to the family, dear. Perhaps it's not in the way I would have hoped, but . . ."

"Hey, now I remember!" Ken cut in. "You're that girl from out at the island. That dancing girl."

"I beg your pardon?" Deanie asked, her eyes widening.

"Yeah, now I remember," Ken snapped his fingers. "Looks like you scored after all, bro. But have you never heard of condoms? They're this really great invention -"

Russ's fist connected squarely with Ken's jaw, sending him sprawling into a nearby planter beside the couch. "What the hell?" Ken barked. Russ stood over him, ready with fists bawled for the next round, if necessary. Ken launched back onto his feet, lunging for his younger brother.

"Stop it at once!" Dorothy Graham commanded, her voice rising shrilly.

An all out wrestling match was now in progress, amid grunts and swearing as each brother tried to get the upper hand. The three children, Mark, Samantha, and Greg, came running to see the commotion and stood

146

transfixed in the living room doorway. Greg started to bawl. "You're frightening the children!" Dorothy yelled. Mark stood in wide-eyed silence while Greg had run to cling to his Grandmother's skirt.

Russ was the first to pull away, extracting himself and shoving away from his older brother's grasp. "Don't worry Mother," he said between heavy breaths. "We're not staying."

"But you just got here!"

"Never mind," Ken cut in, straightening his shirt. "I gotta get over to the center before visiting hours are over. I'll be back later for the kids." Ken eyed Russ on his way by. "Nice left hook."

Russ kept his mouth tightly shut.

"Give my love to Kathy," Dorothy called to Ken's retreating figure.

Ken grunted from the doorway. "She'll be some surprised when I tell her the news." He swung out the front door, shutting it with jarring force. An awkward silence penetrated the room once he was gone.

"I think it's best for us to go now, too," Russ finally said gruffly.

"Nonsense!" Dorothy snapped. "It's bad enough you spring this news on me. Now you're going to leave without even letting me get to know my new daughter in law?" Her eyes dared him – any of them – to defy her. "Now, who wants cream?" she demanded, pouring coffee from the decanter into the mugs. Everyone else sat.

Dorothy began passing the coffee, as I everything was perfectly normal. No one dared question her or comment on the surreal atmosphere that had enveloped the room.

"Do you have family in town?" Dorothy asked, holding the tray in front of Deanie. She took one of the mugs.

"Deanie is Jack Burton's daughter," Russ supplied, taking his own coffee.

"You don't say," Dorothy responded, pausing with the tray.

"You've heard of him?" Deanie asked, trying to pretend this was a normal conversation. A normal day with a normal family.

"Of course," Dorothy replied. "My late husband enjoyed listening to a lot of music. He had a record player down basement which he used to like to go and listen to by himself. It was his solitary time. I'm sure he had at least one of your father's recordings."

"Hm. I didn't know that," Russ mused. "I mean, I knew he had the record player and liked to go listen once in awhile, but I didn't know he liked jazz."

"Oh yes," Dorothy nodded. "He liked music of all kinds."

"Cool! Maybe I can listen to it later," Mark piped up. "Since he is going to be my grandpa now and everything."

"Who?" Greg asked. "Am I getting a new grandpa, too?"

"Not today, dear," Dorothy responded, setting the tray on the coffee table.

"How come Mark gets a new grandpa?" Greg asked, just the slightest hint of a whine in his voice.

"You're so dumb," Samantha said, rolling her eyes.

"Why don't you children go play?" Dorothy suggested.

Mark looked over at his father, his eyes begging to stay with the adults.

"Go along," Dorothy urged. "Granny needs some time to talk to your father."

Mark gave his father one last pleading look.

"Take another piece of cake and then go," Russ directed. "Grandma is right. We've got adult stuff to discuss."

Mark sighed, but took another piece of cake. "At least I don't have to keep it secret any more."

"You mean you knew all along?" Dorothy turned to her grandson. He just nodded, his grin from ear to ear. "You stinker!" she exclaimed.

Cake in hand, Mark headed for the basement with the other two children. Deanie caught the words, 'my new mother' as the children headed down the stairs.

"So? When is your baby due?" Dorothy asked, surveying her new daughter in law over the rim of her coffee cup.

Deanie sputtered in her coffee then swallowed hard. "Um. The end of May, I guess." She dabbed at her mouth with the napkin Dorothy had provided, keeping her eyes lowered.

"It's funny you didn't bring Deanie around a little sooner, Russ," Dorothy commented. "It would have been lovely if she'd joined us for Christmas."

Russ scowled. "Mother. Not now," he clipped.

Deanie set her mug down with a clatter. "Um, maybe you two need a few minutes alone," she offered, standing. "I know this is all quite a shock. I mean, I don't blame you if you have questions. I know I had some explaining to do with Jack. Why don't I head downstairs and see if I can find some of those old records? The kids might like it."

Neither Dorothy nor Russ argued and Deanie beat a hasty retreat. Poor Russ. He was in for a grilling, if she was reading things right. Good. Serves him right. At least she wasn't the only one suffering. She descended the stairs into the finished rec room, careful to watch her step since she was having difficulty seeing her feet. The décor was dark, with retro wood paneling and out dated furniture.

"Hi," Mark said, replacing a photo album on the shelf. "What're you doing down here?"

"Well, I thought we'd look for some of those records," Deanie said.

"Cool!" Mark responded, jumping from the couch and heading for several milk crates that were stacked next to a cabinet style stereo system. "Grandma keeps all the records over here."

"This is fun," Deanie stated, starting right into sifting through the LP's. "There's lots of cool stuff in here."

"Let's play tag," Greg suggested.

"Not now," Mark said. "We're looking through Grandpa's music."

"But this is boring," Greg whined again.

"Go play with the lego," Samantha instructed like a mother hen, joining in the search.

"Aw!" Greg turned and shuffled to the toy area.

Samantha peered into one of the crates. "What are we looking for?"

"Anything with 'Jack Burton'," Deanie answered. "Jack Burton Band, Jack Burton Quartet . . . "

"That's my *new* Grandpa," Mark informed.

They looked for several minutes until Samantha called out, "I think I found one! Is this it?" She pulled out an LP and handed it to Deanie.

"Yes! Oh, I remember this one!" she exclaimed.

"Which one is he?" Mark asked, squinting at the picture on the cover. It portrayed a much younger group of musicians.

"The one with the saxophone," Deanie replied. "Here." She pointed and smiled. "Of course he's a lot older now."

"They sure had funny clothes," Samantha noted.

"Come on. Let's play it," Mark said, jumping up and taking the record out of its protective cardboard sleeve.

"You know how to run this thing?" Deanie asked, gesturing to the record player.

"Of course," Mark said, rolling his eyes slightly. "I come down here all the time."

He carefully placed the record on the turntable, set the needle and hit the play lever. The arm swung and descended with mechanical solemnity onto the vinyl. A few seconds later the heady whine of a saxophone filled the basement. They all listened for a few moments, even Greg, until Deanie started to sing along.

"You know the words?" Mark asked in surprise.

"Sure," Deanie laughed. "And when I don't, I just make them up."

"Wow. I didn't know you could do that," he said in awe. They listened again until the next song began to play. "Um, Deanie?"

"Yes?" She blinked, bringing herself back to the present.

"What am I supposed to call you?"

She focused fully on his face for a moment. "Deanie, I guess," she shrugged. "I mean, I'm not really your mother, so that doesn't seem right."

"Oh," Mark said, looking down. His crestfallen body language spoke volumes.

"Hey," Deanie interjected. "I call my own Dad by his first name, so I guess I'm just more used to that."

"Okay," Mark nodded. He seemed satisfied with the answer. "Deanie?"

"Yes?"

"Is it okay if I think of you as my mother, even if you're not?"

Deanie laughed. "Of course. I am married to your dad, after all."

Mark smiled. "Right. I'm glad you married my dad and not Rita."

Deanie surveyed his innocent boy's face. "Yeah?" Rita. The haughty colleague from the restaurant. So, she was a past flame. No wonder she seemed so miffed.

"She was just no fun at all," Mark continued. "She didn't really have time to talk to me or anything. Not like you."

"I see." Deanie smiled, but inside she could feel the unmistakable pangs of jealousy stabbing. Maybe Russ had really liked Rita and now his plans were spoiled for good. Maybe that's why he didn't want to make love to her last night. Maybe he was still seeing Rita.

No. Russ wasn't that kind of person. She frowned. What did she really know about what kind of person he was? She shook her head. This was stupid. Pointless. She was married to Russ now, for better or worse. She turned back to the crates of LP's. "Hey! Let's look for another record, okay?" She wouldn't let her mind wander in that direction or she was sure to get sick again.

❧

"So. Are you going to tell me?" Dorothy demanded. Her hands were in her lap; her eyes penetrating.

Russ looked away, avoiding his mother's piercing gaze. "I'm not sure where to start," he shrugged.

"How about at the beginning," came Dorothy's sharp suggestion.

"Um . . . yeah. Well, I met her last fall and we just recently met again and decided to get married," he tried. It sounded lame, even to him.

"Russell Anthony Graham," Dorothy stated. "Not one month ago you brought another woman to my home for Christmas dinner. A woman that for all intents and purposes seemed absolutely perfect for you. Now you show up on my doorstep with a mere girl, pregnant no less, and announce that you're married. What happened?"

"It's complicated," Russ sighed.

"I can see I'm not going to get very far," Dorothy said stiffly. "I expected more from you."

Russ was silent. What could he say? That he'd made the same mistake twice? That he married her out of duty? No, that wasn't entirely true. He wanted to be near her for some odd reason, which didn't even make sense. He couldn't get her out of his head, for goodness sake.

"Is the child even yours?" Dorothy asked, holding him with her pointed stare.

"Of course!" Russ shot back.

"Hmph." She took a moment to digest that information. "And where did you meet?"

151

"One of her father's concerts," Russ supplied, weary. "What difference does it make, anyway?"

"Where was she while you were dating that other one? Rita?"

"I'd appreciate it if you didn't mention Rita again," Russ grated. "I'm married to someone else now and that's all you need to know."

"Let me guess," Mrs. Graham persisted. "Knowing you, you married her because it was the 'right thing to do'." When he didn't answer right away she continued in frustration, "Russ! When are you going to learn? That's no foundation for a marriage. I thought you would have learned that lesson already after Miranda. And now you've spoiled your chances with that other nice young woman -"

"I broke up with her, remember?" he reminded, his voice testy.

"I know, but," Dorothy sighed. "It's too late now, obviously. You just seemed so perfect together."

"I said don't mention her again," Russ ground out. "Rita or Miranda." He stood abruptly and started gathering the mugs.

"I'm sorry, dear. Of course it's your life, after all. I just can't believe. . . Oh, never mind." She rose with a sigh and picked up the coffee tray. They moved to the kitchen, mechanical robots programmed to tidy up after themselves no matter the crisis at hand.

Russ set the mugs down on the counter beside the sink. "What if I told you I loved her?" he finally said, looking directly at his mother for the first time since the conversation had begun.

Dorothy scrutinized her son. "Do you?"

He hesitated for just a beat. Did he? "Of course," he clipped, turning back to the dirty tray.

Dorothy surveyed her son for another moment, then shook her head. "Well, I see I've got my praying cut out for me," she sighed. She began to fill the sink with water.

"Great. What is that supposed to mean?"

"Just what I said," Dorothy replied, hands now submerged in the soapy water. She stopped her scrubbing, turning to look fully at her son. "I'm sorry, son. For anything I might have said to upset you. Of course I'm going to accept your new wife into the family. It's not the way I would have liked to see things, but what's done is done."

"Thanks, I guess." Russ picked up a dish towel and rubbed the water droplets from one of the mugs.

"Sometimes we don't understand why things are the way they are, but the good Lord in Heaven knows, and we must trust Him and know that some good will come out of it in the end."

Russ winced. Great. Philosophical mother had taken over for I-have-a-right-to-know-your-business mother. "Sometimes I feel more like God is out to get me."

"Things don't always make sense. But that is where faith comes in. 'Faith is the evidence of things not seen.' We can't always see the outcome, but we must believe that it's all part of God's sovereign plan. When your father died, I wanted to die right along with him. But now I see the hand of God in my life again. I still have time to witness to my children and my grandchildren. That's a gift, and I won't give it up easily." She sighed. "Like I said. It looks like I've got my praying cut out for me."

He'd had enough for one day. "Right," he responded mechanically, setting the dish towel down. "I better go downstairs and see how they're doing." He excused himself after drying his own hands. For once he agreed with his mother. She did have her praying cut out for her.

Chapter Eighteen

"It's about time you came over and paid your old man a visit," Jack blustered. Deanie kissed him on the cheek and pushed past into the apartment. "I've hardly seen you since you off and got married on me."

"Sorry. My car wasn't running again. I had to get Brent to fix it," Deanie explained, surveying an apple that rested in a bowl on the table before rubbing it on her sweater.

"Brent?" Jack asked. "That's your husband's job."

"I think he's embarrassed for me to drive it," Deanie shrugged. She sat down at the table and took a huge bite of the apple before continuing to talk, her mouth half full. "Besides, he's not that mechanical." She swallowed. "Mm. These are good apples. I'm starving."

"What's a matter? He not feedin' ya?"

"Don't be silly," Deanie laughed. "Of course he's feeding me. I just didn't feel like making anything for lunch."

"You better be looking after my grandchild," Jack warned.

"I'm not stupid," Deanie replied. "There weren't any leftovers and I didn't want to make a mess."

"Now you're sounding just plain lazy," Jack observed.

Deanie shrugged. "Russ doesn't really like it when I try to get creative in the kitchen. He says I make too much mess and I put things back in the wrong place."

"That sounds downright ornery. You living under some kind of martial law over there or something?" Jack huffed.

"Can you say 'obsessive compulsive'?" Deanie laughed.

"This is no laughing matter," Jack continued. "Is he treatin' you okay? Cause if he's not..."

"Jack, relax! All I said was Russ doesn't like it when I make a mess. He's used to doing things a certain way, and. . . well, I'm trying not to rock the boat right now. He and Mark have been alone together for a lot of years and it's not easy having another person around."

"That's just pretzel logic," Jack retorted. "Sounds like you're makin' excuses, that's what. I don't care how long he's been doin' things a certain way, he's married now. You're man and wife and it's your house now, too. It's the way things are supposed to be. Marriage is all about compromise. Give and take."

"I guess," she shrugged noncommittally. "In time." She got up and went to the fridge, bending over to peer inside.

Jack furrowed his brow and surveyed his daughter. "You're not one to lie down and play dead. What's going on?"

"Nothing is going on," Deanie replied, spreading some peanut butter on a slice of bread.

Jack scrutinized her more closely. "Why am I having trouble believing you?" he muttered.

"You're being paranoid."

"You think?"

Deanie let out a clipped laugh. "Trust me. When I say there's nothing going on, I mean there's nothing going on." She slapped her sandwich together and lowered herself onto a chair.

Jack was silent for a moment. When he finally spoke his voice was quiet. "Spill it."

"What do you mean?" she hedged.

"You can't fool your old man," Jack replied. "I can always tell when something's not right. So you might as well spill it now than later."

Deanie chewed her sandwich, considering her father's words while he sat across the table from her expectantly. He was right. There was no hiding things where Jack was concerned. She swallowed, took a sip of milk to wash it down, and sighed as she set the glass down on the table. "I don't know how to describe it. Sometimes I just feel like I don't really belong. I mean, it's not like he's mean or anything. He's civil, but. . . "

"Civil?" Jack squawked. "Marriage is about passion! You need more than that. Civil," he repeated the word under his breath and snorted.

"I just feel so useless sometimes," Deanie continued. "He made me quit my job, he won't let me cook or clean. I'm getting tired of watching TV."

"Probably just doesn't want you to strain yourself," Jack suggested.

"Well, maybe. But then in the evenings he spends all his time in his study or doing things with Mark. It's like I'm an outsider looking in. I'm so bored I look forward to the cleaning lady's weekly visit, for goodness sake!"

"You're a passionate person, like your old man," Jack said. "Without it you'll wither up and die. You need to tell him how you feel. That's how it works in a marriage. People get used to doing things one way and they don't realize that other people have other ways of doing things. If you talk about it; tell him how you feel, you'll work it out."

"You think?" Deanie asked, sarcasm lacing her words.

Jack frowned. "You don't?"

Deanie sighed. "This is really embarrassing, but . . ."

"Spit it out, girl!" Jack blustered.

Deanie surveyed her father for a few minutes, considering. "Jack, its not like a real marriage. Not really."

Jack remained silent, waiting.

Deanie sighed and gave a sheepish grin. "The other night, Mark asked why we didn't share a room. Russ told him it wasn't good for the baby. Jack, he sleeps in the spare room! We've only had sex twice since we got married. That's twice in a whole month! And then it was like he couldn't get away from me fast enough after."

"Well . . ." Jack's brow furrowed as he considering this for a moment. "Some men don't like it when. . . you know. When there's a baby in the way. Maybe he's just worried about you," he suggested.

"I don't know," Deanie shook her head.

"Do you love him?" Jack asked candidly.

Deanie nodded.

"Well, then, looks like you're stuck. I'd say just wait for a bit. See what happens after you adjust to married life and the baby is born and what not. I'm sure things'll work out," Jack reasoned.

"Do you really think so?" Deanie asked. She wanted to believe it. Maybe things would change after she had the baby. Maybe he would grow to love her. Another dark thought popped into her mind, unbidden. Or maybe he was still in love with that Rita woman. That was a fear she couldn't share even with Jack. The last thing she needed was for him to go ballistic on her. She took a deep breath and tried to straighten up. Smile. "You're probably right."

"Sure I am. Now, you listen to your old man, girl. If you're bored and he won't let you do anything around that place, you just go right ahead and come over here during the day. I'd love to have the company. Or come and hang out with us at rehearsals. Lord knows we could use the inspiration."

"Thanks. I think I'll start doing that more often," Deanie agreed. "And thanks for being so good with Mark. He's so keen about having you for a Grandpa."

"The kids alright," Jack nodded. "Bring him any time. Maybe I'll teach him to play the saxophone."

"He'd like that. Actually, I better get going," Deanie said, rising. "I have to pick Mark up after school today, since they get out early. I don't want to screw up and be late." She kissed her father on the cheek.

"Don't let yourself get pushed around," Jack said. "You start standing up for yourself, you hear? No daughter of mine cow-tows to any man. Not even her own husband!"

"Okay, Jack," Deanie laughed. "I'll remember that. But I won't be telling him you said so."

Chapter Nineteen

Deanie shoulder checked as she pulled into the school parking lot. It was nice to have her own set of wheels again, despite the fact that Russ didn't exactly approve of the beat up vehicle. He would probably be especially miffed if he knew she was using it to pick Mark up from school. What he didn't know wouldn't hurt him. The last thing she needed was to have to endure her husband's silent recriminations over something so trivial. She wasn't sure what was happening in her relationship with Russ. It was almost like he was afraid to be around her. And when they were together, he seemed so distant. Jack was right. She had never been one to lay down and just take it. Maybe she should just have it out with him. Set him straight on a few things. Like her need to be an equal partner. Or the sex thing. After all, she got herself into this mess, so she might as well be the one to try to fix it.

She saw Mark emerge from the school and waved. Her relationship with Mark was blossoming, at least. It was certainly not anywhere near a 'mother and son' thing, but they were becoming good friends. It was obvious that he was starved for attention, especially from a female. Besides his grandmother, he really didn't have anyone else.

"Hi," Mark greeted as he bustled into the front seat of the small car.

"How was your day?" Deanie asked.

"Okay," Mark shrugged.

Deanie nodded. "I was wondering if you'd like to do something different today. Since it is early and your Dad won't be home for awhile."

"Are we going to Grandpa Jack's?" Mark asked hopefully.

"No," Deanie replied. "I was thinking of something else."

"Oh." Mark sounded disappointed.

"You like rock music, right?" she asked as she pulled out onto the street.

"You bet!" Mark answered enthusiastically.

"Good. Remember when I told you I used to be in rock band?" she asked.

Mark nodded, his eyes wide.

"Well, how about if I take you over to see a real rock and roll band rehearse? I'm still friends with the band members and I know they won't mind."

"Oh wow!" Mark enthused. He sobered almost as quickly. "Do you think my dad will mind?" he asked.

Deanie laughed. "What your dad doesn't know won't hurt him." A slight twinge of guilt fluttered somewhere inside. It seemed to be her new favorite line. "Besides, we'll be home long before he will. He's working late today."

She took the next exit and headed in the direction of the old, three-story house her friends called home. It had been awhile since she'd hung out with them. Too long. To say that Russ disapproved was an understatement. He'd never really met any of them formally. Only that one unfortunate incident in the parking lot. And when she'd suggested inviting them over he had practically exploded then stalked off to his study, slamming the door. It was the one and only time he'd showed any kind of emotion. Maybe his ego was still bruised. In any case, it just wasn't worth it right at the moment.

After her discussion with Jack, she realized it was time she started standing up for herself. She wasn't a doormat, after all. Brent and the others were good friends, and if Russ didn't like it, tough.

They arrived in front of the house and Deanie put the car in park before struggling to get out of the car. This being pregnant thing was a lot of hard work.

Mark looked a bit timid as he joined her on the sidewalk.

"Come on," she encouraged, putting an arm lightly across his shoulders.

"These guys are a lot of fun. You'll love it. But remember, it's our little secret, right?"

Mark nodded.

"Hi guys!" Deanie called out as she let herself into the entry.

"In here," came the reply from somewhere in the house.

Deanie kept one hand lightly on Mark's shoulder as they entered. She knew he was feeling a little awe-struck at the prospects of meeting a 'real' rock group. They made their way into the living room-rehearsal studio, where all four members of the group were already assembled.

"Hey, long time no see," Grant greeted, looking up from his keyboard..

"Yeah, what's up with that?" Brent joined in, setting his guitar aside and giving Deanie a hug. "You hardly ever come around these days."

"You know how it is," Deanie shrugged. "Married life and all that."

"I still can't believe some accountant beat me to it," Grant said shaking his head.

"As if," Deanie laughed.

"You're looking good," Brent noted. "Fat, but good."

They all laughed. All but Lenny, that is. He just nodded in Deanie's direction and went back to tuning his bass.

"This is Mark. He'd like to hang out while you rehearse. That okay?" Deanie asked.

"An audience," Brent grinned. "Guess we better get it right, eh guys?" He counted out the time and rocketed into a song. One bar in, the rest of the group followed.

Mark was perched on a high stool, eyes wide with excitement. "Told you they were good," Deanie leaned over and whispered. Mark just nodded and kept on listening.

Deanie checked her watch. They would only stay for half an hour. Standing up for yourself was one thing, but there was no sense pushing your luck.

Deanie closed her eyes and allowed the music to soothe her ragged emotions. This was exactly the kind of therapy she craved. Brent and the guys had been her life line before and she wondered at how quickly she had let them slip into the background. She needed the kind of loyal and unconditional friendship that she knew she could find right here. That was another thing she was going to set straight. Maybe even tonight once she got home.

※

Josh poked his head into Russ's office. "Hi Russ. You got a minute?"

Russ looked up from the stack of papers on his desk. "What's that? Oh, sure. Come in." He closed the folder and waited as Josh slipped into the small space and sat in one of the available chairs.

"I never got a chance to congratulate you on your marriage," Josh said.

Russ blinked. "Oh. Thanks."

"I thought maybe you and your new wife might like to come over sometime. My wife suggested it," Josh added.

"Um… I'll have to ask," Russ hedged.

"How's your boy adjusting? I suppose it might take some getting used to, seeing as its just been the two of you for so long," Josh continued.

"He's fine."

"Good. Good," Josh nodded. "Kids can be funny that way."

"He's fine," Russ repeated.

"Of course he is. Kids are resilient. They adapt. Probably better than most adults."

Russ glanced down at the closed manila folder, fingering its edge. What exactly was the guy fishing for? He looked up, pinning the other man with his eyes. "Yeah. Look, is there anything I can help you with?"

"No, that's it," Josh replied. He stood, obviously feeling awkward under Russ's pointed scrutiny. Good. Served him right for getting nosey. "Just wanted to, you know, pop in and see how you were doing."

"Fine. We're all fine." Russ's voice did not solicit further inquiry.

"Okay then," Josh gave a stilted wave as he backed from the office. "Let me know when you and your family can come over. And if you ever need to talk, you know where I am."

Russ watched Josh's retreating figure. He could have been more congenial, he supposed. The other guy was probably just trying to be nice. More than he could say for the rest of the people at work. He felt a distinct hush every time he entered a room, the conversation coming to

161

an abrupt halt upon his arrival. He could just guess what they were talking about.

The inner conflict was really starting to wear on him. He was caught in a vortex of mixed emotions. Humiliation and self deprecation swirled alongside anger, at himself and at the woman who was the center of this dark comedy. He knew he was not an easy person to live with at the moment, but even with his best intentions well intact he couldn't seem to show her his other side. The side that wanted to shield her from the ugliness of gossip. The side that wanted to take away the hurt that he saw in her face at times, caused by his own insensitivity.

Somehow they would get through this stage. They had to. With deliberateness Russ reopened the manila folder and tried to concentrate on its contents. The telephone rang, eliciting an oath as he snatched it from its cradle.

"Hello," he clipped into the receiver. "Oh, hello." He cleared his throat, softening his timber considerably. "Yes, this is Mark Graham's father. . . There was an early dismissal today? I didn't know. . . I see. I appreciate the call, but that was my wife picking him up. . . I know you probably didn't recognize the vehicle, but . . . right. Thank you. I realize you're just doing your job. Alright. One can never be too safe. Good-bye."

Russ hung up the phone, rubbing his chin as he considered what he had just heard. It wasn't like Mark to forget to tell him about something like this. He usually took time off to pick him up from school himself if he couldn't make alternate arrangements. At least he could have left Deanie the car so she wouldn't have to show up in that rattle-trap. It was probably nothing. Just a slip.

Except that those nosey teachers at Mark's school were also interested in Mark's sudden acquisition of a 'mother'. People just couldn't mind their own business. Maybe he should call home and see if they were there yet.

Russ dialed the number and drummed his fingers on the desk as he waited. No answer. Maybe Deanie had taken Mark over to her father's place after school. He wasn't exactly excited about the bond that had quickly developed between his son and the aging jazz musician, but what harm could the old geezer do? It was one of the few concessions he'd made. After all, Jack Burton was his wife's father. He couldn't very well expect her to sever all ties.

One more call to Jack's just to satisfy his curiosity. For some reason he felt compelled to know that Mark was safe. It was probably just a force of habit after all their years without another 'parent' in the house. He would really have to learn to loosen up a bit. Mark wasn't a baby anymore.

❧

"Hold up," Brent called over the music. "Somebody's at the door." Notes trailed off into a discordant anti-climax.

A look passed between the men, and for a milli-second Deanie felt a distinct waft of tension.

"Geez," Chris snorted, breaking the spell. "Probably the neighbor again. I don't know what her problem is. It's the middle of the day." The moment passed so quickly that Deanie thought she must have imagined it.

"I'll get it," Grant said, heading toward the front entrance. "Quit bangin'! I'm coming, I'm coming!"

From her proximity in the living room, Deanie heard the front door swish open. Almost instantly Grant uttered an expletive which was soon lost on her as Russ strode into the room. Ice blue eyes met hers. "What are you doing here?"

Behind him, a silent Grant threw up his hands in a 'I haven't a clue' gesture.

"Russ," Deanie exclaimed. "I -"

"I got a call from the school," Russ interrupted.

"We forgot to tell you, that's all," Deanie replied. "No big deal. As you can see, Mark is safe and sound."

"Hardly," Russ muttered.

"Excuse me?" Deanie asked, her voice betraying the offense that was building.

"Mark, get in the car," Russ directed at his son.

"Okay," Mark said, scrambling off the stool.

"Would you chill out for a sec?" Deanie managed, an embarrassed titter betraying her agitation. "You're hardly making a good first impression.

163

This is Russ, by the way. My husband," she gestured to the others.

"We've met," Brent said. His eyes were surveying Russ warily.

"We didn't think you'd be home for awhile," Deanie tried to explain. "And I thought Mark would like -"

"We'll talk about it later," Russ clipped, focusing all his attention on Mark. "Let's go." He turned to leave, his arm steering his son safely in front. He stopped abruptly, turning to face Deanie. "You coming?" he asked.

She blinked. Enough was enough. "No," she stated with quiet resolve.

"We need to talk," he said.

"I'll come when I'm ready."

Their eyes locked in a silent battle for several seconds. Finally, Russ simply turned on his heel and marched Mark out of the building.

An awkward silence followed as each band member fiddled with a cord or a button. Finally Chris broke it. "I could rough him up a bit, again, if you'd like."

"No thanks," Deanie said, daring to breath. She knew he was just trying to ease the tension, but she was having difficulty keeping her lip from trembling. "Excuse me," she said, rushing from the room to the safety of the bathroom.

Things could not continue like this. She was living in a prison. It was time Russ Graham realized this marriage wasn't only about him. The trouble was, she wasn't sure he would listen. . . even wanted to listen. When she emerged from the bathroom a few minutes later, everyone was gone but Brent. "Where'd the rest go?" she asked, looking around.

"Just taking a little break," Brent answered. "We figured you needed a few minutes."

"Sorry to ruin your rehearsal," Deanie apologized.

"Hey, you didn't ruin anything," Brent assured. "Come here, kid." He gently enfolded her in his arms. She let out a tiny sob. "It's okay. Cry it out. I know you've been trying really hard. But you can't fool me. Things aren't right with you and him."

Deanie let herself go. She cried all her heartache out onto Brent's shoulder. When she was done except for a few shivering breaths, she pushed back and smiled weakly. "Thanks. Got a tissue?"

"Only the round variety, I'm afraid," Brent laughed. "Listen, you go freshen up and I'll make some tea or something."

She nodded and headed for the bathroom once again. When she was finished, Brent already had the kettle boiling and two cups on the table.

"You deserve better, you know," he stated.

"Brent," Deanie sighed. "Don't."

"Why not? I don't like seeing my best friend get treated like crap. It stinks."

"I just don't know what to do," Deanie shrugged, taking a sip of her tea.

"Could always leave him," Brent suggested, eyeing her over the rim of his cup. "Nobody would blame you, that's for sure."

"You don't understand," Deanie shook her head. "I couldn't do that."

"Why not? Cause you're pregnant?" Brent scoffed. "Guys like that end up abusing their kids."

Deanie frowned. "He wouldn't do that. He's a good father. He's not the abusive type."

"Maybe not physical, but emotional. It's so much better," he added cryptically.

"You don't get it," Deanie sighed. "I love him."

"It's just the baby thing that's got you all confused."

"Would you say the same thing if we were talking about Holly?" Deanie asked.

"That's different."

"Why? Isn't she the one always talking about 'the Lord's will' and 'trusting God' and stuff like that? Maybe this whole thing is part of some master plan. It's that little carrot of hope that makes me want to wait and see. Maybe, just maybe, it could happen. Once the baby is born."

"And if not? Then what?" Brent asked.

"I don't know. . ."

"I'm surprised to hear you talk about God. Thought that was too far out for you."

"Nothing surprises me much anymore, these days," Deanie said. "Listen, thanks for your ear, but I really should get going. Russ looked really pissed and me staying behind didn't help matters. I might as well brace myself and get it over with. No use prolonging the inevitable."

"You sure?" Brent asked. "You don't have to go back, you know."

"Yes. Yes I do."

❧

Deanie pulled into Russ's driveway and parked her car with a jerk. Taking a deep breath, she stepped from the car and made her way to the house. She opened the front door and was greeted by an ominous silence. She went to hang up her coat in the closet and then thought better of it. Instead she tossed it defiantly across a chair.

"Took you long enough," Russ greeted gruffly. He was standing in the hallway, cloaked in shadow.

"Where's Mark?" she asked, brushing past him on her way to the family room.

"Upstairs in his room - where he will remain for the rest of the evening," Russ stated, following her.

"Why?" Deanie demanded, swinging around. "He didn't do anything. This is between you and me."

"He is my son and I will raise him as I see fit," Russ ground out.

Deanie's voice was laced with sarcasm. "Of course. I forgot you call all the shots around here. Whether it makes sense or not."

"What doesn't make sense is you taking Mark somewhere you knew I wouldn't approve of."

Deanie let a sarcastic bark escape from her lips. "That is rich. As if I took him to some den of iniquity."

"That's not the point. The point is you didn't tell me."

"Because I knew you'd make a big frickin' deal out of nothing," Deanie shot back.

"It's not nothing!" Russ countered, barely keeping his voice in check. "I don't know those. . . men, and from what I've seen they aren't the kind of influence I want for Mark."

"Those men happen to be my friends," Deanie reminded.

"Fine. I can't stop you from seeing them, but I can stop you from taking my son there."

"You are such a snob," Deanie seethed, turning her back on Russ and folding her arms. The man was totally insufferable.

"Be that as it may, I know what's best for my son. And I say I don't

166

want you taking him *anywhere* without my permission."

"Great. And should I call you every time he has to go to the bathroom, too?" Deanie asked.

"Now you're being childish."

"And you're being unreasonable."

There was an angry silence.

Finally Deanie sighed. "Look. I can't live this way. I may not be perfect, and I may not know as much about parenting as you, but I'm here now, and I need to feel like I'm part of this thing. I'm tired of being treated like I don't belong."

"What do you mean, don't belong?" Russ asked. "That's just ridiculous."

"Really?" Deanie raised an eyebrow. "Then what do you call it when you're not allowed to make a mess in your own house? Not allowed to touch anything or move anything, or go anywhere without asking first? I'm your wife, Russ, not another child for you to put up with." She held his gaze, waiting for him to deny it.

"You want to move stuff around? Fine. Just tell me what and where," Russ shot back, flailing his arms in exasperation.

"That's not the point and you know it."

"No? Then what is the point?"

"Things haven't exactly been kosher between us. You know that as well as I do. And today you made it pretty clear that you look down on me as a person."

"I never said that!" Russ denied vehemently.

"You said as much when you insulted my friends. You think they're a bad influence on your son, but I'm like them, Russ. I'm one of them. One of 'those kind' of people that you don't want your son around."

"Not the same thing at all," Russ shook his head.

"You're not a very good liar, you know that?" Deanie snorted, derision in her voice. "I can see it in your eyes. The way you look sometimes when you think I don't see. All sad and humiliated and angry at the same time. Like you're fighting a major battle with yourself and losing. Like you've just taken a bite of the worst tasting food in your life, but you can't spit it out for fear of offending the hostess. I'm that food, Russ."

"Now you're over dramatizing," Russ scoffed. "I married you, for goodness sake."

"Sure, because you got caught up in the moment and didn't want to look bad in front of your son. But now you regret it, I can tell. You won't even make love to me. What kind of marriage is that? Sometimes I feel like you can't stand the sight of me."

"What you're saying is ridiculous and just. . . not true at all," Russ sputtered. "Besides that, you're pregnant and -"

"No! Just stop," Deanie interrupted, holding up her hand. "I don't want your excuses."

"I'm not making excuses," he cried, throwing up his hands. "But it hasn't been easy for me either, you know, adjusting to someone else around the house. Explaining to everyone."

"Poor Russ," Deanie mocked. "All the humiliation you've had to deal with. What about me? I'm the one with the fat stomach."

"Granted. . ."

"Just what are they saying at work, Russ?" Deanie continued. "Has Rita been around to offer her condolences?" It was a catty, childish remark and she knew it. But he was hurting her and she wanted to hurt him back.

Russ's jaw tightened. "Of course not. Is that what you think of me?"

"Well?"

"I could make the same accusation about you and your band of male friends," Russ countered.

"Don't be dumb."

"Well?" he repeated her own response.

Deanie sighed heavily. The fight was going out of her. "Look, I'm too tired to argue anymore."

"You started it," Russ clipped.

"No, you started it when you freaked out about Mark and me visiting Brent," Deanie reminded.

"And I stand by what I said. Don't take him there again," Russ reiterated.

Deanie squeezed her eyes tight, pinching the bridge of her nose between her thumb and forefinger. She was near the breaking point and knew it. With a sigh she opened her eyes again. "You know what? I need a breather. We'll talk again when you're done being so pig-headed." She pushed past Russ on her way to the stairs.

"You're just going to go to bed angry." It was a statement, not a question.

Deanie turned. "No. I'm going upstairs to get a few things. And then I'm going to Jack's for the night. Where I'm wanted."

"Running away."

"If you like," Deanie shrugged. "I told you. I'm too tired to argue with you anymore, Russ. When you're ready to talk to me as an equal, then you know where I'll be."

"What am I supposed to tell Mark?" Russ asked, frowning.

"You're the one with all answers. Figure it out."

Chapter Twenty

Russ knew he should call Deanie. It had been two whole days and she hadn't come home. Hadn't called. It was plenty of time to think about what she'd said and he had to concede that she was right on several accounts. He did need to lighten up. Maybe they could go shopping for some new furniture or something to make her feel like his home was her home, too.

As far as her friends went, he supposed he could try giving them a chance. He wasn't totally comfortable with the idea yet, especially with their 'past history', but he had definitely over reacted the day he'd found Mark there. Maybe they could host some kind of a party before the baby was born. Sort of a post wedding get together for all their friends and colleagues. It would be a gesture of peace as far as Deanie's friends went, and it might actually help dissipate some of the office gossip. Kind of throw it back at them. A picture of the long haired quartet hob-knobbing with Josh Fredrickson came to mind and Russ smiled. He could sick the over zealous Josh on the foursome and see how long they stuck around.

And then there was the matter of their intimacy . . . or lack there of. This was one he couldn't quite figure out. She thought he wasn't attracted to her, but nothing could be farther from the truth. Then why, when evening rolled around, did he suddenly put the brakes on? Was it guilt, pride, or self punishment? It was something he could not explain, even to himself.

Explaining Deanie's absence to Mark was a little easier. She just had some family stuff to take care of and would be back soon. Mark seemed satisfied, although Russ suffered definite twinges of guilt at lying to his son. He hoped his words were true. That she would be back in a couple of days. Otherwise he would have some real explaining to do. Which brought him back to his original thought. He should just call her and apologize.

🌺

The telephone rang shrilly, as if on cue. Deanie's stomach tightened in anticipation and she took a deep breath before answering. She had been waiting for Russ to call, almost stooping to call him herself a couple of times. But she had some pride. And some stubbornness, too.

"Deanie?"

She blinked, letting out a gust of air. Brent. "Oh. Um, hi."

"Geez. You don't sound too happy to hear from me," Brent said, bemused.

"What? Oh, sorry," she apologized. "Just tired. You know how it is."

"You did the right thing," Brent said.

"You think?"

"Sure," he affirmed. "I take it he still hasn't called?"

"Obviously, since I'm still here," she sighed. "I don't know. . . I was thinking of calling him."

"Stick to your guns," Brent advised.

"Easy for you to say."

"You're not alone are you?" Brent asked.

Deanie frowned. That was a strange question. "No. Jack is here. He'll be going out in a little while with the guys, though. Why?"

"Oh nothing. Um, listen. I was wondering, maybe you'd like to get out of the house," Brent suggested.

"What's up?" she asked. She did need to get out of the house. She was going stir crazy.

"Well, I was, that is, Holly and I were wondering if you'd like to come with us. To church."

"Church?" Deanie asked, frowning. "Is it Sunday?"

"No," Brent laughed, "but there's been a bunch of services over at Holly's church all week. It's been pretty cool, actually. Lots of good music. Thought you might enjoy it."

"Well . . ." Deanie hesitated. "I've never really been to church before."

"Come on," Brent urged. "You'd like it."

"But. . . church really isn't my thing."

"How do you know that if you've never been there?"

"Well, I don't have anything to wear," Deanie hedged.

"Now you're making excuses. Just wear what you have on. Everybody does."

"Well. . . Brent!" Deanie ended in exasperation.

"What? Are you afraid or something?" he baited.

"Now that isn't fair! Of course I'm not afraid, and of course you know that I can't let a challenge like that by."

"Good. Pick you up at 6:30, then," Brent laughed. He clicked down the receiver before Deanie could make any further comments. He knew exactly how to manipulate her, she mused with a smile.

❧

Russ dialed the number and let it ring six times. He was just about to hang up when a breathless Jack barked a hello into the mouthpiece. Russ winced, moving the receiver slightly away from his ear. "Um, hello. This is Russ. I'm looking for Deanie."

"Just missed her," Jack replied. "She left a few minutes ago with Brent."

Anger mixed with mistrust surged through his chest at the mention of the other man's name. So. She'd gone right back to the tribe, had she. The ones who had started this whole fight in the first place. His earlier concessions in regard to Deanie's friends seemed to have disappeared.

"Hello? You still there?"

Russ brought himself back to the moment. "Yes, I'm still here."

"I told her marriage is about give and take, on both sides," Jack said. "The sooner you work this out the better."

"Right. Can you tell her I called?" Russ asked.

"Sure thing," Jack agreed. "I'll tell her the minute she gets home. But the rest is up to her. She can be stubborn, that one, when she wants to be."

Russ hung up the phone, reflecting on what Jack had said. She wasn't the only one. He'd made the first move. Now it was her turn.

Deanie, Brent and Holly arrived at the large church on the outskirts of the city a few minutes before the event started. It was more like a building complex, Deanie noted, with a large gymnasium attached and a high rise apartment on the same property. Not like any church she'd imagined.

"No need to be so nervous," Brent chided in her ear as they entered the spacious foyer. "You'll like it. You'll see."

Deanie couldn't believe how uncomfortable she felt. It was rather strange. She'd performed in front of hundreds of people before and never experienced the jitters she felt at that moment. Brent on the other hand, seemed totally at ease in this strange environment. He even greeted several people in passing.

The sanctuary itself was tastefully decorated in muted colors and was full of removable, cushioned chairs, not the hard bench seats she was expecting. That was a blessing. Sort of. Now she wouldn't have an excuse for leaving if it got too claustrophobic. At the front was a large platform, outfitted with a full band in the midst of tuning up. They had some pretty nice sound equipment, her well-trained eye noted. She focused on these familiar objects, willing herself to relax. Brent must have noticed the change, for he leaned over and whispered, "Just wait until the music starts." She smiled weakly, clutching the back of the chair in front of her.

A man came forward and welcomed the now packed auditorium. He said a short prayer and then introduced the band. After the first several bars she began to relax in earnest. Brent was right. Music was her element. Even though they were singing about God, this was something she could relate to.

The songs were lively and upbeat and Deanie found herself clapping along. About halfway through the singing, though, the mood in the room changed. It went from lively jubilance, to reverent worship. These songs were beautiful and Deanie heard her own voice blending with the hundreds of other voices. Maybe this was what heaven was like. . .

She was jolted back to reality when the speaker for the evening came forward. His prayer was long and sent shivers down her spine. Then he began to preach. She'd never heard anything like this before. Whenever anything like it came on TV, Jack had quickly turned the channel. She didn't understand what he was talking about, although some of his words were things that Holly had shared. She looked desperately around the room, focusing on the tops of people's heads in an attempt to shut out what he was saying. But something kept drawing her back to his words. He seemed to be speaking directly to her. And she could not ignore it.

"We're all sinners. The Bible says 'For all have sinned and fall short of the glory of God'." Didn't she know it? The shame of her past as well as the predicament of the present flooded over her. Her belly tightened and she thought for a moment that she might be sick.

But now what was he saying? "There is a way to be free. To be washed clean of any guilt and shame. Jesus is that way. He told us, 'I am the way the truth and the life. No one comes to the Father but by me'." Oh to be free! Not just for her sake, but for the sake of her unborn child. For the sake of Russ Graham, the man she couldn't help loving. She wished that she were the kind of guiltless woman that he could be proud of. Then maybe he could accept her. Love her.

Just accept Him now. . . Jesus. . . Deanie felt her heart reaching out. Something snapped inside. Her mind recoiled even as her heart cried, *"Yes!"* This was ridiculous - a fantasy. She'd let herself get carried away by the music. She had to get out of here. Fast.

She glanced desperately at Brent, ready to ask him if they could leave. But. . . Surely those weren't tears in *his* eyes? Had he been sucked in by the skillful words of the preacher, too?

The man at the front was calling for people to come forward to accept Jesus as their personal Savior. Brent was rising. He looked to Holly for support, and she stood with him, taking his hand. They walked forward, along with many others, and made their way to the front of the church.

Deanie sat numbly in her seat. She was shaking like a leaf. Part of her wanted to go forward with Brent. But another part scoffed at the emotionalism of the whole thing. She jumped to her feet, but instead of joining the others at the alter, she fled toward the back entrance and pushed her way through the exit, gulping at the cool outside air as if she had been submerged under water for a very long time.

A middle aged woman emerged from the building right behind Deanie. "Is there something wrong, dear?" she asked in a concerned voice.

"No," Deanie replied a little too sharply. "I mean, I only need some air. It was a little stuffy in there."

The woman nodded, understanding in her eyes. "Yes, I suppose for someone in your condition it - "

Deanie cut her off mid sentence, "How much longer will they be in there?" She gestured toward the sanctuary.

"That depends," the woman said. "There is usually some one-on-one counseling and prayer time afterwards. We also have some fellowship and coffee, too. Would you like to come back in with me and wait? Perhaps have a cup of coffee?"

Deanie hesitated, but realized she couldn't very well wait outside in the cold. "No thanks. Um. . . is there a way to get a message to my friend? I'm really not feeling that well and I think I'll just take a cab home."

"Of course. Just follow me."

Deanie followed the woman back indoors and made her arrangements with another attendant. Then she called a cab.

She felt angry with Brent for coercing her into coming to this place. He was all she had at the moment, and now he had abandoned her too.

Deanie let herself into the old apartment. It was deathly dark and quiet. The baby jumped inside of her, signaling that he, at least, was alive and well. She placed a gentle hand across her abdomen. Too bad Russ hadn't felt that yet.

There didn't seem to be anyone home to greet her. Jack must still be out with the boys. But that was funny. His boots and jacket were lying crumpled by the door where he always dropped them. He didn't usually go to bed this early.

"Jack," Deanie called, not too loudly just in case he was sleeping. Nothing. "Jack!" she called again, a little bit louder this time. Then she heard it. A strange groaning sound coming from down the hall.

Deanie rushed to Jack's bedroom and switched on the light. He was half lying on the bed, clutching his chest, a contorted grimace on his face. With a scream she rushed to his side and tried to haul him up onto the bed. The only response that came was a painful, gurgling moan. "No, Jack. You can't leave me, now, too," she whispered.

FOURTH MOVEMENT:
Crescendo et al Fine

Chapter Twenty-One

The bright lights and bustling noise of the emergency room only increased the numbness that Deanie felt as she sat waiting. Both Brent and his father Benny were there with her. She was grateful for every shoulder to lean on at the moment. She just didn't think she could take it if Jack didn't pull through.

"Everything's gonna be all right, Kiddo," Benny consoled, perhaps more for himself than anyone.

"You didn't see him. He was so white . . ." Her lip started to tremble almost uncontrollably.

"Hey! Sh," Brent soothed, putting his arm around her shoulder as she leaned into him.

"It's like I have nobody left," she whispered.

"You've got me," Brent replied.

"Do I?" Deanie asked, surveying him with doubtful eyes.

Brent frowned, but didn't say anything. The doctor was approaching, and he stood up, along with his father, Benny. "How is he?" they asked, almost in unison.

"As you probably know, he had quite an extensive heart attack. We've got him stabilized and are moving him to the intensive care unit," the doctor explained.

Deanie began to cry in earnest, and Benny put his arm around her. "Its okay, girl. Its gonna be okay." Tears also gleamed in his eyes. "You're old man is tough. He'll pull through."

"Yes, I'm fairly confident of that," the doctor agreed. "Although the first twenty-four hours are always the most crucial."

"So we just wait it out, then?" Deanie asked.

"There's really nothing else for you to do at the moment," the doctor said. "My advice is to go home and get some rest. I'll call you if there are any significant changes. Your father is going to need you tomorrow."

"He's right," Brent agreed. "You're exhausted."

With a final nod, the doctor took his leave. The threesome watched him as he retreated down the hall.

"I'm not sure I can sleep even if I go home," Deanie admitted.

"Need some company?" Brent asked.

"Would you?" The relief she felt was mirrored in her eyes.

"Of course. It wouldn't be good for you to be alone."

❧

Banging his fist on the desktop, Russ rose from his chair and stood to look out his study window. A light beamed softly into the darkness from the neighbor's window. Other than that, there was only the slightly orange-ish glow from the street lights that canopied the night sky. He should be in his bed, fast asleep. But that was an impossibility. Why hadn't she called?

He felt helpless, like a man being tossed at sea. He could not seem to reconcile the hope he felt with the anger and hurt. Yes, he still wanted her; felt that same softness inside that wanted to nurture and protect. But the jealousy, the suspicion, the mistrust . . . they were powerful forces. It was a battle, plain and simple, and it was one that he wasn't sure he could win.

Maybe he should just risk it all and call again. Surely she was at home by now. Then again, it was kind of late. Calling at this hour would make him sound desperate. Maybe he was.

With deliberate accuracy he dialed the numbers, hovering between hanging up and continuing until the first ring sounded in his ear. Two more and he would hang up for sure.

"Hello?"

Russ's body stilled, reaching into the recesses of his mind to recognize

178

the voice. "Hello?" Russ repeated the greeting. "I think I might have the wrong number."

"This is the Burton residence," Brent informed.

"Oh?" Confusion clouded Russ's brain. It didn't sound like Jack.

"Sorry," Brent laughed. "You caught me off guard. Is this Russ?"

"Yes it is."

"Brent here. There's something I think you should know -"

Russ cut him off. "Is Deanie there?" he clipped.

"Sleeping. Look, she's had a hard day and she was kind of upset, so I offered to stay the night -"

Russ cut him off again. "You what?"

"Look, man. It's not like that. It's just -"

Russ didn't wait for the explanation. Jealousy was no longer warring for a place within him. It had taken the front lines.

Chapter Twenty-Two

"Any luck?" Brent asked as Deanie approached. He was standing outside Jack's door in the intensive care unit.

She shook her head. "No. He's still with a client, apparently."

"He'll call back," Brent assured. "Don't worry."

"How could you?" Deanie asked, her brow furrowed and her arms crossed.

"Not this again," Brent sighed, rolling his eyes ceiling-ward. "I thought we had this conversation already. About three times."

"I can't believe you didn't just wake me," she continued with a pout. "You knew I was waiting for a call."

"You needed a good night's sleep," Brent argued, his voice intense, but just barely above a whisper. "You'd had enough without fending off an angry husband, too."

"How do you know he was angry when he called?" Deanie shot back.

"Believe me, he was angry."

"Of course he was, when he found out you were spending the night!"

"He was the one jumping to conclusions," Brent defended. "I tried to tell him about Jack but he hung up on me."

"And now I can't get a hold of him to explain," Deanie sighed. "He's been busy all morning. I'm beginning to think the secretary is just putting me off."

"You left a message about Jack, right?" Brent queried.

"Of course."

"Then he'll call. Don't worry."

"So what's with you lurking in the hall?" Deanie asked, gesturing at Jack's doorway with her head.

"The nurse is in taking his vitals again," Brent said.

Deanie nodded. At that moment the nurse emerged from the room.

"Everything okay?" Deanie asked.

"He's stable," the nurse said. "But very tired. He probably needs some rest. Why don't you two take a break and let him sleep. Go down to the cafeteria for a coffee." She smiled and continued down the hall to the next room, as if it had been settled.

Deanie sighed, and stepped inside the darkened room where Jack lay. He looked so frail. So weak. His eyes were shut and he was breathing rhythmically. She backed out of the room, almost bumping into Brent. "Sh!" she whispered, putting a finger to her lips. "Come on. We might as well go sit in the waiting room for awhile."

They moved down the hall to a small waiting room with two couches and a small coffee table. Deanie plopped down onto one of the couches and let out a wide yawn.

"Look at you," Brent clucked. "You should really be going home for a rest, that's what. I'll go with you."

"And leave Jack? Not a chance," Deanie shook her head.

"I'll keep vigil," Brent offered. "You could go over to my place and grab a nap."

"Why would I go to your place?" Deanie asked. "I have a perfectly good bed at home and it'd be quieter, too."

"I don't know," Brent shrugged. "It's not good to be alone right now. You need the support of your friends."

"So you keep saying."

"Seriously. Head over to my place and I'll stay here. I'll call you if anything changes."

"Hmph," Deanie mumbled.

"What's that supposed to mean?" Brent asked.

"Just that you're not on my list of most reliable people at the moment," Deanie quipped. She was smiling, though.

"I guess I'm not going to live that one down any time soon," Brent mused.

"Nope," Deanie laughed.

"You could just go and talk to him in person," Brent suggested.

"Just show up at his work?" Deanie asked. "That would go over well."

"Why not?"

"I'm not sure how much the people at work know, although I can guess. It would just embarrass him."

"I'm not sure why you're sticking up for the guy," Brent shook his head. "It's not like you got pregnant alone. And besides, if it was my wife, I wouldn't be embarrassed."

"That's because you're you," Deanie pointed out. "You don't care what people think. Well, at least most people."

"I remember a time when you were the same," Brent noted, raising an eyebrow.

"I guess things change. People change," Deanie shrugged.

"I guess."

"Speaking of. . ." Deanie narrowed her eyes, scrutinizing Brent. "My best friend kind of weirded me out last night."

Brent shifted uncomfortably in his seat. "What do you mean?"

"You know exactly what I mean," Deanie said. "You going forward at that church thing. Don't tell me you've gone and got religious on me."

Brent considered this for a moment. "I guess when you put it that way, I have."

"Well, just don't go and change too much. I want my best friend, not somebody with the life sucked out of him."

"You've got it all wrong," Brent replied. "Becoming a Christian doesn't suck the life out of you. It gives you life. New life in Christ."

"You're even starting to talk their language," Deanie rolled her eyes.

"Seriously, I never knew asking Christ into my life would be like this," Brent said.

"No preaching!" Deanie cut him off, pointing her finger. "You promised me."

"Okay, sorry," Brent held up his hands.

"Besides, if there is a God, why did he allow this to happen?" Deanie asked.

Brent shook his head. "I don't know, Dee. I really don't know. All I know is, God is for real. End of story."

Deanie sighed heavily. "I guess I should just be happy for you. Now you and Holly can, well, you know. Move forward in your relationship now that you believe the same way and everything."

Brent frowned. "That's not why I gave my heart to Christ."

"No?" Deanie returned, raising an eyebrow skeptically.

"No!" He stopped and looked around, realizing his voice had become a bit too loud. "No," he repeated more softly. "It's not like that. I just wish I could make you understand somehow."

"Whatever," Deanie shrugged, looking down at her hands. "I have had way too much drama lately."

"Now that, I agree with," Brent smiled.

"Maybe I should slip over to the apartment and clean the place up a bit. Make it nice for Jack to come home to," Deanie mused.

"Since when did you ever care about housework?" Brent asked. "Is this some kind of nesting thing?"

"It better not be," Deanie laughed. "It's a bit too early for that." She cocked her head to one side. "I don't know. I guess I'm getting used to it. We. . . I mean Russ and I, have a cleaning lady. *Had* a cleaning lady." She sighed." It was kind of nice. I liked it."

"You make it sound like things are over for good," Brent frowned. "I'll go over to his work and talk to him myself if you think it would help."

"No, thank you," Deanie quipped. "You've done enough."

"Here we go again," Brent rolled his eyes.

"Yeah, my life pretty much sucks, " Deanie sighed melodramatically. "My father just had a heart attack, my husband isn't speaking to me, and I'm sick and tired of being fat."

"Poor thing."

Deanie laughed. "I need to keep busy. Starting with cleaning the apartment. The more I think about it, the more I think it's a good idea."

"You're pushing yourself."

"Whatever," Deanie shrugged. "I'm restless. Can you blame me?"

"I guess not. I could help you," Brent suggested. "Clean, I mean."

"Thanks, but actually, I think it might be kind of therapeutic," Deanie said. "And despite what you say, some alone time is what I want. To think about what's next."

"What's next?"

"Yeah. What if Russ and I can't make a go of it," She hesitated. "You know, Russ actually said that if it didn't work out we could always get a divorce after the baby was born. Maybe he was just looking for an excuse."

"Bastard," Brent stated.

Deanie frowned. "Never mind. I don't think he meant it. At least not yet, anyway."

"There you go defending him again."

"Somebody has to," Deanie retorted. "He certainly hasn't won you over."

"Right you are."

Deanie hoisted herself from the couch. "Well, if I'm going to get any cleaning done, I better get at it. It shouldn't take long and I don't want to be away too long."

"You're sure you don't want my help?" Brent asked. "I think I should come, too."

"No, I'll be fine. Geez! Why are you acting so weird?"

"I'm not acting weird," Brent denied. "Just worried about you."

"Well, can it, mother hen," Deanie laughed. "I'll be back before you know it. Are you staying here? You could probably use a break, too, since Jack is sleeping right now."

"I'll stay for a bit," Brent said. "Holly starts her shift pretty soon. I might go to emergency and see her before she starts."

"I see," Deanie nodded her head, her eyes twinkling. "Have fun. And call me if anything changes."

"You know I will."

❧

Russ watched the numerals climb ever so slowly above the elevator doors. He'd told the office receptionist to hold all his calls, but he hadn't expected her to take him quite this literally. When he had finally emerged from his office to check his messages it was all he could do to keep from biting her head off on the spot. Stupid woman! Deanie had called – several

184

times – to say that Jack had had a heart attack. If that wasn't reason enough to disobey his orders, he didn't know what was. Then again, he hadn't been the easiest person to work for lately. She was probably afraid of what his reaction might be. Now she knew. The thought of Deanie, facing this alone was enough to make him forget his anger from the night before. Almost.

The elevator swished open and Russ stepped out onto the shiny linoleum of the third floor. He strode in the direction indicated by the receptionist and stopped when he saw a familiar face outside Jack's hospital room. It was that friend again. The one doing all the consoling. That was a husband's job. Although he now realized the reasons for the other man's presence at Deanie's apartment so late last night, he still felt pangs of jealousy. His wife had the kind of relationship with Brent Walters that he would probably never have with her.

"You're here," Russ stated the obvious.

"That's right," Brent replied, his eyes wary. "I take it you got Dee's message?"

Russ nodded.

"About last night," Brent said. "Deanie just needed a friend. There's nothing between us. You know that."

Russ just shrugged.

"Come on man," Brent continued. "She's like my sister. Besides that, I have a girlfriend. If you hadn't hung up on me you would know the score."

"How's Jack?" Russ gestured toward the semi-closed door.

"He'll make it," Brent responded.

"Good. Good."

"I'm not sure if the nurses will let you in to see him right now, though. He's sleeping."

Russ shook his head. "It's okay. Where's Deanie?"

Brent laughed at that. "She went back to the apartment to clean. Apparently something she learned from you."

Russ's eyebrows rose. He remembered the state of the little apartment. That was too big a job for one person. "Thanks." He turned to leave, but Brent was close on his heels.

"I'm on my way over to emerge," Brent said. "Might as well ride down with you."

"Suit yourself," Russ shrugged.

They walked silently to the elevators. Once inside, Brent spoke up. "I figured this was a better place for a private conversation."

So. The other man wanted to talk did he? Russ felt himself instinctively bristling.

"I know you don't like me very much, and to be honest, the feeling is mutual," Brent began. "But since Deanie loves you, I'm trying to make an effort. I think we should start over. Try to get along for her sake."

"Pardon?" Russ asked, his brow furrowed.

"I think you're all wrong for Deanie and the way you've been treating her stinks. But -"

"Not that," Russ cut in. "You said she loves me. How do you know? Did she tell you that?"

"Of course," Brent replied. "I told you. She's practically my sister."

The elevator doors swished open and they stepped out, pausing a few feet away. "Listen, I don't want her to get hurt," Brent continued. "You get my drift?"

"I'm not really sure of your point," Russ replied. "Are you threatening me? Warning me? What?"

"Neither," Brent stated. "Geez! I said I thought we should try to get along. As in get to know each other. Be friends. For Deanie's sake." He threw up his hands.

Russ frowned. This was not what he was expecting and he wasn't sure it was what he wanted, either. He was about to make a reply when he was stopped short by a frantic looking Len Colby, who had just arrived in a rush.

"Whoa, buddy! What's up?" Brent asked, turning to Len.

"Um, can I talk to you for a minute?" Len said, gesturing away from Russ with his head.

"Keep what I said in mind," Brent called over his shoulder, already moving away with Len.

Russ grunted. He'd think about it. He knew his jealousy was unfounded. He knew he couldn't expect Deanie to give up her entire life for him. He knew she deserved better than what he had offered so far in terms of a loving husband. But all he could think of right now were Brent's words. She loved him.

His reverie was cut short. "Hey, Russ! Wait up!" It was Brent, jogging after him as he reached the outside doors. Len was close behind. Russ stopped and turned.

"How fast is your car?' Brent asked.

Russ frowned. "Fast enough."

"Good. We're going for a ride," Brent said. "Over to the apartment. There are a couple of things we need to talk about."

"Oh?"

"Yeah. Not to alarm you or anything, but. . . well, I'll explain on the way."

"Come on, man," Len cut in. "I think we should hurry."

"Hold on," Russ spoke. A deep crease marred his forehead. "Just what is going on here?"

Brent ignored Russ and focused on what Len was saying instead. "Chris is already on his way over there," Len told Brent. "I stopped over at your place cause I thought you'd be there. So Chris went over to Deanie's while I came to get you."

"Wait a minute!" Russ bellowed. "Would somebody tell me what's going on?!"

"Deanie's ex is back in town," Brent said, his eyes never wavering from Russ's. "And he's bad news."

Chapter Twenty-Three

Deanie plodded down the flight of stairs, the two stuffed trash bags bumping behind her on each step. She felt good about what she had accomplished so far. Even Jack was sure to notice the improvement. All that was left now was the vacuuming.

She opened the glass security doors to the building, then backed out, pushing the door wide with her rear end as she hauled the bags out. Just as she turned to walk towards the disposal, she was stopped short, bumping almost headlong into a square, burly chest. She looked up and with a quick intake of air, the garbage bags dropped to the sidewalk.

Before she could even open her mouth to call out, a large, gloved hand clamped over it. One scuffed, booted foot managed to jam itself in the security door before it had time to close. He propelled Deanie through the door and up the stairs, all the while keeping his vice like grip over her mouth with one hand, and twisting her arm painfully up behind her back with the other. "Stop struggling," the gravelly voice commanded, barely above a whisper.

She'd left the door to her apartment ajar. He had only to push it open with his foot and then kick it shut with a resounding slam. "Same old dump, I see," he commented. He relaxed his grip over her mouth somewhat and she began all the more to twist and struggle, muffled screams coming from behind the glove.

"Shut up," he grated and jerked her head painfully as he tightened his hold. Deanie could hardly breathe. His hand covered both her mouth and nose and she had to struggle hard for each breath. Tears had sprung to her eyes, which were open wide in fear. The feeling of helplessness was almost too much. She thought she might faint, and yet knew that such a blessing would not come. Every nerve ending was completely strung up, the terror she felt pumping the adrenaline through her veins like an explosive.

"Put on some music," Brad ordered, propelling her toward the stereo. With fumbling fingers, she chose a cassette. "Not that one!" Brad barked. "Something I like. You *do* remember what I like? Something that can be cranked. Loud." She put in a different tape, and turned it up until he told her to stop. "Don't try anything," he threatened as he released her mouth and spun her around to face him.

She had a chance to look at him fully, now. Brad Kilpatrick. Ex boyfriend. He had changed. Become even more hardened, if that were possible. His brown hair was longer and more straggly and he had grown a dark shaggy beard and mustache. He looked much older than the mid twenties that he was. But the eyes were the same. The same hard glint. And the voice. The same sarcastic, threatening quality that she so well remembered. She shivered convulsively, her lips trembling as she formed the barely audible words, "What do you want?"

Brad smiled - more of a sneer, really. "I've just come back for what's mine. You thought you could get rid of me, but you know that I'm a part of you and you're a part of me. You can never get rid of me, Deanie. Never." The grip that he had on her shoulders was biting into her flesh, and she winced in pain.

"You're hurting me," she cried. Brad shook her once more, then pushed her backwards, releasing her. She stumbled and knocked into a lamp, toppling it to the floor. Instinctively she clutched protectively at her protruding stomach. The movement seemed to draw Brad's attention, and his eyes narrowed as if seeing the truth for the first time.

His voice rose from a low growl to a full-blown roar. "You little whore! You've been cheating on me!" He lunged for her, sending her sprawling to the floor on hands and knees.

Deanie screamed, "No, Brad! No! Please don't hurt my baby!" She rolled and managed to scramble to her feet, missing the cruel kick that had been directed at her abdomen.

"How dare you?" Brad growled, "I should kill you for this. Who's the father? Who is he so I can kill him?"

"Brad, stop! I'm married now. You have no right. Please!"

Brad laughed cruelly. "Married? Ha! Who would marry you? Besides, you're already mine."

"I am not yours. I never was. I'm with someone else now. I'm married to him."

"And you're knocked up. Mine wasn't good enough for you, but you carry his."

"That's not true. I loved our baby."

"You killed it!" Brad roared.

"No! No I didn't. . . please," she pleaded quietly. "Be reasonable."

They had been circling around the room, Deanie trying to find a safe defense, while Brad carelessly knocked furniture out of his path. He looked like a madman, staring without seeing. She glanced toward the telephone and in one fluid motion he snatched it up and jerked it from its connection, cutting off that particular life line.

Deanie backed towards the kitchen. From the corner of her eye she spotted a rather dull butcher knife lying on the counter. With heroic effort, she lunged for the knife, grasped its wooden handle and thrust it in his direction. "Stay back!" she shrieked.

Brad just blinked for a moment and then laughed. With one quick motion he caught the blade with his bare hand, drawing an oozing red line across his palm. Within seconds he had overpowered her and was holding the knife to her throat.

❧

The little convoy sped through the streets of Winnipeg, Len in the lead on his motorcycle, Russ and Brent following closely behind in Russ's vehicle.

"What in the name of hell is going on?" Russ demanded, focusing on the swerving motorcycle just ahead.

Brent sighed. "Did Deanie ever mention a former boyfriend by the name of Brad?"

Russ frowned, reaching into the recesses of his mind. They'd talked about a lot of things that time, back at Hecla. But he didn't remember the specifics, exactly. His mind had been elsewhere. He shook his head. "No, I don't think so."

"Believe me, if she told you, you'd remember," Brent said.

"Get to the point," Russ clipped.

"It's really something that's better coming from Dee herself," Brent hedged. "But under the circumstances. . ."

"Under the circumstances, my patience is wearing thin," Russ growled.

"Edited or unedited version?" Brent asked.

Russ responded with a glare that could melt an iceberg.

"Right," Brent replied, rubbing the back of his neck uncomfortably. "Shit! I thought that psycho was out of the picture for good!" he spat, slamming his palm against the dash.

"Tell me!" Russ barked. "For God's sake, what is this all about?"

"Okay, sorry," Brent countered, holding up a hand. He took a deep breath. "Brad Kilpatrick. Used to play drums for us a few years back. Man, I'm not sure where to begin. The guys a maniac. A dangerous one at that."

Russ tightened his grip on the wheel. "Go on."

"I'm not sure where to begin," Brent repeated. "You better not use anything that I'm gonna tell you against her. She was kind of mixed up then, you know? But she really does love you. She deserves better -"

"Just tell me," Russ fairly roared.

"Okay, okay! Like I said, Brad was our drummer. Damn good drummer, too." He glanced over at Russ and continued quickly before Russ could explode again. "And they were, like, you know, a couple. But Brad was a pretty bad apple. I knew it and I guess I was partly to blame cause I was the leader of the group. But I just couldn't let him go. He was really gifted on the drums. . . Anyway, none of us were completely clean, if you know what I mean. Who doesn't get high once in a while, right? But Brad was getting into some strong shit. It made him go kind of crazy. It kind of scared the living shit out of all of us. But Deanie took the brunt of it. She tried to break it off with him a few times, but he was pretty controlling. He slapped her around more than once." Russ let out a growl. Brent continued. "Anyways, when he found out she was pregnant, he -"

191

Russ sputtered and almost choked, "What? What did you say?" His head was spinning all of a sudden. He concentrated on following Len's motorcycle in front of him.

"Sorry, man. I guess that came as a shock to you." Brent looked out the window, avoiding eye contact.

"Where is the child now?" Russ whispered hoarsely.

"Just take it easy and let me finish," Brent said. "Like I said, Dee got pregnant and when Brad found out he kind of went ballistic. He was already stoned out of his head, and he started beating on her. I mean really beating on her. I guess she told him during one of our breaks one night at a gig. We saw them go out back together, and then the next thing I knew Brad had disappeared. We found Dee out in the back alley. She was a real mess. She was in the hospital for quite awhile. Lost the baby."

The imagery cut deep into Russ's heart, like a knife, twisting and probing into tender flesh. He accelerated, almost rear ending Len on the bike ahead.

"Man, I'm really sorry to have to break all this to you. But maybe now you can see why I'm kind of over protective. She means a lot to me, and I don't want to lose her again."

"She's *my* wife," Russ reminded. He was having some trouble taking it all in. He felt compassion and revulsion all at once. "Why isn't he in jail?" he asked.

"He was. That's what has us worried. He shouldn't be out for a long time to come. Besides what he did to Dee, he's serving time for all kinds of shit. Trafficking, B and E's, you name it."

"So what are you saying?"

"We got word that he might be back in town. That he got out early on good behavior. And then Len actually saw him."

"And?" Russ prompted.

"We're afraid he might try something stupid. Try to get revenge or something."

"Revenge. On who?" The growing sense of foreboding in his stomach told him he already knew the answer.

"He blamed Deanie for everything. The fact that his life was the shits.

That he landed up in jail." Brent looked over at Russ. "He's got a real nasty streak. I don't suppose incarceration has made things any better."

"Does Deanie know he's back?" Russ asked.

Brent shook his head. "No. I didn't want to worry her. She's got enough on her mind right now." He looked sideways at Russ. "No thanks to you, I might add."

Russ grunted his ascent. "You still haven't explained why we're rushing over there now. What else are you hiding?"

Brent shifted uncomfortably. "Yeah, well. . . we have reason to believe he's been watching her. Hanging around the old apartment."

"What?" Russ almost swerved into the other lane.

"Len's been keeping an eye out, but -"

"What do you mean 'Len's been keeping an eye out'?" Russ spat.

Brent looked sheepish. "He's just been doing a little surveillance. We all have. No big deal. Making sure she's okay."

"I can't believe this! I could have you all arrested!" Russ exploded. "You mean to tell me that some psychotic killer has been stalking my wife, and you knew about it, *and you didn't tell me*?!"

"Hey, its not quite that way!" Brent defended himself. "Besides, you haven't exactly been the model husband, you know. You've put her through your own brand of hell lately."

Russ was silent for a moment. He couldn't defend himself on that score. "Has anyone called the police?" he demanded, keeping his voice in check.

"And say what?" Brent snapped.

Russ clamped his jaw tight. He stepped on the gas, accelerating past Len.

Chapter Twenty-Four

Brad held the knife just close enough to feel the now warm metal against her throat. This wasn't the way it was supposed to end. Deanie squeezed her eyes tight, willing the tears that were sure to enrage him further, away.

Without warning, a loud banging sounded at the door. Her eyes flew open as the knife pressed in. "Deanie? Deanie are you in there?" came a muffled voice from the other side.

Deanie managed a stifled yelp before Brad clamped his bloody hand over her mouth. "Shut up," he hissed into her ear. The banging continued for a few more seconds and then all was silent. She felt her body sag in despair.

Suddenly the door came crashing down as Chris Nambert stumbled into the room, shoulder first. He stopped abruptly, taking in the situation. Brad stood with Deanie in front of him, one bloody hand clamped over her mouth while the other held the knife to her throat. Deanie's eyes were wide with terror, but she was unable to make a sound.

"Hey, Brad," Chris said calmly, advancing slowly toward the pair. "Put the knife down, okay?"

"Okay," Brad sneered. He moved the knife so that it hovered, point first, over Deanie's protruding abdomen. "Is that better?" Deanie's eyes widened even more, her nostrils flaring.

"That's not what I meant," Chris continued in the same, calm tone. "Hurting her isn't going to accomplish anything."

194

"Says who?" Brad spat out.

"Says me. Just let her go and we'll talk." Chris's cool behavior was uncanny. Deanie prayed that Brad would listen to reason, but didn't hold out any hope as his grip tightened.

"I should have known!" Brad's laugh was maniacal. "First you take over as drummer, and then you take over my woman."

"You got it all wrong, man," Chris explained, as if to a child. "Deanie's not my woman. Now just let her go and we'll talk about it."

"Ha! Don't try that with me," Brad sneered.

Suddenly Chris lunged for the knife. Equally muscled hands shook as forearms bulged, the knife shaking violently just millimeters from her baby. With a last frantic twist, Deanie was suddenly released from Brad's grasp as his attention was focused elsewhere. She crashed into the stove with the force of her efforts, not stopping to assess the pain as she plunged herself out of harm's way.

Brad had gained control of the knife and lashed out at Chris. He dodged the first swipe, but was not so lucky when the next swing slashed across his upper arm and chest. Bright red blood stained the T- shirt that now hung openly on his body, but he had no time to stop and inspect the wound. The two men, of about equal size and strength, locked forces once again, Chris struggling to keep the knife at bay, until they finally crashed heavily to the floor, rolling and twisting in an Olympic style wrestling match.

Deanie stood frozen, watching the battle as if in a dream. Suddenly, as if awakening from a trance, she bolted for the smashed door and ran down the hall to the next apartment. "Help! Call the police!" she yelled as she banged on the door. An elderly woman peeked out through the chain. "Mrs. Magnuson! Call the police!" Deanie repeated. The woman's eyes were as round as saucers. With a shriek she slammed the door shut.

This was no time for neighbors who didn't want to get involved. With a stifled sob, Deanie dashed back to her own apartment. The two men were still wrestling on the floor, but the knife lay safely off to one side. Deanie kicked it farther away, then frantically looked around for something heavy to use as a weapon. Her father's saxophone stood propped in the corner. She snatched it up, and stood poised, the cumbersome instrument raised above her head, waiting for a clear strike at Brad.

She swiped at him a few times, the unwieldy metal object connecting with a tinny thud against head and shoulders, without much effect. It did, however, provide the momentary distraction needed for Chris to land a resounding blow to Brad's jaw. Brad reeled backwards, and Chris jerked him onto his stomach, applying a half nelson. Chris straddled the other man triumphantly as three more figures burst into the room.

As soon as she saw Russ, Deanie lowered the now bent saxophone and sank shakily to her knees. After one quick sweep of the ransacked room, Russ strode toward Deanie, brought her gently to her feet and locked her in a tight embrace. She began sobbing wildly into his shirt.

"Are you hurt?" he asked with urgency, holding her back from him. "Is the baby hurt?" She shook her head dumbly, unable to reply. Their attention was drawn to the kitchen, where Chris, Brent and Len had hauled a cursing Brad to his feet. Carefully unfolding himself from Deanie's embrace, he stepped toward the kitchen and came face to face with his wife's abuser. With a solid thud, he landed a head jerking blow square in the middle of Brad's face.

"Now *that's* the baby's father," Chris informed with a grin.

Brad spat, landing a string of spittle on Russ's cheek. Hard, cold rage blazed in Russ's eyes. He pulled back, readying another blow when several police officers charged into the room. Mrs. Magnuson scurried in behind them. "Oh my!" she stewed. "They seemed like such nice neighbors."

Russ returned to Deanie's side, putting an arm protectively around her waist. It took several minutes to secure Brad in handcuffs and take statements from all those present. Brad was led away, still swearing vehemently.

Deanie surveyed the shattered room. "Oh! My nice clean house!" she wailed. She stooped to pick up a piece of broken glass, but Russ stopped her.

"Leave it. You're in no shape right now," he said gently.

"But I wanted it clean for Jack!"

"We'll look after it," Russ reassured. "Won't we?" he shot at Brent.

Brent nodded. "Yep."

Russ took her elbow and steered her toward the bathroom. "You might want to clean up a bit before we go to the hospital, though."

"He's right," Brent whispered. "You look like hell, babe."

"Thanks," Deanie replied sarcastically.

"I'm afraid you can't stay here," one of the officer's said to the group. "We need to seal off the area until we've finished our investigation. And after your visit to the hospital, we'll need you to come down to the station." He surveyed Deanie with solemn eyes. "I'd say you were pretty lucky. Kilpatrick is a pretty dangerous man."

Deanie nodded.

"You mean the police knew he was a danger? And you didn't do anything?" Russ asked, his words iced with outrage.

"He was a free man," the officer informed, taking on a defensive edge himself. "We had no authority to arrest him without cause."

"So you just waited around until he did something," Russ fumed. "My wife's life was in danger!"

"Good thing we got here when we did," was all the policeman said. "Now, if you'll hurry along? We've got work to do."

"I knew the Big Man would look after you," Brent offered, striving for lightness as he patted Deanie's shoulder..

"Yeah. I don't know what would have happened if Chris hadn't arrived when he did," Deanie replied, shaking.

"Not *that* Big Man," Brent said. "You know, the BIG Man. I prayed all the way over here."

Deanie didn't know what to say, but gave Brent a weak smile. "Oh. I guess it worked then."

"That and your husband's crazy driving," he joked.

"How did you know?" she asked, looking from Brent to Russ.

"Now that's a long story," Brent sighed. "Maybe one I'll let your husband explain. But right now we need to get the hero down to the hospital," he said, looking at Chris.

"It's nothing. Just a scratch," Chris shrugged.

"Shall I call an ambulance?" the policeman asked.

"Chris?" Brent deflected the question onto the other man. "You need an ambulance or can we make it in your car?"

"I'm not waiting around for an ambulance," Chris stated emphatically.

Brent eyed him up and down. "What if you get blood on the seats?"

197

"Who cares," Chris scoffed. "The things a piece of shit anyway."

"Alright then," Brent laughed. "Keys?" He held his hand out.

"I can drive," Chris mumbled.

"Not a chance, buddy," Brent shook his head. "Hand them over. Even heroes need to know when to call it quits." Chris tossed Brent the keys, despite his continued grumbling. Brent turned to Russ and gave him a firm handshake. "Pretty solid left hook."

"Thanks."

"You look after my girl now," Brent warned, eyeing Russ.

"I intend to," Russ replied, putting a protective arm around Deanie's shoulders. They watched the others exit. Russ looked down at Deanie. "I guess we'd better follow them."

"Do we have to?" Deanie asked. sighing. "I'm so exhausted. Can't we just go back to your place? I'm sure Chris is going to be fine."

"Our place," Russ corrected. "And no. It's not Chris I'm concerned about. I want them to check you. Just to be sure."

Chapter Twenty-Five

Russ stole a glance at his wife, slumped into the passenger seat, looking out the window as they drove. What did he really know about her? Tonight's crazy events; the revelations he'd heard from Brent earlier. . . It was like a soap opera and he wasn't sure he was up for it. Too bad. He'd already jumped in with both feet. And after everything she'd been through, he wasn't about to add to her distress.

"You're quiet," she said, breaking the silence.

"Mmhm. Just thinking, I guess," he responded, trying to keep his voice light.

"You probably have lots of questions," she sighed. "I guess there are some things we need to talk about."

"You don't have to," he said quietly. "You've had enough for one day."

"Where's Mark?"

"He went to my mother's after school," Russ informed her. "I called before I left work. When I found out Jack had a heart attack."

"Yeah, I'm sorry about that," Deanie said. "About the misunderstanding. I'm sorry about everything."

Russ glanced over at her once again and saw her bottom lip trembling. He reached over and squeezed her hand. "It's okay. I was a dumb ass and I admit it. Brent and I had a talk, and . . . well, let's just start over, okay?"

Deanie blinked, tears shimmering in her eyes. "You want to start over? Even after today?"

Russ nodded. What else could he say? She was so vulnerable. He couldn't tell her that the thought of her pregnant with another man's child was like boiling rocks hitting the pit of his stomach. That the thought of her lying in an alleyway, bloody and beaten made him want to throw up. That the thought of whatever else she might not be telling him was enough to make him want to shake it out of her himself.

"So this talk that you and Brent had," she began hesitantly. "What exactly did he tell you?"

"Enough to get the gist of the story," Russ replied.

"Can you elaborate a bit?" she asked.

So. She was going to try to hide whatever she could. Russ frowned, a black cloud descending even further into his thoughts. "He told me about Brad, obviously. That he was a past boyfriend and was out of jail and possibly trouble."

"I don't get that part," Deanie scowled. "Brent said you'd tell me on the way. How did you know that Brad was going to try something like this?"

"Apparently those friends of yours were keeping tabs on him." He looked over at Deanie for her reaction. "I'd say they're all right after all."

Deanie nodded. "I told you."

"Although I'm not happy about the fact that I wasn't told sooner," he added.

"What else did he say?" she asked.

"Why don't you tell me?"

She sat for a minute, contemplating, then let out a big sigh. "Did he tell you that I lost a baby once? Brad's baby."

There was silence in the car for a moment. "Yes," Russ finally admitted.

"Oh." Tears welled up in her eyes, and she turned to look out the side window.

"Why didn't you tell me?" Russ asked, his question barely audible.

She shrugged. "I was afraid."

"Because I'm such an unfeeling ogre," he stated.

"You must hate me," Deanie whispered.

"I didn't say that."

The fact was, he hated himself right now. For all the pain that he had put her through. She could have been killed. The baby could have been lost. And for what? His own foolish pride? The fact that he was responsible for her present circumstances, which so closely mirrored those of her hellish past, was almost more than he could stand.

❧

They arrived at the hospital and Deanie went through the motions of getting checked. She was glad that Holly was one of the attending nurses. She needed her friend's reassuring smile right about now. The extent of her physical injuries were fairly minor – a black eye, swollen lips, and several bruises - although she was sure the emotional wounds would take longer to heal. Russ had been unreadable on the way over. On the surface he seemed caring. Attentive. But she couldn't help worrying about the effects her past revelations would have on their already tenuous relationship.

Chris had been attended to and was waiting with the rest of the group in the lobby when Russ and Deanie joined them. Grant had driven over, so all four of them were together. Chris opened his black leather jacket to display the large sterile bandage across his chest. "Twenty seven stitches," he boasted.

"I can't thank you enough," Deanie said, her voice choking on the words.

"Is everything okay?" Brent asked.

"Apparently," Deanie tried to smile. "Although I am beat."

"I think it's time I got you home," Russ said. He looked at the other men. "Thanks again. For everything."

"Any time. We better get the hero home to bed, too," Brent laughed.

"I'm feeling fine," Chris protested. "We should go out for a beer."

"No way, man," Brent said, gesturing with his head to Len and Grant. All three men gathered around Chris, arms crossed. "The nurse pumped him so full of pain killers he shouldn't be too hard to handle."

Chris gave Brent a friendly shot in the arm, then winced in pain, "Enjoy the advantage while you can, my friend. I won't be down for long."

"Didn't that policeman say we should come by the station?" Deanie asked.

"Not tonight," Russ stated firmly. "It can wait. You need your rest."

201

She was glad Russ was putting his foot down. She really was exhausted and couldn't imagine sitting through another round of questioning.

They all headed toward the exit. Russ put his arm around her waist and she let herself be propped up by his strength. Suddenly Deanie stopped, her feet rooted to the spot. Russ looked at her with concern. "Deanie?" He examined her ashen face more closely. "Are you all right?"

"I'm not sure," she replied, hesitating as she put her hand to her abdomen. She gasped in sudden pain.

"What is it? Is it the baby?" Russ looked around frantically. "Help! Over here, please! My wife . . . I think she's going into labor!"

Holly bustled through the emergency doors to Deanie's side, calling out to the nurse behind the reception desk. "Get some help. A wheel chair, stat!" She turned to Deanie and encircled her shoulders as another wave of pain rolled in. Deanie paused, bending slightly and moaned. An attendant arrived with a wheel chair just as the wave crested.

Deanie paused for another moment, catching her breath, and then lowered herself into the chair. "It's too soon," she whispered.

"Yes, but, you're far enough along," Holly reassured. "Everything will be fine. You're in the right place, anyway. This way," she instructed, gesturing to the rest of the group.

The little entourage hurried down the corridor, Holly pushing Deanie in the wheel chair, followed by five anxious, hovering males.

"Wait just a minute," a stern looking nurse said at the entrance to the maternity ward. "You can't all come in. Which one of you is the father?"

"I am," Russ spoke up, raising his hand.

"I'm sorry, but the rest of you will have to wait elsewhere," the sergeant major in white said.

"You guys go on. Chris needs some rest. I'll phone you first thing," Russ promised.

"You're sure," Brent reiterated. "First thing."

"I promise," Russ said solemnly. "And Brent, Chris - all of you - thank you."

They all nodded, and gave their last well wishes to Deanie, before the maternity doors swung shut. Deanie gave a tremendous wail, and all Russ's attention was focused back on her. "Hold on. It's going to be okay. Like

Holly said, you're in the right place."

Deanie just nodded, then let out another moan as a new wave of pain rolled over her. This was nothing like what she had been preparing for. Another torturous tide seemed to engulf her completely. In the far away distance she could hear a nurse calling out. There seemed to be a sudden swarm of attendants around her, focusing and fading before her eyes. Bright lights. . . prodding and poking. . . a voice calling out Russ's name. Her own, perhaps. . .

Then all was silence.

Chapter Twenty-Six

Russ sat in the front pew of the church. The same church where he had been christened, attended Sunday School as a child, been confirmed, taken first communion. The same church where he had married Miranda, and buried his father. Many memories were woven into this building, meandering in and out among the inlaid pine alter, the smooth polish of the pews, and the dappled colors on the carpet as the afternoon sun filtered through the stained glass.

He had been sitting here for what seemed like hours. Just sitting. And thinking. Letting the memories wash over him, as he stared at the warm and familiar interior. Just why he had come, he wasn't sure. He had so many questions about life. About the meaning of his own existence. About God. He wasn't sure that he would find the answers here, but for some reason he felt drawn to this place. This was God's house. And if ever he needed to find God, it was now.

He thought about the child - his child - that lay in the sterile incubator at the hospital, tubes protruding from her tiny body. He hadn't even been allowed to hold her yet. A girl. He smiled. He had a daughter.

The doctor said she was probably out of danger, although premature. They had feared complications, even brain damage, after the traumatic delivery by emergency cesarean section. But the worst was over now for her. In time, she would grow healthy and strong.

But Deanie . . . Here his mind froze. She had still not come out of the coma. It had been four whole days. Her body had gone into shock, then kidney failure. She had almost died right there during the delivery.

Russ slammed his clenched fist down hard onto his thigh. She had to live! He struggled, trying to remain composed, refusing to give into the despair that threatened to break him. Was this to be his lot in life? Another infant child to raise all alone? And he, never to know the warmth and companionship of someone to love?

Love. The word struck him like a blow. Love! He didn't know the meaning of the word. And yet, there was something that had been growing inside of him. Formless, yet pulsing, warm and alive. It reached out to unite itself with. . . what? It had nowhere to go; nothing to latch onto for sustenance. It was left starving, suffering; twisting in agonizing pain, boring a hole straight into his heart.

Yes. He understood it now. He loved her. Had always loved her. But stubborn pride and self-sufficiency had kept him from admitting it. To himself and to her. And now she might die. He would never be able to tell her.

"Where are you now, God?" he whispered hoarsely. "Where are you now?" He bent forward, shaking violently with all the pent up emotion that now burst forth like water through a broken damn.

"He's been there all the time," came a strong yet compassionate voice. "He's been waiting for you."

Russ looked up through blurred eyes to see the Reverend, not much older than himself, standing by his side.

Sunlight filtered in through the half open blinds of the hospital room. Deanie blinked heavy lids, uncertain of where she was or why she was there. She tried to move and a searing pain shot through her. She lay still for a few moments, letting the pain subside, and then noticed the tubes protruding from her body. She lay in confusion for a moment and then it all came rushing back. Brad . . . the hospital . . . the baby.

The Baby. Her mind stopped short. Where was the baby? She felt panic rising in her breast, but almost as quickly, peace filled her instead. Somewhere between death and life she had seen something. Been somewhere. Felt some presence. Wherever her baby was, it was safe. She knew it. In this life, or in the next, her baby was safe in the arms of Jesus.

Deanie smiled. Brent would be pleased. For now she knew. HE was more than a fairy tale, an ancient myth, or a fantastic fabrication of troubled men's minds. He was real. She closed her eyes and offered up a silent prayer. A prayer of thanksgiving, confession and acceptance of all that Jesus had to offer. She smiled contentedly and drifted back into a deep sleep.

Chapter Twenty-Seven

When next Deanie's eyes fluttered open, Holly was in the room checking her vital signs. Deanie smiled weakly at her friend.

"Well, hello there!" Holly said brightly. "You look like you've seen an angel."

"Maybe I have," Deanie replied, her voice soft.

"You gave us all quite a scare," Holly said with a smile.

"What's all this?" Deanie asked, motioning to the various tubes still attached to her.

"You've been a pretty sick lady. But now that you're awake, I'd better call for the doctor."

"How long?"

"Four days, now, honey," Holly replied. "But there's nothing to worry about now."

"And my baby?"

"A beautiful little daughter."

The news glowed within Deanie's breast. "Can I see her?"

"Not just yet, I'm afraid. But soon."

"Since when do you work in maternity?" Deanie asked.

"Oh, I have my ways," Holly laughed. "You need to rest now while I go get the doctor."

"Holly? One more thing. Russ. Has he . . . has he been here?"

"Hardly left your side," Holly answered, gently patting Deanie's hand.

"Oh. Thanks," Deanie smiled, relaxing back into her pillows. Holly turned to leave. "Wait! One more thing. I did like you said."

"About what?" Holly asked, furrowing her brow.

"I . . . well, I asked Jesus to be my Savior." Deanie looked down at her hands, then brought her gaze back up to meet her friend's.

"Deanie! That's wonderful!" Holly exclaimed. "When?"

"I'm not exactly sure. Sometime while I was asleep, I guess. But I just thought I should tell you. Just to make sure it was for real."

"It's for real, Deanie. Don't ever let anyone try to tell you otherwise."

"But what if I screw up again?" Deanie asked.

"Not 'what if', but when." Holly laughed at the crestfallen look on Deanie's face. "But don't worry. Nobody can live up to God's standards on their own. But now you don't have to try to be good all by yourself anymore. Jesus is there to help you. To carry you through. Being born again doesn't mean you'll never make mistakes. You will, because you're still human. But He'll be there to pick you up when you fall. He's a friend that sticks closer than a brother."

"Even for someone like me?"

"Of course, even for someone like you! The Lord doesn't expect you to become someone you're not. After all, he created you, with all your little quirks included. The Bible says that even the hairs on our head are numbered. But He will begin to use you, faults and all if you'll just let Him and submit yourself to His will for your life. It's all part of the growing process as we learn to walk with Him."

"You mean there's more?" Deanie asked, frowning.

"Much more. You need to get into the word of God every day. It's like our spiritual food. And you need to spend time in prayer. You see, Jesus wants a relationship with you, and like every relationship you have to work at it, keeping the lines of communication open." Seeing Deanie's doubtful look, Holly added. "Listen, don't worry about it. I'll be there to help you every step of the way. And now, I really must get that doctor." She gave Deanie's hand a light squeeze and left the room.

A few minutes later, several nurses and a doctor bustled into the room and began checking Deanie over. Most of the paraphernalia was removed and she was told that she would be moving to a regular ward later that day.

Holly slipped her a small booklet on her way out of the room. It was the Gospel of John.

❦

Russ sat at the desk in his study, hands steepled in contemplation. The release he felt was unimaginable. Like a giant weight had been lifted off his chest and he could finally breathe. But asking Jesus into his heart didn't make Deanie's situation any better. He wasn't sure he had the strength to pray any more than he already had.

He glanced up at the bookshelves running perpendicular to the desk. On the very top, laying on its side as to be almost invisible was a large, leather bound volume. He rose from his seat and reached for it, rubbing a layer of dust off its surface with his palm.

The Bible had been a wedding gift from his parents when he and Miranda had married. It was a reminder of more painful times and so he had put it up there, safely out of reach and away from his line of vision. But the word of God was still the word of God, no matter how it had been acquired. The Reverend said he should start reading it. Russ opened the book slowly, smoothing the velum pages with care. Where did one start?

"Dad?"

Russ looked up. His son was standing in the doorway, looking for all intents and purposes like an orphan. In some ways he was.

"Come here, son," Russ invited. His voice was suddenly choked with emotion.

"Is Deanie going to live?" Mark asked, searching his father's eyes for reassurance.

"I sure hope so," Russ said. "I pray so."

"Me too."

"I was just going to read from the Bible," Russ said. "Would you like to listen?"

Mark nodded.

Russ got up from his chair behind the desk and moved to the other side where he and Mark could sit beside one another. Father and son settled in and Russ opened the book.

Deanie found that once she started reading the little book, she couldn't put it down. A small seed of understanding was beginning to grow. She was amazed at what Jesus had done for her. Her own hardships seemed small compared to the sacrifice that He had made upon the cross to pay the penalty for her sins. The shackles of her past had been broken, and all of her mistakes, both past and present, were washed away by the blood of the Lamb. It was too incredible. She closed her eyes and breathed another prayer of thanksgiving.

It was with this peaceful look of contentment on her face that Russ found her later, lying in her new room. He stood in the doorway for a moment, not wishing to disturb her, overwhelmed with the emotions that were tightening his chest, making it hard for him to breathe. She was alive. Small and frail, yet so very, very beautiful. Like an angel. His angel, sent from heaven to rescue him from himself.

"Sh," Russ whispered to Mark, who was one step behind him. "Let's not disturb her." They each took one of the two chairs, Russ quietly moving his closer to the beside.

Deanie's eyes fluttered open. "Hello," Russ whispered, taking her hand. "You finally decided to wake up." Deanie smiled weakly. He reached out and stroked her cheek.

"Hi," Mark said, coming to stand beside her on the opposite side.

"Hi," Deanie returned, her voice soft. She reached her free hand out toward Mark and he took it in his. "Have you seen her, yet?" she asked.

Mark nodded. "She's small."

"She's beautiful. Like her mother," Russ stated, a tender smile on his lips.

Warmth and hope fluttered in Deanie's breast. She smiled again. "I only saw her for a moment when they moved me. But soon I should be strong enough to go myself. She's so small."

"But she's a fighter. Also like her mother."

Deanie laughed at that. "I haven't much fight left in me at the moment."

"Good. Let's not fight anymore," Russ said soberly.

"Sounds good to me."

"There is something that I think we need to discuss," he continued, then looked at Mark. "Um, Son? Do you think you could go out to the waiting room for a couple of minutes? I need to talk to Deanie. Alone."

"Okay," the boy shrugged. He slipped his hand from Deanie's and gave her a little wave. "See you later," he said.

Deanie waved back. "See you later," she repeated.

Russ waited until Mark was well out of the room. Then he turned back to Deanie and took a deep breath. "Okay. There is something I need to tell you -"

"Wait," Deanie interrupted. "Before you go on, there's something I need to say first. I want to apologize. I should have told you about Brad. It wasn't fair of me not to tell you. But I guess I was afraid that if you found out you would hate me. And I couldn't take that because I loved you so much and. . ." Her voice had become wobbly.

"Sh . . ." Russ put a finger to her lips. "Everything will be all right now."

"No, let me finish," Deanie insisted, trying to prop herself up a bit, and wincing with the effort. "It's okay. You're a good man, Russ, and you want to do the right thing. And I don't blame you if you can't love me in return, but -"

Russ gently pushed her back onto her pillows and silenced her with a kiss. "I love you," he whispered, the truth and freedom of the words spreading like sunlight across his face. Deanie's eyes opened wide in amazement. Russ smiled broadly and repeated the words with confident deliberateness. "I love you. With all my heart, soul and mind."

Tears welled up in Deanie's eyes. "What's wrong?" Russ asked, brushing a tear away. "Don't you believe me? I suppose it's no more than I deserve."

"No. It's just that I'm too happy. It's hard to believe actually," Deanie smiled.

"Well, believe it. I swear to you that I will never knowingly hurt you again. I will be there to protect you for the rest of my days. To love, honor and cherish you. I want to grow old with you, Deanie Graham. My wife." He stared down into her eyes, hoping that she could see there the truth and the depth of what he had said. She reached her arms up around his neck and began to cry in earnest. "I am so sorry for what I've done to you. How

I've hurt you. I have been a stubborn, unfeeling brute. Can you ever forgive me? Can we start over again, only properly this time?"

Deanie nodded her assent.

"Good," Russ shook his head and laughed.

"What's so funny," Deanie sputtered.

"I was just thinking how it took me long enough," Russ mused. "I think I loved you right from the moment I laid eyes on you. But I was too stubborn and pig headed to admit it. And then with all the complications. . . I guess I got things mixed up with the hurts from my past and couldn't see things clearly. I let the resentment I felt towards Miranda transfer over to you. She was an unavailable target. You were right there. It was easier to blame all my own shortcomings on you, rather than to face up to them myself."

"So what happened to change that?"

Russ looked at her candidly. "I guess the reality that I could lose you - forever - woke me up. The fact that you almost died made me realize just how important you are to me. It kind of cut the fog away and I knew that I had to let go of the past and concentrate on the future. Our future." He stopped for a moment, collecting himself. "Deanie, there's more. And I'm not exactly sure how to say this to you. You might not understand, or think it sounds foolish, but . . ." He rubbed the back of his neck, suddenly embarrassed and not quite sure how to continue.

"I'm listening," Deanie encouraged.

"Well, you know that I was raised in the church. Went to Sunday School and all that. And of course, my mother has taken every opportunity to make her views known on the subject," he laughed.

"Yes."

"So, what I'm saying is, I always believed in God, in my own way. But I never really knew. I mean, I didn't know *Him* - God. Not personally. But I met Him today, Deanie. This afternoon. I met God. And I did what I should have done years ago - what I knew in my heart I needed to do for so long, but was too stubborn to do. I surrendered my life over to Him. I made a personal commitment to Jesus Christ."

Russ stopped and looked steadily at Deanie for her reaction. She was completely silent. Interpreting her silence as a negative thing, he hurried on. "Now before you go thinking I'm some kind of religious fanatic, I should explain things a bit. I haven't joined some kind of cult or anything. But you have no idea the relief I felt after saying that prayer. For all these years I've been trying to do it on my own. Trying to be Mr. Perfect for myself and everyone else. It wasn't until this afternoon that I finally admitted I was doing a lousy job with my life. I thought you were dying, and I couldn't do a single thing about it." One tear trickled down Russ's cheek. He made no attempt to brush it away. "But now I've found the answer. And that answer is surrendering - the one thing I always thought made one weak. But instead of weakness I've found strength and I'm ready to build a new future. With you."

"You are not going to believe this," Deanie said, tears streaming down her cheeks. "I understand totally because I prayed and asked Jesus into my heart, too."

"Really?" Russ asked, hardly daring to believe it. "When?"

"Sometime between awake and asleep," she laughed. "I don't actually know, but once I told Holly she gave me this little Bible and I've been reading it." She sighed. "I can't believe it. I was ready for anything, and now God's given me you."

Russ leaned over the bed and they clung to each other, letting the tears flow.

There was a rap at the door and they both looked up to see Mark in the doorway, with Holly not far behind. "Excuse me, but you have a visitor," Holly announced, wheeling a plexi-glass bassinet into the room. "Meet your mom and dad," she cooed as she gently lifted the tiny form from her nest and placed the bundle in Russ's arms.

"She's so tiny," Russ said, grinning like a schoolboy. Mark came around beside him and offered her his finger which she promptly gripped with her own tiny hand.

Russ looked up and noticed the look of longing on Deanie's face. "I think it's time you met the most beautiful woman in the world," he said to the tiny bundle. "Your mother."

With Holly's assistance, Deanie gingerly propped herself up on her pillows. Then with trembling hands she took the warm little form into her arms.

"She's so beautiful. Just like you," Russ whispered in Deanie's ear. "What shall we name her?"

Deanie smiled. "I was thinking that Harmony would be kind of neat." She looked to Russ for approval. "Jack would like it. But now Faith seems kind of appropriate."

"Why not both?" Russ suggested. "Harmony Faith."

"Harmony Faith," Deanie repeated. "I like it."

"Speaking of Jack," Russ said. "I've been up to visit him a few times."

"How is he?" she asked.

"He's doing well," Holly supplied. "When you're up to it, I could probably arrange for some wheels and you could go for a visit."

"Really?" Deanie's eyes were wide with excitement.

"Absolutely. I told you. I've got connections," Holly laughed. "And now, I better get a move on. I'll check on you later."

Russ looked back at his little family, his wife's face flushed with happiness, and his heart swelled with love. She was not a typical woman. But she was his. The one that God had ordained for him. He smiled and said a silent prayer of gratitude.

Their life together would not always be easy, he knew. But thanks to the Lord's gracious mercy, a new path stretched before them. With the Lord's steady hand to guide them, Russ knew they could face whatever lay ahead. Together.

The story continues! If you enjoyed Russ and Deanie's story, read about their son Mark Graham in the suspenseful sequel *And The Beat Goes On,* available in hardcover, paperback and e version.

And The Beat Goes On

By Tracy Krauss

Chapter One

The African sun beat down on his head in the open jeep as Dr. Mark Graham and his companion bumped along what could hardly be called a road. A local man from the Nbedele tribe, hired on as part of the archeological team, drove the jeep along the hazardous path up the mountain. Hair raising switch backs and steep inclines didn't seem to faze the driver as he maneuvered the vehicle with one hand. Some pebbles cascaded off the trail's edge to the ravine below. Good thing he was used to it, Mark decided, or he might have been tempted to bail.

As he braced himself for the next jarring pothole, Mark thought about yesterday's meeting with the Zimbabwean government officials. Everything had gone well – on the surface, at least. They had agreed to continue their sponsorship, and renewed their pledge of faith in his abilities as a leader in his field. Yet there was this nagging sense at the back of his mind that something rippled beneath the surface – something hidden either by neglect or design of which he was not aware. It was an uncomfortable feeling. Probably just his general distaste for dealing with administrators. As meticulous as he was himself, it rankled when unnecessary red tape seemed to get in the way of real progress. Added to that, it was not a trip he relished, unless absolutely necessary.

His crew had been meticulously digging under the site of an ancient temple – a sacred site stringently protected by the government of Zimbabwe. The temple site itself had been unearthed decades before, but legend had led to speculation that an even older civilization had once used

217

the spot. Mark had been honored when asked to assemble a team of specialists to investigate the possibilities without compromising the original excavations. It was painstaking work. But already, after only five months, the team was rewarded with signs that the legends were indeed rooted in fact. Under the temple mount they had discovered an even more ancient burial ground with an intricate system of tombs that seemed oddly more advanced technologically than the layer of simple graves directly above it. This was not entirely unexpected; history often bespoke of a more barbarous people supplanting a superior civilization. But there was more . . . so much more. There was a sense that they were on the verge of something big – monumental, even.

And then the authorities had the audacity to question whether there was any use continuing! They said they were running out of budget and it was taking too long. Fools! Didn't they know there was no way to unearth secrets that had been buried for millennium in just a few short months? These things took time and care. And money.

That was the bottom line. Always was. Mark wished he had the benefit of some nice multi-trillionaire benefactor right about now, instead of a crumbling third world dictatorship. Oh well. For now he had managed to secure another four months contract, having convinced them of the importance of the find to the economic development of the region. But in the end, he doubled it would be enough time and he was a scientist, not a politician.

As the jeep rounded the last corner, Mark spotted one of the tents that had been set up on site as a lab. The archeological site extended over a fairly large area. Several tents and simple wooden structures had been erected to house the necessary work stations and accommodate the crew. Various roped off areas were meticulously squared off for the painstaking process of uncovering tidbits of information, one grain of sand at a time.

Mark jumped from the jeep into the cloud of gathering dust and strode directly to the quarters where he expected to find his coworker, Laura Sawchuk. He left his bags for his Nbedelian assistant.

He had left Laura in charge during his brief absence. Laura Sawchuk, Doctor of Anthropology, was very knowledgeable in a wide field and was also very capable at giving direction and leadership. She had been his colleague on more than one job before and he trusted her judgment and skill for the task at hand. She was also, at present, his girlfriend.

Girlfriend had a somewhat adolescent ring to it, Mark decided. His 'partner' would be a more appropriate phrase – it was the terminology Laura used, anyway. Mark wasn't quite sure how their relationship had advanced to more than just colleagues. Close proximity did that to people sometimes. And loneliness.

He found Laura sitting at a corner along one wall, examining a fragment under a microscope. She didn't look up when he entered. At 36 she was a couple of years older than Mark himself. Her career always came first; a fact that suited Mark, since he shared her passion for work.

"Laura," he greeted her, "What have we here?" He tried to get a glimpse over her shoulder at the tiny fragment she was scrutinizing.

She ignored the question. "I thought you were going to be back yesterday," she said, still not taking her eyes from the eye pieces.

"I was delayed an extra day in Harare," Mark explained as he pulled up a stool and sat down beside her.

"Oh? That good news or bad?" she asked.

"Good. I managed to convince them to give us another four months."

"Four months?!" Laura asked sharply, straightening and looking at Mark for the first time since he had arrived. There was a powdering of dust on his skin and hair which almost made him look like he had stepped out of one of those old fashioned sepia photographs – all monochromatic brown. "We can't possibly be finished in four months." She reached over and flicked a stray twig from his unruly mass of dark curls.

"I know that," Mark shrugged, running a hand through his hair, creating a small cloud of dust. He rubbed his chin thoughtfully. Two days growth of stubble had begun to form. "But for now I had to take it or leave it."

Laura leaned forward and placed a quick kiss on Mark's nose, her streaked brown and blonde ponytail bobbing. "Good to have you back, in any case. Mnanga didn't kill you, I see, with his reckless driving."

"Still in one piece, miracle as that is," Mark nodded with a grin. "What you looking at, anyway?"

"A fragment from some of the plaster leading into the antechamber I

219

told you about," Laura replied, turning back to the microscope. "It seems to have some kind of metal alloy embedded right in it."

"Plaster?" Mark asked uncertainly, his brows furrowing.

Laura nodded. "I'm not sure what else to call it. A coating of some kind. Unusual, I know."

"Very," Mark agreed. "Most tombs are simply hewn from the rock, not plastered over. Mind if I take a look?" Laura relinquished her seat and Mark took his turn peering into the microscope. "Hm. I see what you mean. I've never seen anything like it." He couldn't help keeping the disappointment from his voice. He had wanted to be the first into the chamber himself.

Laura picked up on the tone in his voice, "Don't worry. We haven't made a breakthrough into the chamber itself yet. I knew you'd be disappointed not to be here, so we've held back a bit."

"Oh. Thanks. I appreciate it," Mark nodded, obvious relief in his voice as he continued to peruse the tiny fragment.

"Besides, there's been plenty of other excitement to keep us busy."

"Like…?"

"Like the bone fragments," Laura offered.

"Still no word from the lab?" he asked. He already knew the answer. He'd checked back in Harare.

"Nope. But we are starting to see a pattern emerging," Laura said.

Mark's curiosity was really pricked now. He looked up. "What kind of pattern?"

"Come and see," Laura said, leaving the plaster fragment behind for the time being. She led Mark to a computer station. She sat down in front of the screen and clicked several icons with the mouse. A large blueprint of the dig appeared on the screen. "The strange bone fragments we found first were located here," she pointed to the location with her finger, "alongside the human remains that appear to have been disturbed - either by some type of seismic activity, or by other humans."

"Mmhm," Mark nodded. It was nothing new to him. He had been present during that discovery. "Go on."

"The next grave we uncovered also contained unidentified bone fragments. Only this time," she paused for effect. She glanced over at him, ready to gage his reaction. He raised his brows in question. "I'll bring up a digital photo," she said, clicking the mouse deftly once again. Several windows opened. "Ah, here we are." She punched one more key and a color photo came up of a long curved bone. It was broken in two places, with part of the inner section missing. She hit another key and a second picture came up. This time it showed Laura and Rocco, one of the crew managers, holding the bone between them.

"That's one big chicken wing," Mark whistled.

"Then you do agree that it looks like part of a wing?" Laura asked, surveying him closely.

Mark blinked and peered at the image again. "Yes . . . it does, doesn't it?"

"The humerus is almost entirely in tact, with parts of the ulna attached. It looks to be from a very large winged creature. The parts that are left clearly seem to have been placed with the body, intentionally."

"Large," Mark mused. "How large?"

"Pretty damn big, that's all I have to say. Bigger than an albatross or any present species of bird that I know of."

"You know what this means, don't you?" Mark asked expectantly. He looked over at Laura, obvious excitement burning in his eyes. "We've discovered another Troy – an ancient legend thought to be nothing more than myth." He pounded the computer table and the monitor flickered momentarily. It was the most emotion he had displayed thus far.

"Watch it," Laura warned with a smile. "No hitting the furniture! You're forgetting our power supply isn't the most stable."

"What else you got?" Mark asked anxiously.

"Rocco's team has been continuing on those same graves. He may find the other "wing", so to speak, and by the look of the placement of those two graves, we're speculating that there could be a whole ring of graves surrounding the entrance to the antechamber. Providing you want to disturb them."

"Hmm. Like guards," Mark commented.

"Right. Here's another interesting find from the same grave," Laura said, referring to the next photo. "It appears to be some kind of head piece or mask, probably worn expressly for burial. It's pretty badly decayed and was in danger of disintegrating into dust if we tried to remove it."

Mark just stared at the screen.

"I know what you're thinking, okay?" Laura interrupted his thoughts. "About that legend – don't go spreading rumors until the lab has done a full analysis. I've had a hard enough time convincing Rocco to keep his feet on the ground. You know how he can be. We could all be discredited if we aren't careful. First we need solid lab work as to the type of bone, then solid dating on both the human and non human fragments."

"You don't need to remind me about procedure, Doctor," Mark stated in a business like tone. "I am still chief archeologist on this dig."

"Of course," Laura agreed, giving Mark a sideways glance. "I wasn't trying to offend you. You seem awfully touchy."

Mark sighed and ran a hand through his thick, unruly hair. "My apologies. I guess I'm just tired after the trip."

"More like your nerves are shot after Mnanga's driving," Laura offered.

"Right," Mark agreed with a chuckle. "Plus, I hate being out of the loop. I feel like all the important discoveries are being made when I'm gone."

"You need to relax," Laura said, coming up behind him and kneading his neck with her fingers.

"Hm . . . that feels good," Mark said, closing his eyes.

"Of course. And I'll make it feel even better a little later on," Laura promised with a suggestive smile.

"Oh? That's definitely worth coming back for," Mark said with a smile of his own. He closed his eyes and allowed her fingers to do their magic on the stiff cords in his neck. Suddenly he opened his eyes. "I'd like to take a look, myself," he said, all business once again. "At that bone. It's been stored and numbered with the rest of the artifacts?"

"Of course," Laura shrugged, dropping her hands and walking away with a sigh. She turned back to the computer. "I expected you'd want to have a look at everything. I just thought you might want to wait and start fresh tomorrow."

"With only four months grace, I don't think we can spare the time. I better be off to inspect the rest of the work in progress," he said with obvious relish, rubbing his hands together. He rose and turned to leave.

"Mark," Laura stopped him.

"Hm?" Mark turned.

"I missed you."

His nod of acknowledgement was barely perceptible. He was already out the door.

❧

Mark strode to where he hoped to find Rocco Cortez, one of the crew chiefs. He'd been talking to various other crew chiefs along the way and was brought up to date on most of the developments already, so it was just a matter of seeing it for himself. He was physically weary from his trek, but his mind was on high alert.

By far, the dominant feature of the entire site was the ancient temple ruins. It had been reconstructed in places and consisted of an outer and an inner courtyard, with the chambers of the temple itself in the center. Much of the building had been constructed of rock quarried from the surrounding area. Mostly what was left, after being uncovered, was the foundation, with only a few walls remaining intact. But the location of the altar and several other important features, could be clearly identified from what remained. The original archeological excavations had taken place over thirty years ago. What Mark and his team were interested in now was not the temple itself, but what lay hidden far beneath it.

This type of excavating was very painstaking and precise. In order to get at the layers beneath without disturbing the top layer, the team had to tunnel underneath using an elaborate system of braces, all the while ensuring that they did not destroy a potentially important find. They started well away from the temple mound itself, creating a crater like moat around one side of the site. From here they could open up the side of the hill underneath, exposing subsequent layers as they went. It was backbreaking work with an element of risk, but the thrill of discovery outweighed the drawbacks.

"Rocco," Mark greeted his colleague, pumping his hand vigorously. "I hear there have been some exciting discoveries in my absence." Rocco was a short, somewhat stocky man of Puerto Rican descent. He wore his graying hair in a haphazard ponytail, and sported a thick black mustache.

223

"Hey, my friend," Rocco responded enthusiastically. "She showed you the photos?"

"Yeah. Pretty amazing," Mark nodded.

"See the real thing yet?" Rocco asked, surveying his boss out of the corner of his eye.

"Just heading over there now," Mark informed. The two men started walking together toward the storage and cataloguing compound. "So what do you think?"

Rocco shrugged noncommittally. "You probably don't want to know."

"Come on, Rocco. I trust your judgment." Rocco looked skeptical and kept his mouth shut. Mark smiled encouragingly and slapped the older man across the back. "Don't let Laura scare you off. She even warned *me* about keeping the discovery under wraps until the final analysis report comes in."

Rocco considered his answer for a moment. "Seems obvious to me. In keeping with local legend, plus the size, shape and wing span . . . "

Mark nodded. "I know. I just can't quite wrap my brain around it yet. It seems impossible."

"Wait until you see it," Rocco responded.

"So you seriously think we've unearthed the remains of a long extinct variety of flying dinosaur?"

Rocco nodded. "Very Pterodactyl like. I've seen them before."

Mark grunted and let out a small disbelieving laugh. "No wonder Laura is so paranoid. The sooner we get a positive ID, the better. I just wish I'd been around personally to document the whole thing."

"You don't trust us?" Rocco asked.

"I didn't say that," Mark explained. "It's just that this could either be the biggest scientific discovery of the century or the biggest hoax. We'll either be famous or made to look like laughing stocks. Any slip in procedure and we could be completely discredited."

"They'll try it, don't even fool yourself into thinking they won't."

Mark glanced sideways at his long time friend and trusted colleague. "You sound pretty skeptical. And who are 'they'?"

"The establishment."

"The establishment," Mark repeated sardonically.

"In this case, the scientific community," Rocco clarified.

"Oh?"

"Sure. They accept only what fits into their own preconceived theories. Anything outside the box gets tossed."

"That's hardly fair," Mark laughed. "If that's the case then what's the use? We might as well pack up right now and go home. Discovery is what this is all about."

"There, my friend, is where you are sadly mistaken," Rocco replied knowingly. "It's really about the capitalist regime that rules us all. Money. Profit. Bottom line. That's where the real power is. We're all just pawns in a big game of chess, fed whatever information the powers-that-be think we can swallow. Just enough to keep us quiet and satisfied. It's a conspiracy."

"Someone definitely put something nasty in your cereal this morning," Mark said with a laugh.

"I'm serious," Rocco responded.

"I know," Mark said, sobering. "That's what worries me."

They had reached the compound, a large canvas walled structure. Mark greeted the guard with a perfunctory nod and entered without comment. Rocco followed closely on his heels.

"It's numbered and documented right along with everything else from my quadrant. I did it myself," Rocco said, leading the way now in the dim interior of the make shift compound. It consisted of rows of metal shelving lined with labeled trays and clear plastic bags of artifacts. "Right here." He searched the area with his eyes, squinting. "What the . . . it was here yesterday. I knew you'd want to do the preliminary lab work yourself. What did she do with it?!" he blurted, letting out a string of expletives in Spanish.

"Whoa, whoa! Who do you mean?" Mark asked. "Laura?"

"Has anything been crated for transport to the States yet?" Rocco demanded, ignoring the initial question.

"Is that what she suggested?"

"Yep. I told her to wait until you got back. I told her you'd want to see it for yourself," Rocco spat, shaking his head in frustration.

"I take it you two had some disagreements on the subject," Mark noted.

"You could say that," Rocco admitted.

"So just what else has been going on in my absence?" Mark wanted to know. He wasn't feeling too happy at the moment. Laura had just finished telling him she had saved the bone for him to look at. Why would she lie to him about it?

"Go ask your second in command," Rocco directed with a wave. "She'll tell you what ever you want to hear, I'm sure."

"I don't like the sounds of this. The last thing I need are my two most valuable crew members at logger heads with one another."

Rocco just shrugged, "Talk to her about it. I just did my job. Numbered and documented, just like it's supposed to be."

"I intend to talk to her about it," Mark said, in no uncertain terms. He turned and strode from the compound.

CPSIA information can be obtained at www.ICGtesting.com
Printed in the USA
LVOW060745061211

257940LV00002B/1/P